THE MARK OF THE DEAD

JAMIE JOHANSSON FILES
BOOK 2

MORGAN GREENE

ing, cheering, betting on her life. They drank booze and stuffed their faces with food.

The girl's stomach knotted. First in hunger, then in sickness. These people. They sickened her.

She closed her eyes, not able to look at them as their cheers grew. She knew what that meant, too.

That they were bringing down her opponent. No, not her opponent. The girl they wanted to die. The girl they wanted her to kill.

A girl like her. One stolen and brought to this place.

She swallowed, clenching her fists at her sides, the bandages wrapped around them to spare her knuckles tightening and creaking, darkened with blood. Tears came, the first few times. But no longer. Now, she knew what she needed to do. She needed to kill. Kill to live.

She had learned how to make it quick. How to make it easy. She had taught herself. But when she did that, they beat her. The men with the noose, the ones that brought her here. They dragged her back into her cell and they threw her down and they beat her. Masters of violence. They knew how hard to hit so that it hurt. So that it hurt for days. But never so badly that she couldn't fight again.

Who this girl was, the one she was supposed to kill, she didn't know.

The girl was just brought down the stairs from the room where they kept them, and shoved under the lights, the door closing behind them. She was short. Older. Maybe eighteen or nineteen, even. She had narrow-set eyes and short, thick, black hair, a frightened look on her face.

The girl with the bandages around her knuckles looked away. This was no time for weakness. Weakness meant death. And she was determined to survive.

The cheers kicked up around them, people screaming. Screaming for blood.

The short girl with the black hair cried out, sobbing, mewling, for mercy. For help.

But no help was coming.

And all the girl with the bandaged hands could grant her was a good death.

And so, with the crowd howling like wolves around her, she opened her eyes, lifted her hands, and gave the girl that had been brought to her just that.

CHAPTER
TWO

t was midnight when Alina woke, tangled in clean white cotton bedsheets, the memory foam cradling her sweat-soaked back. She sucked in a hard breath and sat upright, heart beating hard, hands on her chest, the flicker of those bright, awful lights still dancing in her vision. The ache in her knuckles and the taste of blood in her mouth fading as reality set in and she once again remembered where she was.

There was a thud outside the door and her head whipped around to look at it, just in time to see a dark figure advancing quickly across the room.

Alina gasped as the figured climbed onto the bed and reached for her.

She recoiled instinctively.

'Shh, shh,' the woman said. 'It's okay, it's okay. Just another bad dream. I'm here. You're safe.'

And then Jamie took the girl in her arms and pulled her in, holding her tightly.

She felt Alina stiffen in her grasp, and then melt into her embrace, breathing softly, her olive skin moist with sweat.

They'd been staying in hotels for more than six weeks now, their beds separated by just a few feet of space, but a chasm of separation. Alina's nightmares came every night. And every night she woke. And every night Jamie came to her, and held her.

She didn't know how long it would go on, or if it would ever go away. Jamie's nightmares didn't. She just got less afraid of them. Less afraid of going to sleep. Less afraid of not sleeping.

'I heard something,' Alina whispered then, keeping her cheek pressed to Jamie's ribs. 'Outside the door.'

Jamie turned her head to look at it. 'I'm sure it's nothing,' she said. 'Just the guards.' She stroked her hair gently.

There'd been two private security contractors outside their door twenty-four seven since the night that Jamie and her partner Hassan had broken up that underground fighting ring. Since the Armenians – Aram Petrosyan and his men – had slipped through Interpol's fingers and disappeared into the night.

Interpol were hunting them, but they weren't the type to just turn tail and run. And nor were they the type to get slighted and live with it. What Jamie had done, disrupting their operation ... Julia Hallberg,

Jamie's friend and point of contact at Interpol ... she hadn't minced her words: the Armenians would want retribution. In blood. They'd want Jamie's blood. And they'd want the girl's blood.

They'd tried and failed to get her back twice, and Jamie had killed their men. Now it was a matter of principle. Of vengeance. And of their own brand of justice.

Jamie held Alina tighter. Wishing she could take her away from all this. But Alina was a material witness. She'd experienced their horrors first-hand. And when the time came, she'd have to relive it all, giving statements and legal testimonies. And it was up to Jamie to keep her safe until then.

'I really did hear something,' Alina said, pulling away and looking at Jamie. She glanced at the door then, eyes large, lips quivering, her forehead sheened with sweat.

Jamie ran her fingers through the girl's hair, gently brushing the curled strands from her forehead.

'Alright,' she said, standing up. 'I'll go check.' Though she knew she'd only find her two bodyguards standing there, as always. Hell, one of them probably stamped their foot or dropped their phone or something.

Jamie approached the door and laid a hand on it, twisting the handle.

The lock clicked and light came into the room but, as it did, the door was pulled from her grasp, swinging inwards under the weight of the body slumped against it.

Jamie danced backwards as it flopped onto the floor, the lifeless corpse of one of her security detail, throat opened from ear to ear, eyes staring vacantly at the ceiling.

Alina gasped and leapt from the bed, hiding behind it.

Jamie's pistol was already in her hand, ripped from her holster and at the ready.

She steadied herself, listening for any signs of movement, and then peeked, stepping quickly from the shelter of the room and into the corridor.

Her watch glowed on her wrist – three-twelve in the morning.

The hallway was empty except for the second guard, face down about ten feet in front of her, a wide pool of blood spreading from under his body.

'Fuck,' Jamie breathed, turning back and running to the room.

She dragged the body at the threshold into the corridor and then stepped over him, noticing then the strange mark on her door – painted in blood, a smeared and twisted 'S' shape with a split at the top that looked like the maw of a serpent.

But she only let herself get sidetracked for a moment before she darted inside and closed the door, double locking it.

She looked over at Alina, still hiding behind the bed,

and beckoned her from there. 'Come away from the window,' she said, her tone hard enough that she didn't have to say it twice.

Alina rushed towards her, putting an arm around her back as Jamie went to her bedside table and snatched up the two-way radio that the security team had given her. 'This is Primary, come in,' she said, holding the talk button.

A second later, a response came. 'This is Unit Two.' The second pair of close protection officers sitting in an SUV outside. 'Everything okay?'

Jamie resisted the urge to scoff. 'No,' she said, letting out a soft breath. 'Uh, Unit One is ... They're down. They're both down.'

'Repeat that?' The alarm in the man's voice was apparent.

'They're both down.' Jamie felt Alina squeeze her tighter. 'They're both fucking dead.'

CHAPTER
THREE

J amie kept her gun trained on the door until Unit Two arrived, using their pre-agreed knock, and announced themselves.

Jamie let them in and they held the room until the police, the coroner, forensics, and then Interpol managed to get there.

Jamie didn't know what she'd expected – a squad of Armenians clad in military gear bursting in to take or kill them? Something like that. But whoever had dispensed with the two armed close protection officers outside the door, ex-military and highly trained themselves, had done so, firstly without waking Jamie and Alina, who were sleeping just through the door. And in such an efficient fashion that the two men never managed to get a scream out before they were dealt with – never managed to even lift their radios and call for help.

Jamie played it over and over again in her mind – how someone could have done that. No shots fired. Just a blade. And then, to draw that ... *thing* on the door? What did it mean?

Nothing good, Jamie thought. Anything drawn on your bedroom door in the blood of your dead bodyguard wasn't going to be good.

But why hadn't they just burst in the room and finished the job?

As Jamie watched Julia Hallberg pause at the threshold to inspect the strange symbol, holding her hand up to trace the swooping lines of the serpent drawn on the wood, it's all she could think about.

Why were she and Alina still alive?

Hallberg lowered her fingers, then hung her head a little, pushing her hands into the pockets of her slacks, and stepped into the room.

It was gone five in the morning now and light was permeating the sky.

'Jesus,' Hallberg muttered, approaching Jamie. The professional thing to do would be a handshake. But they were way past professionality. So, Hallberg hugged her.

Jamie returned it.

'You okay?' Hallberg asked, holding her by the shoulders as she pulled away.

Jamie nodded, dipping her head towards Alina, who was standing at her side, staring at the door.

'And how are you holding up?' Hallberg asked her.

Alina looked up at her, and then nodded. 'I'm good.'

It had only been six weeks, but Jamie had been teaching her English fiercely. There wasn't a whole lot else to do, and Alina was clearly smart. They'd been practising English, reading together, and watching TV. Jamie had never watched so much TV in her life as she had the last six weeks.

She thought that it gave Alina something to occupy her mind, something to focus on that wasn't what she'd been through. An outlet for her mind.

But Jamie also knew that an outlet for the mind was one thing, but practising prepositions wouldn't cure the anger she felt. Though Jamie knew a good way of channelling that too.

So, Jamie was teaching her to fight. Not to brawl, or to hurt, or to kill, as she had before. But to control herself, to discipline herself. Jamie's martial art of choice was Tae Kwon Do, but she knew how to box, too, knew some Aikido. It was worth its weight a hundred times over to know how to defend yourself in this world. It had served Jamie well, and though she truly hoped Alina would never need to use the skills Jamie was teaching her, they were important to have.

And she seemed to be learning them even quicker than English. She had a deep-seated desire to do so. To be able to protect herself.

No wonder, Jamie thought. And suddenly, she wanted to hold her.

'Your English is really coming along,' Hallberg said, smiling at her.

'Thank you,' Alina said back. 'I am learning ... good.'

'Well,' Jamie corrected her. 'You're learning well.'

'I am learning well,' Alina said.

'Impressive.'

'Im-pressive?' Alina parroted back, then looked at Jamie, not understanding the word.

'It means she thinks you're really smart.'

Alina blushed a little, then looked away.

Hallberg motioned Jamie into the hallway so they could talk, and Jamie followed, gesturing to Alina that she'd be right back. She stepped out over the body now covered by a white sheet, and walked a few steps away from their room.

'You really didn't hear anything?' Hallberg asked as the SOCOs in the hallway documented the scene behind them.

Jamie shook her head. 'No. And I sleep light. Alina woke me up. She has ... dreams,' Jamie said, holding her fingers at her temple, 'nightmares. About what happened to her. Every night. She wakes up, sometimes screaming. Other times she just sits bolt upright in bed. Scared the shit out of me to begin with.'

'Shit,' Hallberg replied. 'I didn't know. Did you get in touch with that psychologist I recommended?'

'Yeah, left a message,' Jamie lied. 'But right now, she just needs ... stability. She needs to feel safe. Not someone poking around in her brain.'

Hallberg narrowed her eyes a little, but didn't say

anything. She knew Jamie wasn't fond of the psychic arts. Mystical or practical. 'So that woke you up? Alina's bad dream?'

'Yeah. I went to her. She said she heard a noise outside, but I didn't hear anything.'

'A noise?'

'A thud. A body hitting the ground, I guess.'

'But nothing else? No groans, shouting, footsteps, nothing?'

Jamie just shook her head. 'Whoever did this was a damn ghost.'

Hallberg looked apprehensive. 'I don't like that mark on the door.'

'You recognise it?'

'No, but we'll find out what it is. Though I think it's pretty clear what it means. This is the Armenians, and they did this as a way to show us what they're capable of. That they can get to you wherever, whenever. That thing on the door, a snake or whatever it is – that's a mark of death. You're marked.'

Jamie exhaled slowly. 'Brilliant.'

'Mm. Not ideal.'

'No, you're right. It's not ideal. So, what do we do now? We can't stay here, obviously,' Jamie said, tsking and folding her arms.

'No, no ...' Hallberg agreed, though she didn't seem to have a better answer.

'What are we supposed to do then?'

Hallberg just met that one with silence.

'Are you any closer to tracking down Aram Petrosyan?'

'We're working on it.'

'I've been a detective longer than you have,' Jamie reminded her. 'Don't feed me lines.'

'Then no. We aren't.'

'Do you know if he's in the country, even?'

'His private plane left a small airfield in Shropshire the morning after the bust at the fighting ring,' Hallberg said. 'But we don't know if he was on it.'

'Great. So, then we just sit on our hands, wait for Interpol to *not* catch Petrosyan, and for the ninja-assassin that murdered two CPOs last night to come back for Alina and me? Is there any point even locking the fucking doors?'

'I can tell you're frustrated,' Hallberg said.

'Something like that. I'm sorry, I'm not trying to take it out on you. I just ... I'm tired. And I hate running.'

Hallberg seemed deep in thought then. 'Have you stopped to consider just why Alina is so important?'

'Because she can identify Petrosyan,' Jamie answered swiftly.

Hallberg sort of shrugged. 'Maybe,' she said, 'but what would that matter? She wouldn't know his name. And they kept the fights going, didn't they, even after she had escaped and she was in custody.'

'What's your point?'

'I don't know,' Hallberg said, sighing a little. 'I just ... We managed to find the families of the other girls, managed to contact people through their embassies, got them home ... for the most part. But Alina ...'

'What are you getting at?' Jamie asked her, a little defensive now.

'I'm not getting at anything. Just that we don't know anything about Alina. That her name didn't come up with any matches anywhere. The name of the village she gave us ... we can't find that, either. There's no record of any epidemic sickness or death like she described ...'

'You think she's lying about that? Lying about her parents dying, her grandfather being killed? About being abducted and trafficked?'

'I can see you're tired,' Hallberg said bluntly then. 'So I won't read too much into your tone.'

Jamie collected herself. 'Sorry, just ... a sore spot. I've killed and almost died for this girl and I've been with her for six weeks straight. I think I know her pretty well by now.'

Hallberg smiled just a little. 'Yeah, no, it's probably nothing. Just my brain. Doesn't like things remaining ... unproven. Comes with the job, you know? Georgia is still rural in places. Really rural. It's not surprising that she could have slipped through the net.'

But the seed was planted, and whether Hallberg rationalised it away or not, Jamie knew that was going to niggle at her.

'There's no point you and Alina staying here now. Why don't you go back and ask her to pack up her things. You can come with me. We'll get some breakfast, look for another place for you.'

'More protective custody?'

'It's pretty much all we can do until we have a case that we can prosecute.'

Jamie nodded slowly.

'We'll close the circle even further. No one will know where you are this time.'

'You said that last time,' Jamie muttered, turning back to the room.

'Hey,' Hallberg called. 'We'll get them. I promise.'

Jamie didn't turn back, just went into the room and told Alina to pack up her things.

As she loaded socks into her duffle bag she glanced up, seeing Hallberg inspecting the serpent drawn in blood on their door. And as much as the symbol scared Jamie, the look of apprehension and worry on Hallberg's face ... that scared her more.

CHAPTER
FOUR

Alina seemed to have developed a deep love of McDonald's. And Jamie could *not* fathom why.

As they rode in Hallberg's car, driving west away from the outskirts of Cardiff, where their hotel had been, Alina pointed towards the services sign that said there was one coming up, yelling so suddenly that Hallberg nearly changed lanes out of shock.

They intended to pass it by, but Alina was insistent – teenagers, Jamie thought – and they eventually pulled in.

Hallberg wasn't much for conversation. She was deep in thought. Which wasn't unusual for her. She'd become much more serious as she'd grown in her role. Jamie still remembered her as a young polisassistent for the Stockholm Polis, where they'd first met. And now she was supervising a multi-national trafficking investigation for Interpol.

The morning was warm, and as Alina sat at a bench outside, choking down a McMuffin like a starved seagull, Jamie and Hallberg queued for coffee from the nearby stand.

'What's on your mind?' Jamie asked.

'I'm just thinking about the call I got this morning,' she answered, staring off into the distance. 'When I saw that number – of the security firm we hired for you – my heart sank. I thought ... I thought you were dead. That they were going to tell me that.'

'We're fine,' Jamie reminded her. 'Me and Alina. We're totally fine.'

'But it could have easily gone the other way. Whoever came after you. They could have killed you.'

'I'd have put up a fight,' Jamie said with a smile.

'I think the guy'd probably have slit your throat while you slept if he really wanted you dead last night. And you wouldn't have even known he was there.'

Whether it was Hallberg's tone, or just the fact that Jamie knew that to be the truth, the conversation became very serious all at once.

'I know,' Jamie said. 'But they didn't. And we *are* okay.'

'For now.' Hallberg shook her head.

'What are you thinking?'

'About what to do next?' Hallberg asked. 'I don't trust anyone. And I know you don't trust Catherine

Mallory as far as you can throw her – and she's still got her fingers in this investigation. Still the NCA's chief Point Of Contact for Interpol on this, after all.'

Catherine Mallory was the intelligence officer who had led the investigation into the initial trafficking case. And while they couldn't prove it, Jamie always had the feeling she was dirty. One of her agents, Ash, had been killed during one of the confrontations with the Armenians. And as far as Jamie knew, Mallory was the only person who could have passed information to the Armenians that led them to the safe house that night. But she couldn't prove that. No one could. And Braun, Hallberg's SO, didn't seem convinced of her involvement either.

But a pattern was a pattern, and Jamie and Alina's luck would run out eventually.

'So where do we go from here?' Jamie asked. 'I can take Alina, we can run. Disappear.'

'Where?' She put her hands on her hips. 'Not like Braun would sign off on that, either. You and Alina are still integral to this case and he wants her on hand when there's a development.' She thought for a moment. 'No, you need to stay reachable, at least. It's just ... we're not going to be able to use proper channels. No security firms. Nothing official. Off the books. Entirely. And ... I know a guy.'

'Hassan?' Jamie asked, hopeful. Mallory had separated them since their incursion at the water treatment facility and was doing all she could to keep them that way.

She insisted it was a matter of professionality, that Hassan's skills were of more use elsewhere than babysitting a witness. But Jamie knew that it was personal. Or at least, she couldn't help but feel that way. That, and she knew how capable Hassan was. And without him there, Jamie and Alina were just that much more vulnerable.

Hallberg shook her head though. 'No, he's still wrapped up with hunting down the faces in the footage you captured.'

'So, who then?'

'We've worked with him before – Interpol, I mean. I was his ... handler. For, uh ... a case.'

'A case?' Jamie read the way she said the word. Like it had been anything but conventional. 'Cryptic.'

'Yeah, not the sort of thing I'm really allowed to expound on, you know? But I trust him. He's capable.'

'Just one guy?' Jamie seemed doubtful.

'Ex-military. Highly skilled. Very discreet. Now, he's a ... *contractor*.'

'Contractor?' She scoffed a little. 'The type that kills people for money?'

The man in line in front of them turned his head and raised an eyebrow.

Hallberg motioned for Jamie to lower her voice. 'No, not ... *just* that.'

'Oh, this is filling me with confidence.' Jamie said,

watching Alina eat. 'But I don't really know if we have another choice, do we?'

'It's my mandate to keep you and Alina alive until we can produce a case that holds water. So ... no. You don't have a choice.'

'Why didn't you bring him up before?'

'He's not exactly ...'

'Not exactly what?'

'He just doesn't respond well to authority, or rules. Or orders. Or anyone telling him what to do. Or how to do it. Hey,' she said then, laughing a little, 'you two will probably get along great.'

'Ha, ha,' Jamie feigned a laugh, stepping up to the coffee stand. 'Large black coffee. Got skimmed milk?'

The freckled barista smiled and nodded.

'I'll take a double-shot latte,' Hallberg added, before turning back to Jamie. 'This guy's not my first choice – hell, I'm still cleaning up the mess he left in his wake. But considering what we witnessed last night, I don't think off-the-shelf security firms are going to cut it. And if you'd seen what this guy did ...'

'Well, I trust you,' she said to Hallberg. 'If you think this guy is our best bet, then make a call, set a meet.'

'Okay, I will,' she said, watching Jamie watch Alina. 'You really care about her, don't you?'

'I do,' Jamie said, seeing out of the corner of her eye that Hallberg really wanted to say something.

The way she just sort of closed her mouth and took

their coffees off the counter instead told Jamie it was something she likely wouldn't want to hear.

So, instead, they just walked in silence back towards the table, feeling the warmth of the sun on their skin, and the cold gravity of the situation on their shoulders.

CHAPTER
FIVE

Jamie sat with Alina as Hallberg walked a considerable distance away and started dialling numbers.

'Jamie?' Alina asked, her accent still heavy, the words coming slow and jilted.

Jamie looked away from Hallberg, who was chewing a thumbnail as she spoke into the phone. 'Yeah?' she said, turning to the girl.

'Where do we going?' She smiled at Jamie.

'Where *are* we going,' Jamie corrected her.

'Where *are* we going?' Alina re-asked, taking the note in stride. She was becoming a real conversationalist, determined to learn the language quickly.

'Somewhere safe,' Jamie responded.

Alina nodded, taking that in. 'We see Nasir?'

Hassan.

'No, I don't think so. But we will see him soon, I promise.'

'Good.' She began picking tiny shards of dried cheese from the wrapper of her breakfast.

As Jamie watched Hallberg hang up and stride back towards them, she rose from the bench and walked out to meet her. 'So?' she asked anxiously.

Hallberg sighed heavily, then gave a nod. 'Yeah, it's, uh … it's set. He's coming.'

'You don't sound thrilled.'

'I'll end up paying for it.'

'He wanted money?'

'Cost isn't always about the price,' Hallberg replied. 'But he appreciates our position. He's dealt with the Armenians before. He knows what to expect.'

'I'm struggling to believe he's going to put his life on the line for us,' Jamie said sceptically. But truthfully. 'Why would he?'

'Because I said I'd do him a big fucking favour if he did. And, believe it or not, he's got a heart. Shit, I don't know. He's trying to right some wrongs? Rebalance the cosmic scales. Hell, maybe he's just got a death wish,' Hallberg scoffed.

'You're really selling this guy to me.'

'Sorry, long night. Long fucking year.' She scoffed to herself. 'Come on, let's load up. Got a drive ahead of us. Few hours to the meet.'

'Want me to drive?' Jamie offered.

'Nah, I'm good,' she said, sounding tired. 'Just ... I don't know how you do this.'

'Do what?'

'Live with the threat of death hanging over your head all the time.'

Jamie smirked, then lifted her hand and beckoned Alina to come to her. 'Oh, you know, you just sort of get used to it. Tune it out after a while.'

Alina approached and put her arm around Jamie.

She looked down at the girl, affording a small smile.

'That, and you've got to find joy in the little things. Right?'

Alina smiled back. 'Right?' she said, not knowing what she was agreeing to.

'I envy you,' Hallberg said.

Jamie looked up at her. 'You shouldn't.'

And Hallberg just took that in and, after a moment, smiled sadly and turned away towards the car.

CHAPTER
SIX

They travelled north, winding through the Welsh countryside.

Alina, full and contented, fell asleep in the back seat. Her resilience to horror was proving to be useful. She seemed to shrug off one event after the next, finding reasons to laugh instead of cry. At least, until the night came.

But for now, she seemed to be sleeping peacefully. Perhaps the nightmares would leave her alone for once.

There was always hope, Jamie supposed.

Hallberg had one hand on the wheel, her other elbow on the door sill, propping up her face as they tracked north through the winding A-roads.

She wouldn't tell Jamie where they were going, but Jamie had faith.

She just wondered who it was they were meeting and what this person was going to be able to do for them. The leash of the investigation felt tight around Jamie's neck, she knew that much. And she knew Hassan and his new team of Interpol agents and NCA intelligence officers would be closing in on some of the faces from that night at the fighting ring. And when they did, Jamie and Alina would need to swoop back to confirm they were there. So, she understood why they couldn't just disappear from the country. But still, the invisible tethers keeping them here felt like they were just trussing them up ready for slaughter. She just couldn't see who was holding the other ends of them.

Richard Rees, her mother's husband, Dyfed-Powys Police Chief Superintendent, the man who'd brought Jamie into this case in the first place, had been released from jail pending further investigation, stripped of his title and suspended indefinitely from his position. Of course, that was Jamie's fault and not his, so said her mother. Despite the fact that he's the one that had hid evidence from the NCA.

Jesus, the finger. She wondered then; did he still have that severed finger in his freezer?

She shook her head and laughed a little to herself.

Hallberg eyed her but said nothing.

Fuck, what a mess, Jamie thought, imagining him in the field behind his house burying the thing.

She didn't know if he was corrupt too, or if it was one of his men ... Aled Parry, his DCI, maybe. Jamie had met him briefly. He'd seemed like a prick. But selling out young girls to the Armenians to be trafficked was a little heavier than being just a bit of a knob.

Jamie didn't know. She really didn't. If it was Mallory who was corrupt, then what was she getting from it? What did she hope to wring out of all this? Or was it blackmail?

So many questions, not enough time to think about the answers.

Alina was all that mattered now. Alina, and surviving.

If there was some lunatic after them that they couldn't see coming ... Well, Jamie just hoped that Hallberg was right about the guy they were going to be employing.

Who was he? Hallberg had kept quiet about that, just said that he'd left a mess in his wake. That he didn't much subscribe to rules. That he was out to right some wrongs, balance some cosmic scales.

God, she missed Hassan. Why couldn't he be here? Together, Jamie and he could protect Alina.

Not this ... mercenary, whoever he was.

Jamie didn't know who she was more nervous to meet. This guy, or the one who left a fucking snake drawn on her door.

She thought about that the whole way there.

And then, after what seemed like an age, in the middle of nowhere, with the first peaks of Snowdonia rising in the distance ahead and to the left, Hallberg slowed and pulled off the main road into a random layby.

'We're here,' she announced, putting the car in park and rubbing her eyes.

Jamie looked around. 'I don't see anything.'

'He'll be here.'

And as if on cue, a Land Rover Defender appeared behind them and pulled in, an imposing figure behind the wheel.

'Was he following us?' Jamie asked.

'No, but I'm guessing he was waiting.' Hallberg opened the door and stepped out. 'Stay here.'

Jamie watched as Hallberg exited and walked towards the back of the car.

Alina roused a little, opening one eye.

'It's okay,' Jamie said softly, twisted around to watch Hallberg. 'Go back to sleep.'

She just closed her eyes then, still exhausted from the night.

The door to the Land Rover opened and a man stepped out. He was over six feet tall, broad shouldered, with thick arms covered in light-coloured hair.

He took a few steps forward, slow and methodical, and greeted Hallberg between the cars' bumpers. Jamie couldn't see his face from this angle, but she could see how he towered over Hallberg. He folded his arms first as Hallberg spoke, listening carefully, and then moved them to his hips.

He reached up then, and put his hand on Hallberg's

shoulder, squeezing softly. She hung her head, shaking a little, and then – to Jamie's surprise – she hugged him. She sort of stepped forward quickly and wrapped her arms around him.

After a moment, he hugged her back, holding her for a second, Hallberg's head on his chest. And then she stepped backwards, wiped off her cheeks and straightened her jacket.

She came back to the driver's door and opened it. 'Okay,' she said, leaning in. 'Time to go.'

'What was that?' Jamie asked.

She flushed slightly. 'What was what?'

'Nothing,' Jamie said.

'Right.' Hallberg ducked back out quickly and now Jamie did wake Alina.

'Come on,' she said. 'We're going.'

They got out of the car, Alina still a little groggy.

The stranger was already carrying their bags from the boot to the back of his Land Rover.

Jamie watched him go, as did Alina, his wide back seeming to fill the gap between the car and the hedge next to him. The duffle he was carrying in his hands had always felt big and cumbersome to Jamie, but in his grasp it looked like a toy.

He threw the bags into the back and appeared in the gap once more, slowing for just a step as he appraised Jamie, and she appraised him.

He was wearing a pair of jeans, a plain grey long-sleeve with the sleeves rolled up, showing off the bottom half of a tattoo on the back of his forearm: a winged dagger. Except it wasn't a winged dagger at all – it was actually Excalibur in flames. Something that most people got wrong.

But not Jamie.

Jamie knew the insignia.

SAS. Special Air Service.

Hallberg said he was ex-military.

He had a wide jaw with a short but thick beard that shone golden in the morning sun. His strong features made him look stern, his dark eyes – the colour of slate – seemingly hiding beneath his thick eyebrows.

Jamie felt Alina move behind her slightly. Frightened. Strange men hadn't been kind to her. She was right to be wary.

The man stopped at the bumper of the mud-splattered Defender and gently lifted his hands, massaging the uneven knuckles of his right with the fingers of his left.

'We should go,' he said, his voice low and gruff. 'Get in.'

Hallberg stepped forward then. 'Jamie, this is Solomon Church.'

'Solomon Church?' she repeated, a little surprised. She looked at the man in front of her. 'Is that your ... real name?'

His jaw flexed. 'You said we're short on time,' he said to Hallberg, ignoring Jamie's comment. 'We need to go.'

'Right,' Hallberg said, turning and walking towards Jamie. She hugged her tightly. 'Be safe,' she whispered in her ear, and then released her before hugging Alina quickly.

Solomon Church stood at the wing of the Defender, hand on the dirty green steel of the bonnet, watching.

Jamie felt uneasy, not least because the first thing out of her mouth had been an insult. Solomon Church? No way that could be real. Could it? Fuck. If it was …

And then Hallberg was walking back around the car. 'Call me if you need anything,' she said, before getting back in. She leaned across the centre console, waved quickly, and then drove away, as if to spare them a long and difficult goodbye.

Jamie shielded her eyes as a cloud of dust rose around them. And then they were alone with this stranger.

'Jamie,' she offered, stretching out her hand.

He took another step forward, looking Jamie up and down like a horse trainer would appraise a mare, and then walked to his own driver's door and climbed up into the cab.

'Alright then,' she said, dropping her hand and looking at Alina.

She smiled weakly, waiting on Jamie. Who knew she didn't have any other choice.

Jamie approached the passenger door and opened it.

'No,' Church said, firing Jamie a cold look.

'No?'

'Back seat.'

Jamie looked into the back, surprised. 'Why?'

'Because I said,' he replied, his cold eyes telling Jamie it wasn't up for discussion.

Her neck felt hot, a sudden burst of anger flooding through her. 'Fine,' she said, teeth gritted, closing the door with a slam and ushering Alina up onto the bench seat.

'Seatbelts,' Church commanded.

'I was doing it,' Jamie half snapped, checking Alina's and then fastening her own.

They were moving then, and fast. He accelerated hard, the Land Rover jerking through the gears as they motored down the road, hurtling through the countryside.

The windows were all open, the wind buffeting inwards and blowing Jamie's hair all around her face. Alina looked like Cousin It, her thick curls enveloping her entire face as she tried to pull them off.

'So,' Jamie called over the roar of the wind, the heavy-duty off-road tyres, and the unnecessarily loud engine. 'Solomon?'

He didn't respond.

'That's your name, right? Solomon?'

No response again.

'I'm going to have to call you something. "Hey you" doesn't really work for me.'

'Church,' he said then, his voice cutting the din.

'Fine. Church,' Jamie said. 'Where are you from?'

More silence.

It was going to be a long ride.

'I don't know if you know what's going on?' Jamie yelled.

He didn't seem to care.

She hated being the talkative one in a conversation. If you could call it that.

'Where are we going?'

He let out a short breath. A show of emotion of some kind? Or just breathing? Jamie's years of detective work seemed to be failing her.

'It'll be easier if we don't talk,' he said then.

'Easier for who?'

He met her eyes briefly in the rear-view mirror and then said, without a hint of sarcasm, 'Me.'

CHAPTER
SEVEN

Jamie didn't try after that. Where he was taking them, she didn't know. How long they'd be there, she didn't know. If they'd be safe, she didn't know. What kind of comforts they'd have, she didn't know. But they were still tearing north at a rate of knots, delving deeper into the craggy terrain of Snowdonia with no hint of slowing down.

And then he spoke, turning his head very slightly, but keeping his eyes on the road. 'I'm going to need any phones and electronics,' he said, reaching into the cup holder between the seats and pulling out a clear zip-locked bag. 'Put them in here.'

Jamie didn't need to ask why, but she still didn't like the idea of being without a phone. Especially if they got into trouble. 'What if I need to call Hallberg?'

'She knows how to reach me,' he responded. 'Phone. Bag. Anything else you have that connects to the Internet or a phone network – iPads, Kindle, smart watches.' He glanced down between the seats at Jamie's wrist. At the watch there; the one that tracked her runs, her sleep, her heart rate and stress levels – the latter of which she thought was probably through the fucking roof right now. 'All in the bag.'

Jamie hesitated. 'You're not going to throw it out of the window, are you?'

He said nothing.

'It's just … it's new. It's the new Fenix.'

He turned his head a little, raised an eyebrow slightly.

'You know what they are, right?'

More silence.

'Fuck,' Jamie muttered, pulling it off and snatching the bag from his hand.

She pulled out her phone too, held the power button until it shut off, and pushed both into the bag, sealing it tightly. She handed it back through the gap and he took it from her, bringing it into his lap.

'Shit,' he growled.

'That's everything,' Jamie said. 'Just my watch and phone.'

He hummed angrily.

'I swear,' Jamie said.

'Sit back,' he snapped then.

The tone of the words was enough to make Jamie snap to attention. Church's eyes locked on the rear-view, the sudden tightening of his hands on the wheel turning his knuckles white.

Jamie jumped backwards into her seat and turned her head, seeing the front of a black SUV closing in on them dangerously fast.

'Is that them?' Jamie asked, knowing the question was as stupid as they came.

'Either that or some rich housewife late for her spin class,' Church said, the comment catching Jamie off guard as much as the SUV ramming into their back bumper.

She swore loudly. Alina gripped her belt. Church wrestled the wheel straight, changed down a gear, and slammed his foot into the floor, the vehicle snaking and then sling-shotting ahead down the road.

'Guess not,' he said, his voice oozing calm.

There was a loud click then and Jamie saw that he already had a pistol drawn, held upside down and pressed to his thigh. He used his jeans to push the slide back and chamber a round.

Jamie pulled her own weapon from the concealed holster in the small of her back and grabbed Alina, pushing her forward so she was doubled over in the seat, out of the firing line.

But before she could even do anything else, Church braked hard and pulled to the side, mounting the grassy verge, the accelerating car behind appearing at their side suddenly.

Gunfire split the air as Church's hand flew out of the

window, his finger rebounding off the grip, muzzle flash leaping from the weapon.

Jamie's ears rang, but her eyes counted three shots.

The SUV swerved away and then back towards them, crunching into the side of their Land Rover before it pinballed into the opposite hedgerow and speared through into the field beyond.

Jamie saw the back rising into the air as it tumbled, and then it was gone, Church accelerating hard once more.

'There's another one,' he called, leaning forward to check the wing mirror an instant before it exploded in a shower of glass shards.

Bullets peppered the front wing as another SUV appeared at their flank.

Jamie twisted around to look, seeing nothing but empty road as the vehicle chasing them swung in behind them just before Church could lean out and fire.

Jamie didn't waste any time though, turning around fully inside the car and firing right through the back window.

The bullet hit the glass and pinged off, burying itself in the headliner twelve inches from her.

She dived down in shock, cursing.

'What the fuck are you doing!?' Church yelled.

'How the fuck was I supposed to know it's bullet-proof?' Jamie called back as the SUV rammed them once more.

The car lurched and skidded but then straightened

out, bouncing down the narrow country road.

Church changed gears, the box grinding as he stamped on the accelerator and tried to get them going again.

But it was too late, they'd lost momentum and the SUV was on them, swinging wide.

Jamie saw him this time, the shooter.

He was hanging from the window, lithe and dark, nearly an old man, his face lined, gnarled, his lips a heavy contrast from his olive skin. He gripped what looked like a sub-machine gun tightly, lining them up, firing without hesitation.

The muzzle spat fire. More bullets hit the front wing.

The tyre blew out and the whole car sagged forward, the rim tearing through the loose rubber. It hammered against the wheel arch, the Defender twisting sideways in the road as Church lost control.

Jamie pushed herself back into her seat, bracing herself as they turned broadside in the road.

The SUV was there, coming at them fast.

Jamie raked in a breath and held it, throwing one hand across Alina's back to keep her steady as they hit.

The sound of rending metal punctured the air, the force of the crash shunting them off the edge of the road. The heavy mud tyres dug into the soft earth and they pitched all at once, suddenly upside down and rolling.

Jamie felt weightless, watching as her hair flew all

around her head and the sky flashed through the window.

And then they landed on their roof and rolled, bounced down a bank and came to rest on their wheels, pinned against a hedgerow on one side, exposed to the road on the other.

Jamie was dazed, choked by her belt. She groaned and coughed, willing her eyes to focus.

She could feel Alina beneath her right arm and rubbed her back, trying to find her voice. All she could taste was blood.

She shook the girl gently but she didn't rouse. 'Alina?' she croaked, her head pounding.

She didn't get chance to ask a second time before the door was ripped open and hands plunged into the cabin.

Jamie tried to raise her gun, but realised it wasn't in her grip anymore.

A big guy with long black hair and a scarred face reached over Alina, going for her belt.

Jamie tried to fight, but she was still dazed. She got her hands on the guy's arm, but he pulled them free and then punched her in the mouth.

Pain exploded through her face and blood poured into her mouth.

She lolled backwards, still trapped by the belt, and choked on the blood, coughing it over her knees as the Armenian unfastened Alina and dragged her from the cab.

'No!' Jamie spluttered as Alina was carried from the

car and back up the bank.

She fumbled with her own belt, the thing stuck. She swore, looking around, seeing she was alone in the car. Where the hell was Church?

But before she could get loose, she realised she wasn't alone.

She looked up, seeing the old, thin man with the dark lips standing in the open passenger doorway. He was staring in at her with mild curiosity, a sleek black pistol hanging in his grip.

A shiver rode through her as he raised the gun, his eyes as cold and dead as the steel in his hands.

It was him. The man who had left that symbol on their door. She knew it. It had all been a show, a show to draw them out of the hotel and into the open.

Jamie swallowed, not a doubt in her mind that she was about to die. That he was about to pull the trigger without a hint of remorse.

And then it came.

A bang that made her jolt. Made her close her eyes. Made her gasp.

Made her feel cold all over.

But she'd been shot before, knew what that felt like.

And this wasn't it.

Jamie opened her eyes. And the old man was gone.

Blood was splattered across the seat in front of her, and then she saw a flash of black through the back quarter window, a bloody handprint left there, smeared towards the boot.

She twisted as best she could, seeing the old man scrambling up the bank towards the road, clutching his shoulder.

More gunfire rang out and Jamie took cover, finally unhooking her belt and diving sideways across the back seat.

Two guys rained bullets down from the road and a loud thud reached her from the front of the Land Rover, Church's head just visible hidden behind the bumper.

He popped up, elbows rested on the bonnet, and fired back.

Jamie shielded her head as bullets pinged off the vehicle. And then engines flared, tyres squealed, and the gunfire stopped.

Jamie was breathing hard, still shielding her head when Church appeared in the open doorway, panting hard.

He reached in, offering his hand, and pulled her upright, blood still running over her chin from where she'd been punched.

Church looked beaten up too, and had scrapes across the side of his face and all down his right arm. 'Are you okay?' he asked, still holding her arm tightly.

Jamie wiped off her mouth with the sleeve of her jacket, feeling the sting of a split lip. Her ribs were smarting too, and her hip bones. From the seatbelt. But she seemed to be in one piece. She nodded. 'They got Alina.'

Church just grunted, then squinted back up at the road.

'Where were you?' Jamie asked, sliding towards the door and gingerly trying to get out.

Church didn't look at her as he spoke. 'I opened the door when we pitched, got thrown clear,' he said, as though it was perfectly normal behaviour. 'Knew they'd want to finish the job.'

'So you jumped out to protect yourself. Thanks.'

'You're alive, aren't you?'

Jamie leant against the seat in the open doorway, spitting blood onto the grass between her feet. 'You kill that fucker?'

He shook his head. 'No, winged him I think.'

'Great,' Jamie grunted, standing upright. Her vision was still a little blurry.

Church pulled his phone from his pocket, sighing as he saw the screen was cracked. It fired up, the display a little wonky, and he jabbed at it, trying to find the right number to call.

'We have to go get her,' Jamie said, closing her eyes, the pain in her body ramping up by the second.

Church didn't respond.

'You hear what I said?'

'I did,' he said. 'But I don't know how the fuck you expect to do that. You can't even stand.'

'I just need a minute.'

He glanced at her. 'Maybe a little more than that. You're a mess.'

'Gee, thanks.'

'Come on,' he said, grabbing her by the arm and damn near carrying her up the slope with one hand while the other held the phone to his ear. There seemed to be no answer.

'Where are we going?' Jamie asked, wincing and hissing her way up the bank.

'Anywhere but here,' he said as they reached the road, lowering the phone. 'I don't want to be stood here waiting if they come back.' He looked left and right, the tarmac empty in both directions, the sound of sheep bleating in the distance the only sound carrying across the open countryside. He chose a direction and began walking, pulling Jamie by the arm.

She pulled it free of his hand roughly and stopped. 'We need to find Alina.'

'The girl? They won't hurt her.'

'You can't know that.'

'I do know that. Because if they wanted to, they'd have killed her in the car. Two bullets, back of the head. You too. It's how these guys operate. This was a smash and grab. They want her alive.' He reached for Jamie's arm again then, to make her walk.

She pulled it out of his grasp, angered by his answer. But knowing he was right. 'I can walk,' Jamie spat, hawking more blood onto the road.

'Good,' Church said, turning his back on her and striding away. 'Then walk.'

CHAPTER
EIGHT

Hallberg called Church back just as they reached a small town called Llanbrynmair.

'We got hit,' was the very first thing he said. 'They got the girl.'

Jamie heard Hallberg swear through the phone and then begin talking, though she struggled to make out what was being said as she was having to basically jog to keep up with Church's long strides. And he wasn't hanging around, either.

The blood had dried on her chin now, but her lips still throbbed with each step.

'No, she's fine,' Church said then, and Jamie guessed that Hallberg had asked about her.

Jamie resisted the urge to scoff. She was sore all over and covered in her own blood. Though she'd almost caught a bullet in the skull. And she guessed she had

Church to thank for the fact that she was still breathing at all.

He ended the call and stowed the phone in his pocket, lifting his arm and circling it, grunting a little as he did.

'You okay?' Jamie asked.

He grunted a little more.

'What'd Hallberg say?'

'She's coming.'

'What else did she say?'

'Not much.'

'How'd they find us so fast?'

No answer seemed to mean he didn't know. Jamie could guess – satellite imaging, phone tracking, maybe they'd been followed since the hotel. She hadn't seen anyone tailing them, but she guessed that meant they were good at their job. Which they'd have to be considering the show they'd put on at the hotel.

But why go through all that trouble? If they wanted Alina, why not take her last night? Jamie didn't have an answer to that one. Not yet, at least.

Church paused at the main road through the village, then made a beeline for the pub on the corner.

Jamie followed as he pushed inside, the interior dim and cool, empty.

The landlord, an older man with white hair, was leaning on the bar reading a paper.

'Not open yet,' he said.

'Not drinking,' Church replied.

The landlord stood up, ready to say something else, but seeing the scrapes and scratches on Church, and Jamie's bloodied face, he seemed to forget what he was going to say. 'Hell,' he said then. 'You two okay?'

'Car accident,' Church said flatly. 'Waiting for the RAC. Mind if we sit?'

The man faltered and Jamie wondered if anyone ever had the balls to say no to a man like Church.

He gestured to an empty booth then. 'Get you anything?'

'Water's fine,' Church replied, giving a brief nod of thanks.

''Course. Bathrooms are, erm ...' He pointed to the left of the bar. ''Case you want to get cleaned up.'

Church gave another nod, then headed for the booth. Jamie elected to use the bathroom, and when she got in there she saw herself in the mirror for the first time and realised just how bad it was.

There was a matching cut on her top and bottom lip, just in from the corner where a knuckle had landed. And the result was a purple bruise that looked like she'd been punched, along with blood all across her cheeks and mouth where she'd wiped it.

'Fuck,' she muttered, bending at the sink and splashing water on her skin. It stung and she swore more, dabbing at the cut gingerly.

The door squeaked then and she looked up, seeing

the head of the landlord in the gap, a hand pressed to his eyes to cover them. 'Sorry to bother you, miss,' he said. 'You decent?'

'Yeah,' Jamie replied, a little thrown by his visit.

He lowered his hand, eyes honing in on the bruise on her cheek. It dawned then.

'Not my place, I know,' he started, 'but I've been in this job long enough to know a mark like that when I see one. Big fella, your husband ...' The quiver in his voice told Jamie he felt being there was a risk. 'You want me to call someone? The police, or ...? I can be discreet, like?'

Jamie smiled, then winced, the fresh edges of the cut pulling. 'Thanks, I appreciate that, but ...' She pulled her own badge then – Swedish NOD. 'I am police.'

The man squinted at it. 'Oh, right,' he said. 'So ...'

'It wasn't him,' Jamie replied, dipping her head at the wall and the bar beyond. He nodded, seemingly relieved. 'But someone did ...' He touched the corner of his mouth.

'Yeah, unfortunately.'

'Right. And who ...?'

Small town nosiness at its finest. Probably the most interesting thing to happen this year was Jamie and Church walking in here.

She just did her best to smile. 'I can't really discuss that. Active case. You understand.'

'Right, right, yeah,' he said. 'Active case.' He winked at her then. 'I get it. So ...?'

'I'm serious,' Jamie said, walking towards the door now. 'I can't talk about it.'

He laughed a little. 'Right, of course, apologies.'

Jamie reached the door then.

He was still blocking it.

'You mind?'

He pushed it wide for her and she squeezed past him at the threshold, wondering why the hell he didn't just get out of the way.

She headed to Church's booth, noticing him sitting there, hands clasped, eyes closed. Meditating? Just thinking? Sleeping? He might as well have been made of wax.

Jamie slid into the booth.

'He ask if I hit you?' Church said, without warning.

'You heard?'

'No,' he replied. 'But I saw the way he looked at your face, then at me. And then he wasn't exactly stealthy about slinking off towards the women's bathroom.'

'You didn't think that was suspicious?' Jamie retorted. 'Some stranger following a woman into the women's bathroom?'

His eyes opened slowly. 'If that was the case – you wouldn't have needed rescuing.' He looked at her for a moment, then closed his eyes again.

Jamie didn't know whether to be flattered or not.

She didn't think it was a compliment. Or at least, it didn't feel like it.

Church parted his hands and then rested them on the table flat, taking slow breaths.

'So, we're just waiting?'

More silence.

Jamie's knee bounced impatiently. Every second they wasted here, Alina was further and further away. They should be out there, looking for her. They knew the direction they went. They could get a car, head that way, stop at every town and village, see if anyone'd seen a black SUV tearing through.

Church seemed entirely unphased by it all. By the attack, by his Land Rover getting totalled and rolled into a ditch. By everything.

'Why?' Jamie asked then, the word coming before the thought fully formed.

'Why what?'

'Why help us? Why answer Hallberg's call and get involved in this? You have no stake in this case, you don't care what happens to Alina.' Just sitting here, clearly, he didn't give a shit. 'Was it the money? How much are you being paid?'

'I didn't discuss a fee,' he replied evenly.

'So, what is it then? Hallberg said you banked a favour for doing this. So, what is it? Why are you here?' She tried her best to keep a lid on her frustration. Actually, that's a lie. She didn't. Her words were biting.

He opened his eyes now, let out a long breath, and looked right at Jamie, his gaze unflinching and heavy. 'I don't like people who fuck with children.'

She wasn't expecting that. Her eyebrows raised in surprise. 'You don't like people who fuck with children? That's your answer.'

He leaned forward a little. 'My answer is that the world is full of people who do what they want without repercussion. They exploit, and they hurt, and they do evil, evil things that you can't even comprehend.'

'Oh, I *can* comprehend.'

'Maybe. Maybe not. The deeper you dig, the worse it gets. And for a long time, I thought I was on the right side of it all.'

Jamie looked at the SAS tattoo on his forearm, lifted her chin at it.

He didn't deny that's what he meant.

'But even what I was told. What I thought was right. People still got hurt. And the ones that needed protecting weren't protected.'

'So, this is all some benevolent mission for you? Righting the world's wrongs, one at a time?'

'This is me taking the chances I have to hurt the people who deserve it. People like this – like the ones who came after you ... They came after me. My family. They tried to hurt them. I didn't let it happen. I hurt them back.'

'Hallberg said you left a trail of destruction in your wake.'

'I did what I needed to. But one good thing doesn't erase a lifetime of averting my eyes.'

'So now you're, what, a vigilante? Some angel of death swooping down on the bad guys?'

'No,' he said, seemingly not appreciating the comparison. 'I just don't like people who fuck with children. Who do bad things to those who can't defend themselves. Because that's who they prey on. The weak. The vulnerable.' He closed his eyes once more, went back to his breathing. 'I am neither of those things.'

Jamie clenched her jaw, watching him. She didn't like vigilantism. It came with wearing a badge. But she'd done plenty of things that her employers had condemned. That hadn't been lawful. She'd always walked that line between right and just. Could she really judge this man for knowing which side he fell on?

'What are you doing?' Jamie asked. 'Meditating?'

'I'm thinking.'

'About what?'

'Everything.'

Jamie scoffed. 'Sure.'

'Everything we'll need to do.'

Jamie thought on that. 'We? You're sticking around? You're going to help get her back?'

He didn't respond.

'Church?'

'I'll try.'

'How?'

'Jesus Christ,' he said then. 'Don't you ever shut up?'

'Not when someone's life is hanging in the balance, someone I care about.'

'Then it's going to be a *very* long few days.'

'Yeah,' she said, glowering at him. 'Sure seems like it.'

CHAPTER
NINE

t seemed like it took Hallberg a very long time to arrive.

When she finally walked in, she seemed a little taken aback by the tired interior, though she shrugged it off quickly and approached the booth with a sizeable tablet in one hand, and her phone in the other.

She slid in opposite Church. 'Well, I hoped I wasn't going to see you two again so soon.' She looked at each of them. 'Still in one piece though?'

'Did you find her?' Jamie asked immediately.

Hallberg stared back for a second before answering. 'No. We put out word to every local police force, ordered road blocks, scoured the crash site of the first vehicle ... but nothing. Looks like they picked up their dead or wounded, then torched the car and left. It was just a burnt out wreck by the time we got there.'

'So, she's gone?' Jamie asked.

'For now. But we'll find her. I promise.'

'How?'

Hallberg looked at Church for a second, then back at Jamie. 'It's what we do, alright? I know that it's not what you want to hear, but—'

'Not what I want to hear? They fucking *took her,* Julia. Gone. Disappeared. Who knows what the fuck they're doing to her right now—'

But before she could say anything else, Church took her by the wrist and squeezed, hard enough that it hurt.

She shot daggers at him, but he didn't seem phased.

'Calm down,' he said.

She felt her cheeks flush, anger flooding through her. She made an attempt to pull her hand free, but his grip was iron.

'Stop,' he said again, voice cold.

'You stop. Get off me.'

He tightened his grip. 'Be smarter, then.' He seemed to read in her face that the comment only made her angrier, because he gripped even harder, so much so that Jamie thought her wrist was going to snap in two.

She hissed suddenly, holding out as long as she could before her other hand leapt instinctively to his, trying to pry his fingers off.

He released, keeping his gaze fixed on her.

'Control yourself,' he ordered. 'You want to find her, don't attack the people trying to help you.'

She massaged her wrist, glaring at him.

Hallberg cleared her throat. 'So, uh ... I do have something.'

Jamie turned back to Hallberg, feeling Church still watching her, her fingers still throbbing. He'd have broken her wrist, she thought. Without hesitation. And she got a sense then of just how dangerous he was.

'The guy who attacked you,' Hallberg went on, tapping the screen on her iPad. 'Well, I did some digging, made some calls, and ... He's been on Interpol's radar for a while.'

'How long's a while?' Jamie asked, still holding her wrist.

'Uh ... Forty years. Give or take.'

'Did you say forty?' Jamie practically scoffed.

Hallberg nodded. 'He goes by the name of The Nhang.'

'Nhang.' Church repeated the name, pursing his lips in thought.

'It's a mythical creature from Armenian folklore. A river-dwelling serpent monster that can shape shift and drinks the blood of its victims.' She looked up at Jamie. 'Of course, the real Nhang is just a man. But this symbol?' She turned the tablet around to show Jamie a photograph of the same symbol drawn on her door now scrawled on a wall somewhere. 'It's been seen dozens of times across four different continents and four different decades. We know of at least thirty deaths connected to this case file.'

'Shit,' Jamie breathed. 'And now this lunatic is after us?'

Hallberg looked at Church, then back at Jamie. 'Well ... *you.*'

Jamie closed her eyes. 'Why me?'

'Because you disrupted the Armenians' operations, and embarrassed Petrosyan.'

'So, he hired The Nhang to kill me?'

Hallberg just nodded. 'Seems like.'

'And what's with the drawing, the symbol? A calling card?'

'It's a mark. From the reports on file, it seems like his MO is to get close to begin with, and then place this symbol as a way of ... *starting.*'

'Starting what?'

She seemed to fish for the words. 'The ... game? The hunt? I don't know.'

'The game? Doesn't seem like a very fun fucking game,' Jamie growled.

'No, but ... that's what he does. He likes the thrill of the chase. He puts down this sign, and ...'

'You run.' Jamie let out a long breath. 'We did exactly what he wanted.'

'We couldn't have known.'

'I should have.' Jamie cursed herself.

'It's a good thing,' Church said.

'How exactly is this a good thing?' Jamie asked.

'We know he's coming. If he gets off on the hunt, on

watching the light go out behind your eyes ... Then we can use that.'

Jamie thought on it. He'd waited for her to look up when he'd pointed the gun at her. He'd waited for her to realise she was dead. He'd wanted to see that look on her face. Jesus. Was he that sick? Was that what this was? Did he just enjoy it that much?

'Look,' Hallberg continued, 'this guy's going to keep coming. That's what he's paid for. And wherever this sign pops up, there's bloodshed. He's well-versed, well-connected, and he's ruthless. And he won't stop until you're dead. We need to bring you in. Full protective custody, get you out of the country. The whole thing,' Hallberg said decisively.

'No.'

But the word didn't come from Jamie. It came from Church.

Jamie and Hallberg both turned to look at him.

'We don't run.'

'You have to,' Hallberg said.

'He's our best bet to find the girl and deal a blow to these people.'

'I agree,' Jamie said quickly.

'He's going to come to us. And when he does, we capture him, and we interrogate him. We make him give up the girl, and the people he's working for. And then we get them, too.'

'That easy?' Hallberg asked. 'Damn, wish we'd

thought of that. We should just capture and question the bad guys. It's so simple.'

'Glibness doesn't suit you,' Church replied flatly.

Hallberg gathered herself. 'Sorry, I just ... Do you know how frustrating it is when your friends actively *try* to get themselves killed?'

'I'm not dead yet,' both Jamie and Church said in unison. And then glanced at each other.

'You rehearse that?' Hallberg laughed.

They looked away.

Church clasped his hands in front of him. 'Let him come to us. We'll be ready this time. And he's weak. I shot him.'

'You shot him?'

'Just in the shoulder,' Church said. 'But it should slow him down a bit. If he's as smart as you say, he won't act rashly. He'll wait until he's ready to fight.'

Hallberg bit her lip.

'We have time,' Church assured her. 'And in the meanwhile, we should focus on getting the girl back. They wanted her alive, so that means she's still alive. The question is why, and where.'

Hallberg looked at Jamie and then Church. 'I'm not even going to bother arguing. Trying to do it with *one* of you is exhausting enough. Both of you just being in the same room is already giving me a headache.' She started tapping and flipping through pages on the tablet, looking for something. 'We don't have any leads on Alina, but through our interviews with the other girls rescued from the water treatment facility, the footage you captured, and the money trails, we have managed to connect the Armenians' operations to a charity organisation with their headquarters in Cardiff.'

'A charity?' Church muttered. 'Typical. Let me guess, for war orphans in the Middle East? Cleft palates in the Yemen?'

Hallberg straightened a little. 'Victims of child slavery and trafficking.'

Church scoffed now; the first real show of emotion Jamie had seen from him. He folded his arms and sat back in the booth.

'Fucking animals,' he growled. 'Spitting right in our faces.'

Jamie tried to keep herself calmer, aware that Church seemed to be watching her. And she wanted to avoid another slap on the wrist – literally. She cleared her throat. 'So, what's the plan?'

'Hassan has been running down leads as part of his investigation, and he managed to find a woman working inside the charity who's willing to cooperate – an event organiser and PR liaison. Apparently, she's known something's off for a while – misappropriated funds, off-the-books vehicles and properties, the usual corruption bullshit. And when she tried to take it up the chain, they paid her off. Took care of her mortgage, sent her on a three-month holiday to the Caribbean ...'

'And she didn't think that was suspicious?'

'She called it a *lapse in judgement,*' Hallberg said.

'Took the money first, and then I guess by about week eight of lying on a beach sipping rum from a coconut, the guilt started to kick in. Maybe she thought, *hey, maybe these greasy fucks lining their pockets with the charity's money aren't such stand up guys after all.*'

'Does she know the full extent of what's going on?'

'I don't think so,' Hallberg said, shaking her head. 'But Hassan's had no trouble twisting her arm. Even an accessory charge in a trafficking case like this means serious jail time. And hell, even if we don't get that to stick, embezzlement is no joke. And, let's put it this way, she's not exactly cut out for jail. And she'll do anything she can to avoid it. Hassan's had her digging into the charity's hidden finances and dealings, and let's just say that she's coming up with gold.'

'Why didn't you tell me about this this morning?' Jamie asked.

'This morning Alina was safe. Now, she's not. And if there's any chance of getting her back ... I think this is it.' Hallberg reached out and touched Jamie's hand.

She held her fingers. 'Okay. So, what's next?'

'She's cautious,' Hallberg said. 'Rightly so. She knows who she's working for now. And she knows she's being watched. So, you're going to have to meet her in person. Somewhere a conversation won't seem out of place. We can't reach out to her beforehand, but we know where she's going to be, and when.'

'Where?'

'The charity is throwing a fundraising gala this

weekend. Hassan was supposed to meet with her there, get the next load of data. She's supposed to hand over a USB stick to him with the charity's financials. But it's just a simple drop. I can sub you in.'

'To a charity gala?'

Hallberg nodded. 'Yeah, just approach her, thank her for hosting and all the work she does, give her the key phrase, take the USB. Hopefully, you'll have a minute or two alone with her. Explain the situation, ask for her help. Maybe she can point you in the right direction. Give us something.'

Church spoke now, arms still folded. 'Sounds like a lot of *maybe* to hinge this whole thing on.'

Hallberg offered a shrug. 'We're trying. But these guys are slippery. And they're smart. They've had this operation going for who knows how long and we didn't even know it existed until six weeks ago.'

Church grunted a little.

'I think it's a good plan,' Jamie said.

'It sounds like it's our only plan,' Church muttered.

'If she doesn't know anything, you get out of there, we go through the data. And we're one step closer anyway.' She shook her head, almost apologetic. 'I'm sorry, that's all I have.'

'No, no,' Jamie said, squeezing her hand. 'It's great. It's something. It's a start.'

'It's thin,' Church said, leaning his elbows on the table, wringing his hands under his bearded chin. 'But it's something. And something is better than nothing.'

He looked at Hallberg. 'But there's still one more thing.'

'What is it?'

'You bring your Interpol cheque book?'

'Cheque book?' Hallberg asked, brow furrowing. 'Why?'

'Because you two,' he said, pointing at Jamie and Hallberg. 'Owe me a car.'

CHAPTER
TEN

The Park Plaza Hotel in Cardiff was just a few minutes from the National Museum, where the Stand Against Child Slavery fundraising gala was taking place.

Hallberg already had eyes inside, watching through the security cameras, making sure that the place was free of any significant Armenian presence – which it was – but also, that their contact was there. Caroline Lewis was fifty-two years old, with curly chestnut hair and bright red lips. It was hard to miss her in her long, red ballgown, diamonds sparkling on her neck. Nothing says 'save the kids' like amuse bouche on silver platters, champagne on ice, and a bunch of rich people standing around discussing the best way to dodge taxes.

But they weren't here to tear down the capitalist agenda, they were here to make contact with Lewis and find out where Alina was.

There was a knock on Jamie's door.

'Two minutes,' Hallberg said.

'Okay, one sec,' Jamie replied. She'd been standing in front of the mirror in her hotel room for nearly half an hour now, ready, but completely unprepared.

They'd given her a black gown – an 'A-Line' Hallberg had said. It had a split neck that revealed her breastbone in a way that Jamie did not like. She preferred that part of herself to be covered by a ballistic vest, and at the very least some sort of clothing. The dress pinched in at her waist, and then billowed over her hips. It made a swishing sound as she walked, and dragged on the floor unless she was in heels. Which they insisted on.

Her split lips were covered by makeup and a dark lipstick. Hallberg's handiwork. You couldn't even notice now.

Jamie didn't like it, but she knew it was necessary.

If the Armenians were also watching, this had to look right. Nothing out of place. They had to blend in.

And that meant an A-Line and heels.

Jamie tugged at the fabric, puffed a strand of curled hair from her face, and then muttered to herself. 'Screw it.'

She headed for the door and pulled it open.

Hallberg was leaning against the opposite wall. She stuck out her bottom lip, then nodded. 'Good.'

'Good?' Jamie asked.

'You want a better compliment?'

'I want to be wearing running shoes and underwear that isn't halfway up my—'

She cut herself off as the door next to Hallberg opened and Church stepped into the hallway in a tuxedo, fiddling with his cuffs. He paused upon seeing Jamie and stared at her for a moment. Then he looked at Hallberg, nodded in approval. 'Good.'

'Good,' Jamie repeated. 'Good. Everything's good. Can we go now?'

'Relax,' Hallberg said. 'People are supposed to enjoy these events, alright? You're going to have to smile.'

Jamie pulled as wide a grin as she could.

'You just look constipated,' Church said, straightening his jacket.

'This experience is about as unpleasant,' Jamie answered, dropping the smile. And then she pulled up the front of her dress and headed for the lift.

THE WALK WAS SHORT, AND AS SOON AS THEY left the Plaza, Hallberg peeled off and headed for the surveillance vehicle parked down the road from the museum.

As Jamie and Church walked, they fell into step with other gowned and tuxedoed guests. They all sauntered, arm in arm, laughing and smiling, rich in every way, here to have their egos stroked by other sycophants.

As Jamie judged them, she felt Church scoop her

arm from her side. She pulled it away but he held tight and after a moment Jamie just relaxed and let him have it. Just for appearances, she thought.

He had his arm crooked at the elbow, Jamie's laced under it, pinned gently against his ribs.

They approached the steps and took them slowly. Jamie was still sore from the crash, but Church helped her stay steady, keeping his head turned towards her a little, bracing her weight on his arm as she managed her way upwards.

Despite the fact that he'd been *flung* from the wreck as they tumbled, he seemed ... fine. Or at least he was better at hiding it than Jamie. Though she suspected his training had taught him to endure pain.

The steps weren't long, but it seemed to take an age to reach the top. And when they did, Church stepped ahead and then turned so he was facing Jamie.

He reached upwards and lifted her chin gently so he could get a better look at her lips. A slight nod seemed to signal that he was happy that the cuts weren't visible, the bruise adequately hidden by the makeup.

'Ready?' he asked.

'Yeah,' she said, sighing a little.

'Nervous?' He smiled, amused.

'I'd take a shoot-out or a high-speed car chase any day over this shit.'

He chuckled slightly. 'Just try and enjoy it. Fancy food, expensive drinks. Pretend to be normal for a night, huh?'

'Nothing about this is normal,' she muttered, watching the guests filter in around them.

'True. But it's the job – good days and bad. It's a far cry from Kisangani or Kandahar, I know that much.' He stared over Jamie's head at the city behind them. 'Remember the pass-phrase?'

'How was Maria's wedding?'

'Good.' Church nodded. 'Ready?'

'Guess so.'

'Alright then. Shoulders back, chin up. And smile.'

Jamie obliged him.

And they went in.

THE LOBBY WAS ABUZZ WITH PEOPLE STANDING around, sipping champagne from flutes, chatting and mingling as the staff ushered them slowly into the main hall.

Church led Jamie inside, showing their tickets at the velvet rope, and then stepping deeper into the lion's den.

In the centre of the room, a long-necked dinosaur's skeleton was on display, looming above the partygoers. For a fundraiser meant for victims of slavery, it sure did look like an excuse to drink and rub shoulders with rich friends.

Jamie wanted nothing more than to be out of her dress, and out of there.

'Any sign of her?' she asked impatiently.

'Not yet,' Church said easily. 'Let's do a loop, keep things relaxed.'

They made their way through the crowd, with Church plucking bites of food off every passing tray, slotting them between his big teeth and seemingly swallowing them without chewing.

'Hungry?' Jamie asked.

'Always,' he said, taking a pair of champagne glasses off a tray. He handed one to Jamie.

'I don't drink.'

'I know. Just hold it.'

He knew? How?

Church guided them around the dinosaur, casually surveying the room, and drew up next to a pillar. He positioned himself so he could easily see half the room. While standing opposite, Jamie could see the other half.

There seemed to be no sign of Lewis yet.

'How did you know I don't drink?' Jamie asked, turning the glass slowly in her hand.

Church took a sip from his. 'I checked up on you. After Hallberg called me and made me agree to babysit you.'

Jamie didn't know which she disliked more – that he'd looked her up, or just referred to her as requiring babysitting.

'So, you know all about me then?'

'I know enough,' he said, glancing at her briefly.

She narrowed her eyes. 'What's that supposed to mean?'

He just smiled. 'Honestly, nothing. I just like to know what I'm getting myself into before I get into it.'

'And what were you getting yourself into taking this job?'

'A mess. They seem to follow you wherever you go, don't they?'

Jamie's grip tightened on her glass.

'You don't like to stay put. I know that much. Don't like to put down roots, make too many friends or attachments.'

'You can spare me the psychoanalysis.'

'It's not an analysis, just an observation.' He sipped his champagne, watching her over the rim of the glass. 'And nor is it a criticism. It's smart. Serves a purpose.'

'And what purpose is that?' Jamie asked, trying not to sound too blunt.

He chuckled through closed lips. 'Now you're asking for the psychoanalysis?'

'Just curious as to how you think you know me so well.'

'Oh, I don't,' Church said, eyes fixed on Jamie. 'I don't think anyone knows you. I don't think anyone could. And if they tried, you wouldn't let them.'

She squirmed a little, clearing her throat and looking away, folding her arms tightly.

She noticed Church noticing her do that and promptly unfolded them. She didn't want to give him any more ammunition. She needed to turn the tables. 'What about you, then? Ex-military, SAS, right? How did you end up on Interpol's radar? Hallberg said you worked together?'

'Not exactly. I was ... *working.* Interpol were ... aware of the situation. Hallberg and I crossed paths. She didn't like what I wanted to do, but I think she realised that there wasn't much she could do to stop it. So, it was more of a mutual courtesy. I cleared the path, and they ... laid the road.'

Jamie stared at him. 'I have no idea what any of that means.'

'Good.' He sipped more champagne. 'You're not supposed to. Just know that Hallberg trusts me, and that should be good enough for you.'

'Mm. Weirdly, when someone says 'trust me', I tend to do the exact opposite.'

He chuckled again. 'Funnily, me too.' He lifted his glass to cheers her then. 'To getting fucked over by the people we trusted the most.'

Jamie lifted her glass, almost reluctantly, and the two flutes *tinged* off each other.

She couldn't figure him out. She felt like she knew so much, but so little about this man. And in that moment, she rolled everything over in her head that she knew. About who he was, how Hallberg had described him, what he'd mentioned. Kandahar and Kisangani ... That was in ... Africa, right? DRC, maybe? Jamie wasn't sure. He'd been deployed here there and everywhere, it seemed. Betrayed by those he trusted the most ... His own team? He said that he had cleared the path and

Interpol had laid the road. That he'd not worked with Hallberg and Interpol, that she hadn't liked what he wanted to do. But that they couldn't stop it. So, had he done something that Interpol couldn't? Hallberg said he'd left a trail of destruction in his wake. But what, where, and why? He was trying to right wrongs, rebalance the cosmic scales ...

Jamie's head spun with it all.

What had he said in the pub? That he didn't like people who fucked with children. That he'd seen some heinous shit, thinking he was on the right side of it. But he wasn't.

She doubted that asking would gain her anything. All she could hope for was to piece together more about him as they went.

Jamie didn't especially like putting her life in the hands of a stranger. But she already knew him to be capable. And despite herself, and knowing nothing about him, she did trust him. He didn't seem like the sort of man who could be bought or swayed. He was on his own track, and she doubted anyone could sway him from it. At least without killing him.

'I think I see Lewis,' Jamie said then, the chestnut hair swimming out of the crowd, her bright red dress a beacon in a sea of black and white.

'Alright then,' Church said, turning and standing next to Jamie. He lifted his arm for her. 'Shall we?'

She hesitated for a moment, looked up at him, smiled, and then took it.

CHAPTER
ELEVEN

Caroline Lewis was beset with potential donors, so Jamie and Church queued up, shuffling forward with the procession until they neared the front, watching as sequinned and perfumed gentry shook hands, thanked her for her work, waited to be thanked for their money and generosity, and then headed off to discuss the best ways to evade taxes or which Cayman Island was the best for real estate investment. Or whatever it actually was that millionaires discussed.

They were in front of Caroline Lewis then and the woman looked at them each in turn, a little thrown. Perhaps she could smell it on them that they didn't belong here, that they were imposters. Like an antelope drinking at the creek does a log that isn't really a log.

Jamie extended her hand. 'Caroline,' she said warmly, familiarly.

The woman shook Jamie's hand, putting on a forced smile.

'It's been so long,' Jamie said brightly. 'How are you? How was Maria's wedding?'

Lewis faltered for a second, then realisation dawned. 'Oh, right, yes. Of course,' she said. 'The wedding was wonderful,' she replied, a slight waver in her voice. As she spoke, she reached down and opened the flap of her clutch bag, reaching inside. 'The ceremony, it was, uh …' She began to stammer as she rummaged.

'Just lovely, I imagine,' Jamie interjected. 'Understated but elegant, knowing Maria. I'm sorry I couldn't be there.' Jamie watched as she withdrew something from the bag and held it tightly in her fist. 'I'm sorry, how rude of me,' Jamie said then, 'this is my …' She looked up at Church, deciding what to call him, lie or otherwise.

'Husband,' he said fluidly. He reached out his hand to shake Lewis'. 'John Jones.'

Lewis once again hesitated, but then took his hand.

Church grasped it with both hands, allowing her to release the USB stick into his grasp.

He withdrew it, pocketing his hand casually. 'This is a beautiful venue,' he added, looking around.

'Yes, yes,' Lewis said, clearing her throat, a little more at ease now but still clearly rattled. 'After you've made the rounds,' Church said, playing his part brilliantly, 'we'd love to bend your ear for a moment about a potential business matter. If you would be amenable?'

Lewis looked at the few people standing behind Jamie and Church, deciding whether she wanted to, or more likely, if it was within her power to turn down the invitation.

Jamie and Church's wide smiles and unflinching looks seemed to signal it wasn't a polite request.

'Sure,' she said. 'As soon as I have a moment.'

'Great,' Jamie said. 'We'll just be right here.'

She and Church stepped away, staying in earshot of Lewis, but moving far enough away that they could speak without being overheard.

'You get the USB?' Jamie asked.

His eyes widened. 'What? No. I thought you were getting it?'

Jamie had a flush of panic before she saw the corners of his mouth curl up and realised he was joking. 'Asshole,' she muttered, shaking her head.

'I got it, don't worry,' he said easily. 'That's the first part done with.' He glanced around casually. 'Security doesn't seem too tight, honestly,' he said. 'Couple of bouncers. Can't see any of our Armenian friends.'

'Don't speak too soon,' Jamie said. 'I'm sure they're around.'

He shook his head. 'Don't think so. They wouldn't want to draw attention to themselves, not now at least. Not with so many eyes watching. They'll be tightening up on all fronts. I wouldn't be surprised if they pulled the plug on this whole thing.'

'The charity?'

'Sure. Snakes live under rocks. And when you flip a rock on them, you know what they do?'

Jamie shrugged a little.

'They slither under a different rock.' He made a little snaking motion with his hand. 'They don't like the light. And if you want to keep them in the light, make them fight. You gotta be fast, get them by the tail.'

'That method served you well in the past?'

'I'm still standing here, aren't I?'

'And the snakes you've faced ... they're not?'

'Standing?' He laughed. 'No, not many of them. And the few that are, are now doing it inside a six-by-six box, shitting in a bucket.'

Jamie looked up at Church, trying to envision the things he'd seen. She'd like to hear about them, she thought.

'We're on,' he said then, nodding at Lewis, who was excusing herself from her meet and greets, looking at Jamie and Church as she did.

They started walking, following her as she strode towards the back of the room, under the stone arches and towards a secluded corner of the main hall.

Once they were out of the public eye, Lewis' nerves became all at once apparent. She looked drawn suddenly, shadowed and graven, eyes bagged, the skin around her fingers raw from nervous picking.

'What?' she asked quickly. 'What now? I did what you asked,' she said, looking from one to the other. 'I can't do any more. If they find out, Jesus – if they find out what I'm doing. They'll kill me. You understand that? Do you?'

Church quelled her with a motion of the hand. That, and the look in his eyes.

She clammed up pretty quickly.

'This is about something else,' Jamie said. 'A girl.'

'A girl? I don't know anything about a girl,' Lewis said. 'I don't see any of the ... the *kids*.' She found the word tough to say, the reality of what she was helping cover up starkly apparent when she mentioned the victims themselves.

'She's an integral witness to the investigation, but they ... took her back,' Jamie said. 'They came for her. And we don't know where they're holding her.'

'And you think I do?' Lewis' eyebrows raised. 'Everything I could get is on that stick I gave you. Now, I have to get back before—'

Another of Church's Jedi hand waves kept her where she was.

'Anything will help,' Jamie said. 'You must know something – somewhere they might be holding them. A vehicle they use. The name of someone involved. Someone who might know more.'

Lewis kept her mouth shut, hoping her silence would reiterate how little she knew.

Jamie was losing patience. 'I know you know what they're doing. That they steal children, and that they force them to fight. To the death. Children, killing each other for sport, while you're sunning yourself in the Caribbean.'

Lewis flushed with shame.

'And if you think what's on this USB stick is enough to exonerate you, then walk away. But even if it is, and you get away with what you've done – are you ever going to sleep at night? You're going to be called to the stand to testify when this goes to court. You're going to have to tell Interpol *everything* when they get you in a room. So, if there's anything you know now, tell us. You can help the children you condemned, save their lives. Save one that's hanging in the balance right now. Think, Caroline. There must be something. Anything that can help us. Just put us on the right track. Do that, and I'll make sure that Interpol know you did all you could to help us. And you'll know that you did everything you could, too.'

As Jamie finished speaking, she was aware of Church watching her.

Caroline hung her head, shaking it gently. 'I don't know. I … just … the only thing I can think of … Hell, I don't even know what it means. I think it's a name, maybe? I heard one of them talking in the office once – on the phone. He kept saying it, he sounded angry. I picked up a few words here and there, you know?'

'What is it?' Jamie urged her.

'He kept saying *"vortegh e"* – Armenian for "where is" – but the next word, I didn't recognise. It was *vira … vira … virabuyzh,* I think. I'm not sure. But maybe it's something? I'm really sorry. I ... I have to go. Good luck,' she said, ducking past them and into the light.

'Virabuyzh?' Jamie repeated back.

Church seemed to be racking his brain but coming up with nothing.

'What does that mean?'

'I don't know,' he said, 'But Hallberg will.' He looked over his shoulder. 'You get your fill of duck pate and seared scallops? Think it's time to go.'

Jamie took one last look at the crowd, clad in their designer suits and dresses, dripping with jewellery and diamonds worth more than the children they were here to save would see in their entire lives.

'Strangely,' Jamie said, meeting Church's eye. 'I'm not hungry.'

CHAPTER
TWELVE

They slipped from the party quickly, heading back towards the hotel. Church clutched Jamie's arm tightly, head on a swivel. Jamie followed suit, making sure they weren't being followed or watched.

Across the street, Hallberg stepped from the surveillance van and began walking parallel with them in the same direction.

Once they were far enough away, she crossed the street, leading them by thirty feet or so, and entered the hotel.

She held the lift open for them to get in, and they rode up together, exiting onto the floor with their rooms.

Church flashed his card against the reader and they went in wordlessly, waiting for the lock to click before anyone spoke.

Jamie immediately kicked off her heels and sat on the bed. Church loosened his bow tie and undid the top button of his shirt.

Before Hallberg asked, he was already presenting her with the USB.

She took it and nodded, then folded her arms and looked at Jamie. 'So?' she asked.

Jamie thought for a moment, rolling over the words that Caroline had given them. 'She swore she didn't know anything, but when we pressed her, she said 'Vira-buyzh.'

'*Virabuyzh,*' Church corrected her.

'That's exactly what I said,' Jamie clapped back.

He just lifted his eyebrows slightly and averted his eyes.

'Virabuyzh?' Hallberg repeated back, making sure she had it right. She put her hand to her mouth, looking pensive.

'You know the word?' Jamie asked.

Hallberg just shook her head.

'She said she overheard: *vortegh e virabuyzh.* Though I doubt I'm saying it right,' Jamie added.

Hallberg looked at her. 'Where is ...' She pulled her phone out and began typing, sounding out their mystery word as she went. She seemed to land on a list of words and scrolled through them, pausing at one. '*Virabuyzh.* Surgeon.' Hallberg looked up again. 'Where is The Surgeon?'

Everyone looked blank. But Jamie's blood had run cold. The Surgeon? Only one person leapt to mind. One name. Elliot Day. The serial killer who'd claimed dozens of lives. Jamie's first murder case, and a man that had plagued Jamie for years. Who'd stalked her and nearly got her killed multiple times ... But who'd also saved her life multiple times. He was a bad smell she couldn't shake, a shadow following her everywhere she went. Cropping up again and again, wreaking havoc in her life and twisting her arm every time he did. She knew things about him that would put him in prison for life ten times over. But he also knew things about her that would have her stripped of her badge and never working in law enforcement ever again. Hell, she'd probably never see the outside of a jail cell ever again too if he spilled his guts.

They'd never been partners, but reluctant allies several times. Much to Jamie's chagrin. Though working with him was like knowingly infecting yourself with a disease. A deadly one. He worked his way into your system like a parasite, eating you away from the inside, weakening you until you were just vulnerable for him to strike.

The danger with Elliot was as much mental as it was physical.

She dreaded crossing paths with him again; mainly because he seemed to have an unhealthy obsession with Jamie. Some sort of fixation, this twisted idea that they were one and the same. That they were ... meant to be. Or some sick shit.

'Jamie?'

She looked up at Hallberg.

'You okay?'

'Yeah, why?' Jamie asked, smiling.

Church interjected. 'Because you look like you just smelled some actual shit.'

'You were ... grimacing?' Hallberg added. 'That name, The Surgeon. It mean something to you?'

It couldn't be Elliot Day, could it? He couldn't be involved in this? With these people? Of course not. And yet ... He had cropped up in Sweden, working with the Russians, his fingers in their trafficking operation, hired by some high-ranking Bratva to do an organ transplant and save his life ... And the Armenians were connected with the Russians, two Bratvas at the fighting ring. Fuck.

'Jamie.' Church snapped his fingers in front of her face. 'What's with you?'

'I don't ...' she began. 'I don't feel well. Uh ... I think ...' She stood suddenly, a little wobbly on her feet. Her knee jerk had been to fake sickness, but she did actually feel nauseous at the thought of Elliot Day being back in her life. 'I think I need to go to bed.' She didn't wait for a response before she ran out of the room, fumbled her key card from her stupid little handbag with shaking hands, and let herself into her own room.

She told herself she was wrong. It couldn't be him. It couldn't.

And yet, as Jamie threw herself onto her bed and buried her face in her pillow, she could only think one thing —

Knowing her luck, it would be Elliot Day.

And that was only going to make things worse.

CHAPTER
THIRTEEN

J amie decided that burying her head in her pillow would be the best way to survive the night. But she just tossed and turned, snatching sleep here and there.

She rose before the sun came up and changed into her running gear, needing to clear her head.

Out of the hotel the air was cool and she felt like she could breathe. She didn't know the area well, but she let her feet guide her, thoughts of Elliot swirling in her mind.

She cut through Bute Park and ran the River Taff until Castell Coch rose on the hill above. She slowed as she reached it, taking it in, resting her hands on her hips. The sun was coming up and she felt sore all over, still battered from the accident in Church's car.

Images of Alina burnt in her mind, anger coming with them. The face of The Nhang filling her vision.

The darkness of the barrel of his gun. Alina's screams as they took her away.

Her lip quivered, and despite the pain, she ran on, fuelled by it.

An hour passed before she got back to the hotel, sweating and hot. She'd not outrun her mind, but she'd gained some ground on it. Some perspective. If it was Elliot, then so be it. She'd faced him before, and she would again. And, hell, her old partner may not have seen through his lies, his act. But Church would. And he'd kill him where he stood if he needed to.

That pleased Jamie somewhat.

By the time she got back to her room, there was a sticky note on her door that just said 'Need You' – JH. Julia Hallberg.

Jamie paused, turning to Church's room. She hovered at the door for a moment, hearing voices inside.

No time for breakfast then she thought, before she ducked into her own room, showered, and practised her shocked face for when Hallberg inevitably said the name Elliot Day.

She thought it looked sincere. She hoped Hallberg would too.

Though every time she practised it, it seemed to get worse, so she just took a few deep breaths and decided to cross the bridge when she came to it.

She was at Church's door all of a sudden then and knocking.

Hallberg opened it almost instantly and beckoned her inside, where she found Church and another man sitting at the desk opposite the bed. There were no less than three laptops in front of him and he seemed to be flitting from one to the other as he worked.

'Where'd you go?' Hallberg asked, breezing past Jamie and back into the room.

'Just got a run in,' Jamie said, playing it off as nothing.

'Everything okay?' Hallberg stopped and looked at her. She knew Jamie, knew her well enough to know that a dawn run meant she hadn't slept, that something was on her mind. Why did she have to surround herself with damn detectives?

'Yeah, just ... worried about Alina, that's all,' Jamie said. Luckily it was the truth. She hoped she was okay, was trying to convince herself of Church's intuition, that they wanted her alive and well. But that hope was waning by the day. It was all she could do to put it out of her mind.

She could feel Church watching her closely, great arms folded, eyes like little diamond-tipped drills, boring into her, searching for the truth.

She did not elect to look at him, instead targeting Hallberg, hoping that pushing the conversation onwards would take the pressure off her.

'Found anything about this mystery figure?'

'The Surgeon?' Hallberg asked. 'Yeah. We made

some calls, scoured our records and files, and dissected everything that Caroline Lewis gave us.'

'And?'

'We've pieced some stuff together – The Surgeon doesn't seem to have a name, or at least not one that we know. He's referred to by the moniker in several languages; cropping up mostly in Russian, Arabic, Armenian, Turkish. That seems to be his operating area. Though there have been whispers of him appearing in South America, even Japan and China. There's been chatter about him for the last few years now, though who he is we can't say. He flies under the radar, seemingly has ins and outs for every country; slips through the nets without detection, appears for a job, then melts into the night like he was never there.'

Jamie tried to keep her voice even as she asked the next question, each piece of information sounding more and more like Elliot Day to her. 'What kind of jobs?'

'Uh, surgeries, mostly. Unsurprisingly. A high-ranking Bratva gets stabbed, needs life-saving care, so up pops The Surgeon in Moscow. A Turkish businessman drinks himself into liver failure, then gets a new one inserted. A Yakuza boss takes a bullet to the spine and needs a miracle. Enter The Surgeon. You get the idea.'

'Mhm,' Jamie said, looking pensive, Church's gaze still weighing on her. 'So, what do the Armenians want with him?'

'Lewis came up with the goods – their phone

records, emails, texts, and search history have allowed us to compile a picture of the work that he's doing. Seemingly keeping their prized fighters in fighting condition.'

Jamie swallowed.

'We know of the network of fights here, but it's not limited to the UK. Every high-ranking scumbag seems to have a stable of fighters and they get traded, bought, sold like cattle. The Surgeon seems to be on retainer and his presence was requested in the UK. We're not sure why, but—'

'It has something to do with Alina?'

'We can't say for sure,' Hallberg admitted. 'But to bring in The Nhang to go after you and bring Alina back, and to call The Surgeon in at the same time? Seems a little like coincidence. And like you always said, a leap and a lead—'

'Are only one letter apart,' Jamie finished for Hallberg, remembering it was something her dad always said. She didn't realise Hallberg had taken it so to heart.

'Did you find anything else out about Alina? You said you weren't sure her story added up – do we know why she's so important to these people?'

Hallberg just shook her head. 'The girl's a blank spot in our information. She doesn't exist. Or at least, Alina doesn't.'

Jamie paused for a second, unsure what Hallberg meant. She seemed to read that in Jamie's face.

'There's a good chance Alina isn't even her real name,' Hallberg said.

'Why would she lie?' Jamie asked.

'Why does anyone lie about their name? They want to conceal their real identity. But if that's the case, and she lied to us ... We should try to figure out why that is. The Armenians obviously know more than we do about who this girl really is and, hopefully, we can find out what they know once we get hold of some of them.'

'So, what's the plan?' Jamie asked. 'What do we do now?'

Hallberg sank onto the bed and rubbed her eyes. Jamie noticed how tired she looked, wondered if she'd been up all night working on this. She wouldn't be surprised.

'We still don't know where the leak came from that led to The Nhang tracking you to that hotel. So far, no one's burst through the door here trying to kill you, so we can assume everyone in this room is safe. But the jury's still out on Klaus here,' Hallberg said, pointing at the guy in the chair. He stopped clacking on his keyboard and looked over his shoulder at Hallberg, then Jamie, eyes wide. 'Jesus, Klaus,' Hallberg said. 'I'm kidding. Go back to work.'

She shook her head at Jamie.

'Klaus was born without a sense of humour,' Hallberg added. 'But he's a damn good intelligence analyst.'

Klaus cracked the tiniest smile, but kept his eyes

focused on his screen. That comment probably made his whole week.

'As such, we're going to keep this whole operation in the dark. Far as Interpol know, we're still just data gathering. They know that the Armenians snatched Alina, but since then I've given no updates. Far as anyone knows, you're still in hiding with Church here,' Hallberg said, hooking a thumb at him.

He was a statue, arms folded, eyes still on Jamie. She felt like she was under a spotlight.

'And we're going to keep it that way. We think we know how to reach out to The Surgeon, and since he's already in the country, maybe a lucrative offer might lure him out of the shadows. We can set up a meet, and then you and Church grab him.'

'Simple as that?' Jamie asked, a little sceptical.

'The Armenians don't know we know this guy even exists. So, we play it carefully, make him an offer he can't refuse, and then once he's in play, all you need to do is subdue him.' She looked at Church and then at Jamie. 'You two can handle that, right?'

'Then what?'

'Then, you can ask him some questions. He'll know where Alina's being held if our theory holds up. So, if you ask nicely, he might tell you.'

'Ask nicely,' Jamie parroted back. 'Right. And you're okay with that? With this being ... need to know? Unofficial?'

Hallberg let out a sigh. 'No, but the last time we did

it officially, you almost got killed. Twice. And a girl got captured to be sold back into slavery. So – and excuse the language – but *fuck* official channels. You never much subscribed to them and you always got the job done, right?' She looked at Jamie.

'I don't know if I'm the best example to follow,' Jamie admitted.

'Well, then you make the call. You know where I stand.' She fished her phone from her pocket and held it up. 'Either we do this quietly, and stand a chance of it actually working. Or we call it in, and roll the dice on it getting back to the Armenians before we can get The Surgeon, and have him slip through our fingers. And ... if that happens ... I don't have any more rabbits to pull from hats on this one. I think we'll be pretty much done at that point.'

All eyes seemed to fall on Jamie.

She knew Hallberg was right. Call it in and The Surgeon would never show. They'd never get a chance at him again, probably.

But if they did this under the table, and by some miracle they were able to contact, and then meet him ... well, there seemed to be a very distinct possibility that Elliot Day would walk through the door. And then what?

Would he help Jamie get Alina back?

Would he kill Church if he tried to grab him?

Would he refuse to help Jamie out of sheer professional courtesy to the sick fucks that hired him?

A wheel of possibilities spun in her head.

But she knew that it was the only choice they had.

'Put that away,' Jamie said, nodding at Hallberg's phone. 'Reach out to this guy, set the meet.' And then she finally turned her eyes to Church, who'd not stopped watching her the entire time. 'We'll do the rest. Right?'

'Right,' Church replied, stare intensifying such that it made Jamie squirm. 'You can trust us.'

But despite the positive words, Jamie couldn't help but feel like that was a question for her.

Or, worse – an accusation.

CHAPTER
FOURTEEN

Hallberg's humourless analyst managed to find a web address from the data that Lewis provided that led to an old web forum whose primary concern was cabinet restoration. This was the method of contact for The Surgeon, and a deep dive and scrape into the history of the site revealed a pattern that Klaus, an apparent savant, had no trouble cracking. Handle replacements, hinge repairs, framing work, shimming ... they all had specific connotations and related to specific procedures, while the gauge of screws and hardware referred to the time frame and urgency of the matter at hand.

Once a suitable cabinet question had been formulated, it was posted.

Jamie was in her room, rolling over in her head all the possibilities of what was going to happen when she saw Elliot Day again, while they worked their magic.

She didn't know if it was going to take days or weeks, but considering it was a relatively small procedure – an appendectomy – they hoped for a quick nibble. The story was that a criminal wanted by Interpol on drug trafficking charges was in the country illegally after a drop, and was suffering from appendicitis. He was due to leave on the boat he came in on, but the trip back to South America was too long to risk the trip pre-surgery. Unable to go to a hospital, he needed the procedure done quickly, and quietly. Money was no issue.

They hoped that this may appeal, and it seemed like it did. Because just a few hours after it was posted, they got a message from a newly registered user – the same MO that had been used multiple times before. The users could delete their accounts, remove their posts. But they couldn't erase the digital footprint left behind. Apparently, Klaus was very good at this sort of thing, and was practised, too. Shitbags used defunct forums like this all the time for communicating about nefarious things in mundane ways.

So, though Jamie was surprised when Hallberg called her back into the room, no one else was.

She walked in and found Church in the same position he had been earlier, arms folded, gaze still fixed on Jamie. Though she'd been alone for hours, he'd not come in to speak to her, to say what seemed to be on the tip of his tongue.

'Meet's set,' Hallberg said without wasting time. 'We have an apartment here in the city that's owned by

Interpol. It's not currently in use, so we can utilise that. We already sent the address to The Surgeon. No response, but that's typical. You and Church need to head over there and wait. He could show at any time, so best to just be there. We don't want to miss him.'

'Uh,' Jamie said, looking at Church. 'Okay then.' She tried on a brief smile but Church just sort of bunched his lips disapprovingly. 'I'll get my stuff together.'

Jamie exited the room, feeling his eyes on her, and headed back to her own. When she got inside, she leaned against the door, shaking. She tried to steel herself, clenching her fists, willing the blood to flow through them. She could feel it, thundering in her veins, making her fingers vibrate and stiffen. Her chest constricted, choking the air from her, her heart beating fast and light. She gasped short, stunted breaths, dizziness coming.

And then there was a banging right behind her skull. Someone knocking on the door.

She swallowed hard, lurching from it and turning. 'One second,' she squeezed out.

The knock came again.

A deep thudding she knew had to be Church.

And making him wait would only make things worse.

She reached for the handle and opened it, knowing there was no hiding what she was feeling – which she was pretty sure was a panic attack. Or a heart attack.

She almost favoured the latter. It seemed preferable to facing down Solomon Church.

The door swung inward to reveal him, standing there, staring down at her.

He stepped inside without invitation and closed the door behind him.

'Sit down,' he said to her, taking one look at her flushed cheeks and hammering pulse. 'Before you fall down.'

Jamie couldn't really speak, and certainly not in a way cogent enough to lie. So instead, she backed up and sat on the bed, clenching her fingers into the fabric.

Church disappeared into the bathroom and ran the tap, appearing a moment later with a glass of water. He handed it to Jamie and then pulled the chair out from under her desk and sat on it, leaning forward so they were face to face.

'In-two-three, out-two-three,' he ordered her. 'Small sips.' He snapped his fingers in front of her then to get her attention. 'Look at me, talk to me, it'll take your mind off it,' he said, the words far from soothing.

Jamie just nodded, her jaw aching. Yep, panic attack.

'What do you know?' he asked.

She took a sip, trying to speak. 'I don't—'

'Don't lie to me. Don't insult me.'

She stared at him, then nodded.

'What's going on? The second Hallberg said the words 'The Surgeon' last night, you damn near keeled over. You know this guy?'

Jamie bit her lip, wondering if she could lie, but knew she couldn't. 'I don't know,' she croaked, drinking more water. 'Maybe.'

'Maybe? Who is he?'

She let out a long, shaky breath. 'I'm not sure, but ... he could be someone from an old case. My first murder case when I was working for the Met. Homeless people were going missing, a teenager had turned up dead, murdered. It was a rough investigation, but eventually we tracked it back to a guy called Elliot Day. A doctor who was supposedly helping homeless people, but he was actually just sizing them up, and ... and he was killing them. Kidnapping them and ... and selling their organs,' Jamie said, the words coming fast now, and sickening as they were to say, each one was an ounce of weight off her chest. 'He slipped through our fingers and disappeared before we could get him. But then, he came back.'

'He came back? Came back how?' He seemed to read the pained look on her face. 'Tried to kill you?'

'No, no,' Jamie said. 'He tried to ... help.'

'Help how?'

'I was working a murder – a sex worker gunned down in London. She escaped from the brothel she was working at after falling pregnant with the child of a wealthy John. They found her, and killed her. I'd never even have known about the case if Elliot hadn't contacted me about it. It led down a rabbit hole, trafficking, corruption inside the Met, the whole thing.'

Jamie collected her thoughts for a moment as Church listened. 'He ... he tried to help. Or at least I thought he was helping. But he led me into a trap, set me up, almost got me killed. Then, swooped in, saved me. They had me tied to a chair, and—' She cut herself off suddenly.

'And what?' Church asked.

'I just ...' Jamie blinked a few times. 'I've never told anyone this. Jesus. No one even knew I was there.' She shocked herself, revealing that. 'He ... he came in, and killed a detective inspector. Shot him, right in front of me. Saved my life. But ... fuck. I ... I never told anyone that.' She looked up at Church, as though for some confirmation that her secret was safe, but he was stoic. Unphased, seemingly.

Jamie cleared her throat a little. 'He disappeared on me again then, but came back, again. And again. The last time I saw him in the UK was four years ago. I was in Scotland, on leave, getting my shit together. I held a gun to his head, and told him I'd kill him if I ever saw him again.'

'But you didn't pull the trigger.'

'No,' Jamie said, taken aback by the bluntness of his words.

'Hmm,' Church said, sitting up and shrugging a little. 'You don't point a gun at someone unless you're ready to pull the trigger.' His eyes flashed then. 'Were you?'

Jamie dodged the question. 'He left. As I told him to.

But then, in Sweden, a few years later, my partner and I were tracking down a missing person. Turned out to be linked to a bigger case, being handled by Interpol, linked to human trafficking again.' She elected to leave out the fact that he showed up at her house, posing as her half-brother to ingratiate himself with her partner. 'We managed to find the missing woman, but in the process we crossed paths with Elliot Day again. We ... we got captured, held ... the people behind it all ... they tried to ... they tried to hunt us. Like animals.' Jamie's mind cast back to it, and frighteningly, the thought of what had happened seemed to alleviate her anxiety, not deepen it.

'But Elliot Day saved you,' Church said, nodding.

'That's right.' Jamie watched him, looking for some sort of hint that he already knew that.

'Lucky guess,' he said, as though reading her mind. He rubbed his hands along his thighs. 'And you think The Surgeon is him. Which means that when he shows up and sees you ...'

Jamie didn't know what to say.

'This is the part where you tell me what's going to happen so I don't get killed expecting something else.'

'I don't know what's going to happen,' Jamie said truthfully. 'But I know he's dangerous. I know he's smart. I know he's ruthless, and he kills without remorse.'

'And that he's in love with you.'

Jamie stiffened, the anxiety flooding back. 'What?'

'He's clearly in love with you. Why else would a wanted murderer on the payroll of the worst people in the world betray them? Why would he knowingly put himself in danger by reaching out to a police officer when he's being hunted? There's only one thing that drives a man to do something that stupid. And that's love.'

Jamie set her jaw, not saying a word.

'Okay,' Church said, letting out a long breath, slapping his thighs. 'Do you love him?'

'No,' Jamie practically scoffed.

Church had stilled all of a sudden. 'Do you love him?'

Jamie looked right at him. 'No,' she said more firmly.

'So, if he pulls something and comes at me, and I have to put a bullet in him, are you going to do something dumb?'

'No.'

'I don't believe you.'

'I won't.'

'You'll let me shoot him?'

'The idea is to capture him.'

'That's the idea, yeah. But things don't always go to plan. They rarely do, in fact.' He lowered his head to catch her gaze. 'So?'

'No, I won't stop you.'

'Good. And if we do capture him, and I have to hurt

him to get the information we want. Are you going to stop me?'

'Trust me,' Jamie said, 'if there's anyone that wants to cause him physical pain, it's me. I'll be the one twisting the knife, I promise you that.'

'Mmm,' Church said, seemingly unimpressed. 'Remember why you're doing this. Think about it while you pack. Think about Alina.' He gestured to her clothes on the bed, and then he got up and headed for the door. He slowed halfway there, and turned back. He stood in silence for a few seconds, as though thinking about what to say. Or maybe just whether to say it. Then he sighed, softening, becoming human.

'Life is messy,' he said. 'We don't get to choose how we feel. But when the time comes, and you have to make a choice, you can't let your emotions get the better of you. You just can't. You have to think. And you have to act. There's no time for feeling. You're smart, Jamie. And I hope you stay that way.' He opened the door then, turning away. 'Alive, and smart.'

And then he left Jamie alone.

With thoughts of Alina.

And thoughts of Elliot.

CHAPTER
FIFTEEN

Jamie stepped from her room feeling tired.

Church was standing there, duffle bag in hand, waiting for her in the corridor. 'Ready?' he asked.

Jamie just nodded and followed him down the corridor. He seemed to know where he was going, so Jamie didn't ask, just walked with him. Into the lift. Out of the lobby. Onto the street and right.

There were people around, milling through the city as they do. Going somewhere, anyway. Everyone living their own mundane lives, oblivious to the darkness, the evil threaded between them. Oblivious to the killers and rapists that wore skin suits and looked at them like prey. Oblivious to the human traffickers and slavers who thought of people as objects to be used and traded. Oblivious to the man and woman, walking silently, headed for an Interpol safe house where shortly a serial killer would arrive, be subdued, and then be tortured.

Jamie grimaced, sliding past a group of women out to get an early start on a hen do. She guessed that's what it was because they were wearing cheap paper glasses in the shape of erect penises, their eyes staring through the testicles, the ... thing ... stretching up their foreheads, veins and all.

Church cast her a quick glance, cracking a smile at her discomfort as they ploughed on wordlessly.

They covered the ground quickly, arriving fifteen minutes later. Church headed for the stairs and Jamie followed. They went up, and up, and up, headed for the third floor, and then stepped into the corridor. It was clean but dated, the apartment two doors down on the right.

Church lifted the lid of the keypad and entered the code Hallberg must have given him.

It beeped and then swung inwards, revealing a sparsely decorated apartment. Ikea furniture, plastic plants, nondescript art on the wall. Some random abstract thing that reminded Jamie of water, and a pot of flowers. Original.

It smelled like no one had been there in months. But Jamie still hoped there was coffee.

She headed for the kitchen and began rummaging, finding an old bag eventually, and a dusty cafetiere. She set about making a pot, aware that Church had pulled up on the small breakfast bar separating the compact kitchen from the rest of the one-bedroom apartment, and was once more watching her.

When she turned back, his elbows were rested on the surface, his hands clasped loosely under his chin.

'It's rude to stare,' Jamie said. 'Your mother never teach you that?'

'I find it an effective method,' he replied coolly. 'You see a lot when you really look.'

'I don't know what else it is you want to see. I told you everything.'

'If you say so,' he said.

'So, what are you looking for?'

'Maybe I'm just looking.'

Jamie locked eyes with him, his unflinching gaze unnerving more than anything else. The way a wolf just stands and watches its prey.

'You want a cup, at least?' Jamie asked, filling the kettle with water from the tap.

'I'm good,' he said. 'Caffeine makes me jittery. I want to stay clear for this.'

'Well, I'm going to have one,' Jamie said, turning back to the counter and muttering under her breath. 'Think it's the only way I'm going to get through the day.'

THE NERVES JAMIE FELT GREW AND DISPELLED like the ebb and flow of waves. Rolling over her and then drawing back. After the coffee, she paced the apartment, checked out the books on the bookshelf, then looked around the apartment again, before eventually sinking into the sofa and picking up the TV remote.

While she'd walked around, Church had laid out their plan. It was simple, but effective, and not up for debate. Jamie would answer the door when he arrived, inform The Surgeon that the patient was in the bedroom, and upon entering, Church would subdue him.

Jamie told him that the plan was stupid. If it was Elliot, he'd never fall for that. That, upon seeing Jamie, he'd immediately know it was a trap. In which case, Church said that she should pretend it was just her in the apartment, the whole thing a ploy to see him. That she should lure him inside, get him talking, relaxed, off guard, and then Church would jump him.

Jamie told him that plan was *also* stupid.

But she didn't have a better one, and Church was adamant that whoever this person was, he could take him.

Jamie had seen Elliot do some impressive things physically, but she'd studied martial arts, and she knew one thing – size does matter. Big beats fast nine times out of ten. And Church was both big, and fast, and skilled, and pretty fucking scary. So, Jamie didn't really think he'd have much trouble.

Still ... she was under no illusion that Elliot wasn't supremely dangerous. And when it came to a viper versus a lion, she didn't know who her money was on.

And though the hours ticked by slowly, when there was a knock at the door it seemed to be entirely too soon.

Jamie sat up on the sofa suddenly, turning to face the door.

Church pulled back from the window, arms folded, and looked at Jamie. He gave her a firm nod, and then headed for the bedroom, stepping inside and pulling the door to the jamb.

Jamie wiped off her sweaty palms and stood, heart pumping hard.

She headed for the door, wondering if this was going to be Elliot.

Hoping it wasn't.

Knowing it was.

She stood at the door and pulled in a shaking breath, doing her best to calm herself.

She reached for the handle, gripped, and then pushed down, pulling the door towards herself.

Her eyes widened.

Elliot?

No. Not Elliot. Not even close.

Elliot was in his forties, tall, lithe, with sandy hair, green eyes.

This man was in his sixties, the same height as Jamie. He was clearly Middle Eastern, with a bald head, grey hair around his ears, and thin, round glasses perched on his large nose.

He was wearing a brown jacket and a rumpled shirt, a leather doctor's bag in his grasp at his side.

It took Jamie a moment to gather herself. 'H-hello,' she stammered.

The man looked her up and down, keen eyes narrowing behind his glasses. He looked past Jamie into the apartment, leaning out a little to see past her shoulder. 'The patient?' he asked, his voice accented.

'Right, right, of course,' Jamie said, still a little thrown. She pulled back from the door, pointing to the bedroom. 'He's in there.'

The little man stepped inside cautiously, looking around. 'How did you know to contact me?' he asked then, not proceeding far enough so that Jamie could close the door behind him.

'I, uh ... I didn't. My husband, he made a call, and one of his contacts gave him the information,' Jamie said. 'I just followed the instructions.'

The man nodded slowly. 'Your husband.'

'That's right.' Jamie watched him.

He removed his glasses slowly, folding them and tucking them into his jacket breast pocket. 'The message said he was your boyfriend.' The man's head turned and he looked at Jamie, his dark eyes, now naked without his glasses, were lifeless and cold.

Something glinted in his hand.

Jamie caught it just out of her periphery, dancing backwards on sheer instinct and reflex just as the scalpel whipped through the air, missing her throat by an inch.

It sailed under her chin and she stumbled, hitting the wall behind her, swearing as her head thudded against it.

Her eyes went to the open door and she threw her foot out, kicking it closed just as The Surgeon came at her again.

Jamie threw up an arm block, the scalpel coming down, aiming for her face, his wrist impacting on hers.

He grunted, dropping his case, and slung a punch with his other hand into Jamie's gut.

She wheezed, doubling, and then lashed out with a front kick to give herself some room.

The Surgeon stumbled back and Jamie wound up, stepping forward and throwing her weight into a spinning kick, heel leading right at The Surgeon's temple.

But he was fast, and Jamie was used to throwing that higher, at taller opponents.

The Surgeon ducked under it and then wound up to come in for another attack.

But before he could, the bedroom door opened to Jamie's right and Church came charging out.

He dwarfed The Surgeon, who tried to redirect his attack now.

Church's arm cocked back and then shot out. He drove his open palm through The Surgeon's wrist, the scalpel flying through the air and landing behind him.

In one swift movement, Church swept behind him

and scooped him up, tangling his neck in his thick arms, pinning him in place in a fierce choke hold.

Jamie watched, thinking that was it. No escape from the death grip.

But then The Surgeon's hand was in his jacket, then flying through the air.

It whipped over his head towards Church's face. He swerved the blow, The Surgeon's hand striking him on the trapezius muscle.

Church grunted loudly and when The Surgeon's hand came away, Jamie could see a syringe sticking out there, the plunger sunk to the barrel.

The big man swore loudly, loosening his arms for fear of more tricks, and grabbed The Surgeon by the back of his jacket before he could get away, stepping forward and throwing him into the middle of the room like a rag doll.

He tumbled through the air, letting out a little squawk of shock, and then disappeared headfirst over the back of the sofa, landing with a loud thud that sent the coffee table skidding across the floor.

Jamie and Church stood still, waiting for him to get back up. Waiting for a sound to emerge. But there was nothing.

'Mother fucker,' Church said, grabbing the syringe and pulling it free of his neck. He tossed it on the ground, cupping the injection wound with his opposite hand, and then lumbered forward, swaying as he did.

Jamie walked forward too, until she could see the

soles of The Surgeon's shoes sticking up in the air, his body sprawled awkwardly over the cushions, head pinned to the ground by his own weight, neck at an awkward angle.

There was a dark pool of blood slowly seeping into the carpet beneath his head.

Jamie swallowed as Church reached out and poked his shoe.

The man's foot waggled limply, but he didn't move or respond.

'Shit,' Church muttered.

'He's dead, isn't he?' Jamie sighed.

'Pretty much,' Church replied, his speech slurring a little. He drew his hand away from the injection site and looked at it. 'Well, fuck,' he said, turning his head to look at Jamie.

And then his eyes rolled into the back of his head and he collapsed where he stood, rolling onto his back at Jamie's feet, breathing softly.

She put her hands on her hips, looking down at him, his chest rising and falling steadily, a soft snore escaping his lips.

'You said it,' she muttered, looking at the sudden carnage around it. 'Well ... fuck.'

CHAPTER
SIXTEEN

Church came to with a start.

He sat bolt upright on the floor with a gasp of air so sudden it made Jamie jump.

He looked around, instantly alert and ready to fight.

But there was no one to fight. Just Jamie sitting at the breakfast bar eating a bowl of granola, and a dead Middle Eastern man wrapped up in an area rug with a bin bag over his head to stop his blood going all over the floor.

'Sleep well?' Jamie asked, crunching her granola.

'What the fuck?' Church asked, rolling onto his hip and getting to his feet. He wobbled a few times then steadied himself. He rubbed his shoulder where he'd been injected and hissed a little at the pain. He looked at Jamie then. 'Didn't think to call someone?'

'You were fine,' Jamie said, fiddling with the screen of her phone. She was playing chess. And losing.

'I was fine? Pretty sure I collapsed after being injected by a mystery substance. That might be cause for concern for some people,' Church said, seeming a little peeved. He leaned against the sofa, rubbing his head. No doubt the drugs were still riding in his system.

'I checked the doctor's pockets after you went down. Found a little bottle – Amobarbital. I looked it up. Just a sedative,' Jamie said, taking the computer's rook. And then immediately losing it. 'Like I said – you were fine.'

Church didn't respond to that, but instead looked at The Surgeon. 'Did you call Hallberg?'

'No,' Jamie said.

'Why not?'

'Because I didn't think that telling her that you threw our one lead on the Armenians into a coffee table like a rugby ball, promptly cracking his skull and breaking his neck, within thirty seconds of him walking in the door ... was a very good idea.' Jamie looked up at him. 'Do you?'

Church grumbled a little. 'He was littler than I thought. Lighter. I didn't mean to throw him that hard.'

Jamie closed the app, her king firmly in check and her defences seriously overwhelmed, and then got up. 'But you did. And you killed him.'

'You don't sound too upset about it,' Church answered, homing in on her.

'Oh, I am,' she responded. 'But I've had a few hours to think about it. To process it. And I may or may not have kicked you a few times in the ribs to let off some steam.'

Church rubbed them instinctively.

'And now ...' She stopped in front of him. 'And now ... we're pretty much fucked.'

He began reaching for his phone. 'Better get this over with then.'

Jamie reached for his hand. 'No. We're not calling Hallberg. Not yet.'

'Why not?' Church's brow crumpled.

'Because ... we still have another option,' Jamie said, sighing.

'And what option is that?'

She struggled to say it. 'Elliot Day.'

'Your psycho-stalker boyfriend?' Church was genuinely surprised.

'He's not my boyfriend.'

'But he is a psycho stalker, and a serial killer.'

'Yes,' Jamie said. 'But ... He's also a very skilled surgeon who's well known by the same undesirable sort that hired this motherfucker.' She pointed to their dead guest. 'The same undesirable sort who are now without a doctor, and will no doubt be looking for a suitable replacement.'

It clicked for him. 'You want to contact him. Play him against the Armenians.'

'I don't *want* to. But seeing as you killed our actual lead, I don't see we have much of a choice. Interpol doesn't have a photo of The Surgeon. They don't know who he is or what he looks like. Who's not to say that it was Elliot Day that walked through that door.' Jamie lifted her chin towards him. 'That we didn't manage to broker a deal with him, and get him to help us.'

'You think he will?'

'If I ask nicely he might,' Jamie replied.

Church's knee bounced as he mulled it over. 'And we don't tell Hallberg about this?'

'That we killed someone in an Interpol safe house? No, I'd rather not. I'm not sure it's something that she could easily keep to herself. And we're supposed to be doing this quietly. Far as I'm concerned, this guy never existed.'

Church bit his lip, thinking. 'You give your word you won't say anything?'

'I don't need any more professional embarrassments. And I'm very good at keeping secrets.' Jamie kept his stare.

'Okay then,' Church said, getting to his feet slowly. 'So, what should we do about the body?' His eyes slowly turned to the man in the rug.

Jamie laughed a little, clapping him on his huge shoulder. 'Oh, that's for you to figure out,' she said, heading back to finish her granola. 'You're the one who killed him.'

CHAPTER
SEVENTEEN

Jamie didn't know how long it took to dispose of a body, but Church seemed efficient about it.

He left after dark, then returned an hour later, came inside, picked up the body, rug and all, slung it over his shoulder wordlessly, and then walked out.

Jamie watched him do it, but didn't ask. But nor did she offer to help.

Though, after he left, she was a little worried that he'd been caught lugging a dead body through the streets of Cardiff.

Eventually though, well past midnight, he returned, slick with sweat, his hands black with dirt, and let himself into the apartment, scowling.

'All okay?' She was still awake, waiting up for him. Or the inevitable call from Hallberg asking why Church had just been arrested.

'Nghh,' was all she got in reply as he headed for the bathroom.

Jamie heard the shower turn on and the shower curtain slide across.

There was a gentle thud as Church climbed in and steam began to drift through the slightly open door.

Jamie approached cautiously, hanging back at the jamb. She knocked lightly on it, leaning against the wall facing into the living room. 'What happened?' she asked.

'Took care of it.' The response was blunt.

'How?'

'Does it matter?'

'Just want to know whether you dumped him in the bay or just left him in an alley?'

'Neither,' he said. 'Buried him.'

'Where?'

'The woods.'

'How'd you get there?'

'Stole a car.' His voice got more frustrated with each answer.

'How'd you bury him?'

'What's it matter?'

'I just want to know how likely it is that he's going to be found.'

The water creaked off and Church stepped from the shower, pulling the door open swiftly afterwards. He was wrapped in a towel, still scowling.

There was a large burn scar across his chest and

onto his right shoulder. His left was decorated with a sizeable tattoo. Jamie thought the style was Japanese, a large tiger crawling down onto his chest. His skin was a patchwork of scars. It had seen mileage, but still looked strong.

'He won't be found,' Church said flatly.

Jamie opened her mouth to speak, to ask how he could be sure, but he cut her off.

'Because that's not the first body I've buried. And the others haven't been found yet. That's how.' His voice was brittle. 'Now, I'm going to bed. You're on the couch.'

And with that, he strode into the bedroom and snapped the door shut behind him, leaving Jamie standing in a puddle of water.

JAMIE COULDN'T SLEEP, BUT SHE NEVER COULD when she worked. Though she seemed to have forgotten that when she was working in Sweden. The last year she worked for the National Operations Department, she was hunting down serial killers, but she'd been detached from it. She was running a team, telling people what to do, where to go. She was free to think and to work how she wanted. And, as terrible as it sounded, she really didn't care about the victims all that much. The job pleased her. It made her happy. Because catching bad guys and solving puzzles really checked all her boxes. It rarely got her heart racing, but it was enough. She was detached. Without a partner. Without friends or family around. And for the first time, she'd been content. Just floating, skimming through life. And she was sleeping well.

But now, with thoughts of Alina running through her head, blood on her hands from her own actions over the last month and a half, she was back to tossing and turning.

So, after a few minutes of sleep here and there, Jamie got up. Knowing what she had to do, but dreading it.

She had no way to contact Elliot. Not directly. No phone number or email address, nothing. But Jamie knew that he knew where she was. That he was keeping tabs on her. He'd found her in the depths of Sweden. And it was the *depths*. A place you could barely even find on the map. And you'd have to squint to do it. But he'd shown up at her door like it was nothing. Same with Scotland, where he'd cropped up in Machir Bay, the furthest, most remote reaches. But he'd found her. He always would, she thought. All she had to do was call out for him.

She thought Facebook might be too on the nose. Especially seeing as she didn't have it.

Where did women go these days when they wanted to find a specific man?

The question was which dating site would be the right one. It seemed ludicrous that it would even work, but underestimating Elliot was the thing that tended to betray people. So all she could do was try, and see. And cross her fingers. Which were already hovering over the keyboard. She googled the biggest sites, then headed to the number one hit. It felt alien. She'd never online dated. Never dated, actually. Kjell Thorsen, her old partner, was the closest she'd come to a relationship in … years.

Jamie and stable romantic entanglements didn't really mesh well. She wasn't … easy to be with. That much was clear. Everyone seemed to detect that fact from the off, and have no problem vocalising it. And not being able to keep a professional partner, let alone a life partner, reassured her of that. Not that she wanted one anyway. She was happy being alone. The thought of worrying about someone else all the time seemed exhausting. She couldn't believe anyone wanted to do that. That they knowingly entered into the agreement that you'd consider someone else's feelings at all times. That you'd alter your life, shape your decisions and choices around what someone else wanted. God, it sounded awful. And massively inconvenient.

'Woman seeking man …' Jamie typed as she reached the part entitled 'What are you looking for in an ideal partner?'

She paused, then hit backspace. Fuck, this was harder than she thought. Okay, keep it simple.

'Tall …' she wrote, thinking about Elliot. 'Doctor. Uh … serial killer?' She cracked a smile, then deleted that last part. 'Tall doctors who …' She thought of the perfect line then. Something Elliot never failed to remind her of when they saw each other. 'A tall doctor. Someone who knows the real me.'

That'd get his attention.

'About you … What are your best qualities?'

Jamie thought on that, then sighed. The list was apparently very short. 'I can run a twenty minute five-K.' She nodded to herself. 'That'll do. Next … What's your perfect first date?'

Oh fuck. Skip? *"Fields cannot be left blank."*

'You're fucking kidding me,' she muttered. 'Okay … uh … You cooking me dinner in my apartment,' she typed, mouthing the words. 'After you broke in there,' she said, not writing that part. True story though.

She waded through the endless boxes, grabbing her personnel photo taken for her ID at the NOD as her profile picture – not flattering, but it didn't really matter. And then she entered the dating pool as Jamie J.

'And now we wait …'

Her running shoes called to her from the sofa.

So she closed her laptop, got up, put them on, and hit the road, doing her best to outrun the terrifying idea of inviting Elliot back into her life.

And the wholly unwelcomed feeling of nervous excitement that came with it.

CHAPTER
EIGHTEEN

By the time Jamie arrived back at the apartment, Church was already up and cooking what seemed to be a twelve-egg scramble in the biggest pot in the cupboards.

It looked like he'd nipped to the shops while Jamie was out. But she wasn't complaining. She was hungry.

'Smells good,' she said, pausing before she headed to the bathroom to shower.

Church kept facing the cooker. He didn't reply.

Okay then, Jamie thought, sighing a little.

She showered quickly, but by the time she came out, Church had already finished eating. He'd left her a bowl though – filled with scrambled eggs and avocado slices.

At least he knew how to look after himself. Though he was nowhere to be seen to be thanked, and with the bedroom door closed, Jamie figured he must be in there.

There wasn't a whole lot to do but wait. She guessed

Hallberg was giving them time to break The Surgeon, but eventually she'd call for an update. And Jamie really hoped she wouldn't have to lie when that call came. That she'd have an answer for her.

She sat on the couch, her laptop open on the coffee table in front of her, dating site open, inbox being refreshed every few minutes.

She never watched TV, but there wasn't much else to do right now, so she threw on a documentary about doping in road cycling, trying to keep her mind occupied, but becoming more and more aware of the fact that this plan was paper thin and about as flimsy.

Several times the computer pinged with an incoming message, but each time it wasn't Elliot. Just some random man offering to cook her dinner in her apartment – as she put as her first date – which she was now regretting. Or it was some inappropriate line about her claim to be able to run a twenty minute five-K. The worst one was; *"Five kilometres in twenty minutes? You must be fit ... but I bet I could still wear you out! And it'll definitely last longer than your runs ...'*

Deleted and ... blocked. Sorry, Phil. You're not the one I'm looking for. And also ... yuck.

When Church walked in the front door, Jamie was surprised. She thought he'd been in the bedroom this whole time.

He approached the sofa and paused behind it, a shopping bag in his hand. He took one look at the TV screen, and then at the laptop screen.

He hummed disapprovingly. 'Looking for love?'

'Looking for our replacement surgeon.'

'On match-dot-com?' He raised an eyebrow. 'And how's that going for you?'

Another ping went off and Jamie glanced at it briefly, trying not to sound too dejected. 'Early days yet.'

'Mm. Fending off the masses I see,' he said cuttingly, nodding at the inbox that now had *one* new message in it.

'I've been deleting them as they come in,' Jamie replied, a little defensively.

He scoffed a little. 'Internet dating,' he muttered, folding his arms. 'Pile of shit.'

'Lemme guess, you like to woo women at bars by buying them drinks and feeding them lines?'

'That how I strike you? As the kind of person who cruises bars looking for women?'

'I honestly hadn't thought about it. But now that I am, no, probably not. You're not exactly a strong conversationalist, you know?'

'People talk too much, generally. They like the sound of their own voice. Silence is beautiful. As is solitude.'

'Ah, so you *want* to be alone. Congrats, you're doing all the right things to stay that way.' She gave him an emphatic thumbs up, wondering how this conversation had got so bitter so quick.

'You must be rubbing off on me,' he replied without

missing a beat. 'I hear you're a pro at keeping people away.'

'Years of practice,' Jamie responded. 'Suits me just fine.'

'Great. Least I know we're both aiming for the same thing then.'

'To go our separate ways and never see each other again?' Jamie harrumphed. 'Oh yes. Since I met you, I've been in a car accident, had a gun put to my head, and killed a man.'

'You're forgetting it was your impetuousness that put that psycho on our trail – and got us run off the road, and got my truck wrecked in the process. And I think you're also forgetting that I *saved your fucking life*. Twice.' He counted them off on his fingers. 'Once at the side of the road. And then again last night!'

'Last night?!' Jamie almost yelled. 'You broke his fucking neck! You threw him into a goddamn coffee table!'

'You were about to take a scalpel to the fucking jugular!' Church began to rise now too, his voice booming.

'I had that firmly under control,' Jamie protested. 'I certainly don't need you to protect me.'

'No? So what the hell am I even doing here? Because that's the *exact* reason that Hallberg brought me into this. To protect you and the girl.'

'And a phenomenal job you've done of it.' Jamie

looked around. 'Alina? Alina?' she called. 'Where are you? Oh, that's right! You were fucking KIDNAPPED!'

Church laughed, putting his hands on his hips. 'Jesus Christ. You are a piece of work, you know that? I've *never* met someone so fucking arrogant. So blind to their own numerous and obvious shortcomings. Hallberg told me you were difficult, but my fucking God. If I'd have known ...'

Jamie felt the cold fire of fury burn inside her. Hallberg said she was difficult? 'If you'd have known, then what?' she said, teeth gritted.

'Then I would have kept well away. Let you sabotage your own life, and deal with the consequences of your actions for once. And not put that blame on everyone else. Like you always do.'

'You think you know me, but you don't.'

'I know enough.' He sneered a little, then paused, looking down at the computer screen. 'Maybe I should forewarn Charlie Smith, before he regrets sending you a fucking message.' He flicked his hand at the laptop and then turned away. 'He'll need it.'

'What?' Jamie said, doing a double take. She whirled around to look at the computer screen. 'Charlie Smith.'

'Yeah, maybe he'll put up with your shit. Be glad to save your life and then listen to you bitch and moan about it,' Church growled, walking to the kitchen and snatching up the pan he made eggs in. He slammed it into the sink and ran water over it.

'Shut up,' Jamie said, opening the message fully.

'Shut up?' Church chuckled. 'Oh, that's mature.'

'No, seriously, shut up,' Jamie called. 'This is ... this is him.'

The water stopped suddenly, but Church didn't move or say anything.

'Fuck,' Jamie breathed, her heart hammering. 'It's him. It's Elliot.'

Church turned slowly. 'Seriously?'

'Yeah. Charlie Smith was the fake name he used in Sweden. Holy fuck, this is actually him,' Jamie repeated, re-reading the message:

"Hi Jamie J, sounds like we have a lot in common. Would love to meet. The Nook, 2 pm."

'2 PM TODAY?' CHURCH WAS STANDING BEHIND her suddenly.

'Uh ... I don't know. I guess,' Jamie said.

'What the hell is *The Nook?*'

Jamie was already googling it.

'How can we be sure it's him?'

'It's him,' Jamie said.

'Could be anyone.'

'He's pretty confident if he's putting a time and place to meet before he even says hello.'

'Online dating's a weird thing.'

She looked up at him. 'Thought you never tried it?'

He folded his arms. 'I have friends who have.'

'You have friends?'

He grumbled a little. 'Anything about this place?'

'The Nook ... few hits. Looks like there's a café and bookshop called that in Crickhowell. That's the only hit that's even remotely close by.'

'How would he know you're in Wales?'

'I don't know. But I'm sure he does. I did think he'd implanted a tracking chip under my skin at one point.'

'Sounds like a perfectly stable guy.' Church licked his lips. 'If he knows you're in Wales, then he knows why. And if he knows why, he knows you're working with Interpol. So, he's surely not going to show himself just like this?'

'If we showed up with Interpol, he wouldn't. But he's been on their most wanted list for years and they've never even had a whiff of him. He knows what he's doing.'

'For someone you supposedly hate, you seem pretty complimentary about the guy.'

Jamie stiffened slightly and readjusted her position. 'He's our only option right now. Unless you want to tell Hallberg the truth? But either way, he's our only chance at finding Alina. So, whether you're coming or not, I'm going.' Jamie closed the laptop screen and got up.

Church was still, arms still folded. 'Fine. But only because you'll probably get kidnapped too if I *don't* come.'

'I don't need you to protect me,' Jamie reminded him. 'I survived this long without you looking over my shoulder.'

He smiled a little. 'I'm honestly hoping it's just some random Internet dater who shows up so I can laugh my arse off watching you have the most awkward first date ever.'

'You know,' Jamie said, letting out a long breath. 'Part of me wants that too. But we also need to find Alina. So maybe hope that this thing is real, instead.'

Church took that in, and nodded slowly. 'We'll find her,' he said then, sincere all of a sudden.

Jamie swallowed, met his eyes in the quiet of the apartment, and offered a brief smile. 'I know we will,' she said. 'I just hope it's not too late when we do.'

CHAPTER
NINETEEN

I t was a little before two when Jamie walked into
The Nook. It was a sweet little bookshop and café
combination that had the kind of quiet comfort
that all bookshops seemed to have. The smell of new
paper, combined with the smell of freshly roasted
coffee.

The bell above the door dinged as Jamie entered,
looking around briefly, but knowing Elliot wouldn't be
there.

She let her eyes drift over Church, who was standing
not too conspicuously at the back in the corner,
perusing the non-fiction section. He seemed to stand
out wherever he went due to his stature, but he'd positioned himself between two stacks so that he was only
partially on show.

He cast a quick glance over his shoulder, not

acknowledging Jamie, but standing sentinel all the same for when her 'date' showed up.

Church wasn't convinced it was Elliot at all, but on the off chance it was, he wanted to be there anyway. Jamie had refused initially, but he seemed adamant that he wasn't about to let her walk into a meeting with a known serial killer with no backup. And despite her assurances that she knew how to handle Elliot Day, he wasn't budging.

Jamie was more worried that Elliot would spot Church and be scared off.

She was doing her best to put Alina out of her mind, but it was getting harder and harder by the hour. She might be out of the country already, or worse. They needed to close in on her and fast, and if Elliot was warded away by Church's presence, then she wasn't going to be happy.

The café was relatively empty. Half a dozen tables clustered in the middle of a space down a small staircase in the middle of the store, with the counter at the back, and bookcases of old books hemming the tables in from each side.

Jamie picked the furthest and left-most table, so she'd have the best view of the store and whoever was walking in. While it was hopefully going to be Elliot, she was still distinctly aware that The Nhang was likely still hunting them. Church had winged him, but he had his helpers, and she doubted that they'd let an injury like that dissuade them. If anything, it was likely to spur them on. They'd probably take it as a slight, and come back harder than before.

They'd found them once, and Jamie thought they'd be able to again if they wanted.

She put that out of her mind and went to the counter, ordered herself a black coffee.

The young barista served it with a smile, and though it was burnt to all hell coming out of the espresso machine, Jamie took it gladly and went to the table.

By the time she sat, it was already past two. And no sign of Elliot.

He was usually very punctual, so Jamie guessed that if he wasn't here by now, he wouldn't be. Though she promised to give it until she finished her coffee, at least.

The upper level at the front of the store was visible from where Jamie was sitting. The stack that Church was standing behind had no back, so between the rows of books, she could see him loitering.

How the hell he managed to get into the SAS being the size and shape of a steroid-fuelled giraffe, she had no idea. The thought of him sneaking in anywhere was almost comical.

'He does rather stick out, doesn't he?' came a voice from Jamie's shoulder. A voice she'd never forget.

Her head whipped around to see Elliot standing right next to her, sipping out of a tiny espresso cup. She blinked, did a double take. She'd been facing the door the whole time. Where the hell did he come from?

As if reading her mind – which seemed to be Elliot's party trick, he said, 'Back door.'

She looked up at him, still in shock.

'May I?' he asked, gesturing to the chair next to her so that they'd both be sitting in full view of Church.

He was eyeing them both.

'Sure,' Jamie said, her mind casting back to the last time they'd crossed paths. In the remote north of Sweden, in the dead of winter. Jamie injured and half starved, Elliot doing what he did best: playing his own maniacal game while everyone else fought for their lives.

She swallowed, forcing herself to think about the task at hand instead of all that had passed between them.

'So how long have you been online dating?' Elliot asked, putting his coffee cup on the table and crossing his legs. He lifted a hand to Church who quickly averted his eyes, knowing he'd been made.

Jamie swallowed. 'Uh ... about twelve hours, I guess.'

'Hmm,' Elliot offered. 'How's it going?'

'Lousy.'

He chuckled through closed lips. 'I always preferred the face-to-face approach. Really get a sense of someone when you look them in the eye, you know?' He stared at her, his sandy coloured hair and narrow face as youthful as she remembered, his sharp green eyes as keen and intelligent as ever. He looked a little more tired than she remembered but, hell, they were all getting older.

'How's my dog?' Jamie asked then, sipping her own coffee. The last time they'd crossed paths, he'd taken a particular liking to Elliot. And when he'd made his grand escape, he'd taken the dog with him. Without asking. Though it wasn't wholly unwelcomed. Jamie rescued the mutt, but they'd never seen eye to eye.

'Hati?' Elliot said easily, smiling as though recalling him. 'He's well. A friend is looking in on him while I'm working. He spends most of his days curled up in front of the fire.'

There was a lot to unpick there. A friend? Working? In front of the fire?

He answered her questions once more without her asking. 'I have a little cabin,' he said. 'Tucked away. Modest. Quiet. Lake view. Snowy in the winter, but not too much. Stays cool in the summer.' He shrugged. 'It's not much, but it's home.'

Jamie cleared her throat, feeling a little melancholy at the thought despite herself. Elliot had often spoken of them going away together. And though he was totally psychotic, she had to admit the cabin on the lake did sound nice. And she did miss the dog, despite the scars he'd left her with. Both physical and mental. 'Is that what you're doing?' she said then, keen to get the conversation away from Jamie and Elliot's dream home by the lake. 'Working?'

He finished his coffee, tipping it into his mouth as

the girl who'd served Jamie at the counter circled it and walked up into the store with a take-out cup in her hand. She went around the stack and offered it to Church. He shook his head, but then the girl pointed to Elliot, who raised his empty cup in 'cheers'.

Church scowled, then accepted the coffee. He strode around the stack and down the stairs, parking up at one of the tables at the far side of the room. He made no effort not to stare directly at Elliot.

'A little brutish for your tastes, surely?' Elliot asked Jamie, not looking away from Church.

'I don't have tastes,' Jamie replied. 'And don't dodge the question. What are you doing here?'

'Having a coffee with my online date.' His eyes flashed and Jamie looked away. 'How do you think it's going?'

'I didn't come here to make jokes. What are you doing in the UK?'

'I believe it was *you* who reached out to *me,* if I'm not mistaken. I assume because you want something. Help, if history is deigned to repeat itself.'

Jamie shifted a little in her chair. 'You going to tell me what you're doing in the UK? Following me, I'm guessing?'

He smiled. 'Is it that you think I've got nothing better to do with my time, or that you're just that full of yourself?'

'Oh, I just assumed. If history is deigned to repeat itself.'

He laid his hands on his ribs and feigned being stabbed. 'Sharp as always. No, actually. I live here.'

'You live in the UK?' She was shocked. Interpol had a red notice out on him. She figured Eastern Europe would be the best bet. The most remote.

'I do.'

'Where?'

'Wouldn't you like to know.'

'I would, actually,' Jamie said.

'So you can come and visit the dog?' He grinned at her.

She let out a long breath. 'We're getting off topic here.'

'Oh, come on, the witty repartee is the whole reason I came.'

Jamie leaned forward on her chair a little. 'You said you were working. What on?'

'This and that.'

'Anything you can't put on hold?'

'For you? Sure. But my fee went up since the last time we spoke.'

'Of course it has,' Jamie said tiredly.

'What do you need help with? It wouldn't be anything to do with a certain black-market surgeon mysteriously vanishing, would it?'

Jamie stiffened a little. 'What do you know about that? *How* do you know about that?'

He met her eye and she all but shivered. 'I hear things. It pays in my business to keep my ear to the ground. And when my ... contemporaries are in-country, well, that often means they're taking food right out of my mouth. And I don't particularly like that.'

'So you know what he was doing?' she asked, feeling a cool surge of anger. When you were with Elliot it was easy to forget who he was, what he did. What he had done. And who he'd done it to. What he was doing last time you met him, or the time before. He was the definition of a wolf in sheep's clothing, and he had a way of lulling you into a sense of comfort. Right before he put a blade between your ribs.

'I do.'

'And who for?'

'I do.'

'And he took that job from you?'

'I actually turned it down,' Elliot answered dryly.

'Why?'

'Because I don't like Petrosyan and his enclave. I don't like how they operate, and I don't like how they treat people. They're rude, and abrasive. And they're cheap, too.'

She all but scoffed. 'How *they* treat people? You know what it is *you* do for a living, don't you?'

'Yes,' he said measuredly. 'But at least those who go under my knife do so with dignity. They don't suffer. At least not when that's within my power. As much as you convince yourself otherwise, I don't enjoy inflicting pain on people. Quite the opposite.'

'If you tell me you're helping people, I'm going to

ram this teaspoon in your eye,' Jamie said, taking one from the mug in the centre of the table.

'I'd like to see you try.' He smirked devilishly.

'I'll have help, remember,' Jamie replied, lifting her chin at Church.

Elliot let his gaze drift there slowly. He sized Church up – who was now all but glaring – and then looked at Jamie again. 'You think he could take me?'

'I do.'

'Hmm. Perhaps we'll find out. I must say, though, I don't like him as much as I did your last partner. Kjell was a good man, and a good friend. A little confused, but you do have that effect on people.'

Jamie felt a little twinge of anger, of guilt, of something else. She did her best to shrug it off, knowing that this was all Elliot's mind games. This is what he did. Got you all turned around, twisted up, your guard down. She wasn't going to fall for it.

'Perhaps we will,' she said then. 'What else do you know about the Armenians?' She was keen to get back to the matter at hand. Finding Alina.

'I know they're angry.' He looked at the girl behind the counter and lifted his cup, asking for another. He fired the girl a wide grin, and then thanked her. She blushed horribly, hiding her own grin. Not knowing the man who was looking at her, who was making her feel what he was making her feel. What he'd made Jamie feel the first time they'd met. Like she was the only person in the world. His eyes came back to Jamie suddenly and she almost jumped. 'I know they were cut off at the knees six weeks ago. That someone hit them where it hurt. I know they've been scrambling, and that they're trying to rebuild. And they're looking for revenge.'

Jamie shifted uncomfortably.

'And I know it was you who did it.'

'And how do you know that?' Jamie asked, her voice a little thin.

'Because the man they brought in to reap that revenge doesn't get called up unless it's serious. And ... because they provided a description. Plus, I know you. I know you like to stick your foot in things. Regardless of the consequences.'

'What was the description?'

'You don't want to know.'

'I do.'

'They called you ... *that blonde pig-bitch.*'

'Charming.' Jamie's shoulders raised defensively.

'That's the literal translation. In Armenian, it has a little more poetry to it.'

Jamie sipped more coffee. 'And how exactly did you hear about this?'

'As I said, I keep my ear to the ground. When people speak, I listen.'

'What have you got, a people-trafficking chat room? Where all the sickos and criminals get together?'

He chuckled. 'Chat room? What is this, 2001?'

'But I'm not far off.'

'You're not far off.' Elliot paused as the girl came over and brought him another little coffee. She put it down, hovering for a moment until Elliot thanked her. She did a little awkward curtsy, then left, shaking her head at herself.

Elliot spoke again then. 'But I suppose you know that they've been hunting you. Still *are* hunting you. And you no doubt already had a run in with them. It was lucky that they had that two-bit back alley hacksmith already in-country for an upcoming event to fix him up.'

'What event?' Jamie asked quickly.

'Was it you who shot him, or King Kong over there?'

'What event, Elliot?' Jamie asked again.

'You only winged him, though. He'll be back on his feet soon enough. Even with the second rate job that *surgeon* did.'

'What event, Elliot?' Jamie asked more firmly then.

'You know what event, Jamie,' he replied, just as firmly. 'I understand you're anxious to get things moving. But it's been a while since we spoke. We can't have a civil five minutes before getting down to business?'

Jamie growled in frustration. 'No, we can't. Now are you going to help me or not?'

'Why else would I be here?' he asked. 'Now what exactly is it that you need?'

Jamie let out a long breath, trying to still her anger.

'There's a girl. Alina. When they came for us, they took her.'

'The Nhang,' Elliot said. 'The man they sent for you?' He seemed interested all of a sudden, focused and serious, his easiness dispelled.

'Yes. They ran us off the road, tried to kill me. But they took the girl.'

'How old?'

'Fourteen, we think.'

He bunched his lips. 'And what do you want from me?'

'You said they brought The Surgeon into the country for an event. Is it another fighting ring?'

'You could call it that,' he answered slowly. 'But it's ... shall we say, the main event. The fighters they have aren't cannon fodder. No, these are prize fighters. And while only one fighter leaves, they need someone on hand to ensure that the victor lives to fight another day.'

Jamie nodded, trying not to picture Alina going back in the ring. 'Is it just the Armenians?'

'It's everyone. The Russians, Armenians, Romanians, Africans, Arabs, the Chinese. Everyone.'

'When?'

'Soon.'

'Soon when?'

'They don't give an exact time and place until the night. Not like they send out save-the-dates.'

'Okay,' Jamie said. 'But it's soon. Right. And they brought The Surgeon in for that. And he would have access to Alina. Presumably to make sure she was fit to fight?'

'I would think so,' Elliot said, watching Jamie carefully.

'Okay, so you know what I need you to do?'

'I can make a guess.'

'And can you do it?'

He sipped his coffee a little. 'Can I get her back?' He thought about it. 'I could. But I need something from you first.'

'Anything,' Jamie said quickly. 'Whatever it is, I can make it happen.'

A smile began to spread across his face. 'Oh, Jamie,' he said, draining his coffee and placing it on the table. 'I was so, so hoping you were going to say that.'

CHAPTER
TWENTY

Church was unhappy.

After Elliot left, he wasted no time in coming to the table and sitting down. Jamie thought it was interesting he chose a different chair from the one Elliot had sat in.

'So?' he asked quickly, elbows on the table, brow pressed down into a deep V in the centre.

Jamie took her time, still reeling from the whole encounter. 'He ... wants to take me to dinner.'

Church raised a doubtful brow. 'I'm sorry, what did you say?' he asked, incredulous.

'He said he wants to take me to dinner.' She met Church's eyes then, his gaze unflinching. 'He can get Alina back, but his price is taking me to dinner.'

'Bullshit.'

'The dinner part or the bit about getting Alina back?'

'Both,' Church scoffed. 'We should put him in hand-cuffs, deliver him to Interpol, and then let him trade his services for amnesty.'

'Last time Interpol tried to apprehend him, he killed two agents.'

'Even more reason to put him in cuffs. I'd settle for one of those Hannibal masks too, just so I don't have to look at his smug face.'

Jamie restrained a little smile at that. Church sure was getting worked up over this. And Jamie thought it certainly wasn't the first time he'd had to bend the law to get what he wanted. 'He said that before The Surgeon was brought in that he was offered the job, but turned it down on account of not wanting to work with the Armenians.'

'What, a killer with a conscience?' Church muttered.

'And what are we, then?' She eyed him but he didn't respond. Jamie went on. 'He says he can make a call, and with The Surgeon suddenly unable to work, they'll be looking for someone to fill his shoes. Elliot thinks he'll have no problem convincing them.'

'And you believe him?'

'He can be charming when he wants to be.'

'I bet,' Church said sourly. 'And the grand price for doing this, for getting in with the Armenians and getting Alina back – which, honestly, I think if you believe that he will, then you're being naïve. I'm just saying.' He held his hands up.

'Well, *don't* just say,' Jamie answered bitterly.

'I just think it's strange that for sticking his neck out and trying to double-cross a group like them, all he wants is a date.'

Jamie let out a slow breath, looking out over the quiet of the bookshop and the patrons slowly moving about. Checking out the paperbacks. Their lives were so simple, so quiet. And here Jamie and Church were, discussing the worst things imaginable.

'Well, I assume the Armenians will pay him hand-somely for his services. So it's not *just* dinner.'

'I still don't like it,' Church protested.

Jamie was growing frustrated now, and she was doing little to hide it. Any interaction with Elliot was exhausting. And now, to have Church jumping down her throat when she'd pretty much solved what was ulti-mately *his* fuck up. Seriously – throwing someone across a room hard enough to kill them? What a mess. What a goddamn mess.

'Honestly,' Jamie said then, pushing back from the table and getting up. 'I don't care whether or not you like it. It's what needs to be done. So, if I have to sit through one dinner to get Alina back, then I'll do it. And if it's such a big problem for you, feel free to call Hallberg and tell her you killed our asset. If not, then shut up and let me work.'

And then Jamie strode away, up through the book-shop and out of the front door, thinking all the time of Alina, and hoping against all hope, for once, that she could trust Elliot Day.

CHAPTER
TWENTY-ONE

The sunlight hit Jamie's face and washed away some of the anger that had built up. It wasn't Church who had pissed her off – well, maybe a little. Mostly it was Elliot. She had the inability to be around him and not grow angry. It was surprising, considering their history. But she did wish she didn't get so worked up. It was just impossible not to. Every conversation with him was intense. It was emotional and exhausting, a game of mental chess. You always felt like two boxers pacing in circles, sizing each other up, looking to slip in a jab to open the guard so you could slot an uppercut through their hands and score your knockout blow.

And yet, as much as she hated him, she couldn't deny that there was a connection there. And that as much as she didn't want to admit it, he did see her in a way no one else did. Did understand her. She never had to censor who she was around him, and she felt like she did around everyone else. She wasn't neurotypical, that much she'd come to accept about herself over the last few years. But she had to try just a little harder to keep a guard up when she was around other people, especially co-workers and those she met during the course of an investigation. And that was exhausting in a different way.

Jamie often had to curb the desire to scream. Or to scream at someone. She felt anger more intensely and more often than she expected others did. She formed obsessive attachments quickly, latching on to people. One, then another, then another. Jumping from partnership to partnership, co-dependent and burrowed into their lives, taking them away from everything else until they finally asked the question: what the fuck is going on?

And that scared the hell out of her. Jamie loved being alone but it frightened her more than anything else in the world. She hated the idea of being in a relationship or being relied on by another person, but couldn't help but sink her claws into whoever was in her orbit.

And it was only with Elliot that she saw someone else just as obsessive and intense, but with that same deep-seated need to not let anyone else in. Not truly. Not fully.

No one could ever see them. Not all of them. Not ever.

Jamie exhaled hard, letting the sun warm her and burn away the quickened throb of her heart.

Her phone buzzed in her pocket then and she pulled it out, seeing a text from an unknown number.

It just gave an address.

Elliot, she thought. Had to be. She hadn't given him her number, but she'd come to accept his ability to find her anywhere she went.

What was this place? A restaurant? Did he want to do lunch instead?

She clicked the link and it popped up on her maps app just a few hundred metres away.

Curiosity got the best of her, but with a forced sigh – just to make herself feel a little better – she started walking.

Though when she arrived, she realised it wasn't a restaurant at all. 'You've got to be kidding,' she mouthed, standing in front of a small clothing boutique, the mannequins in the window wearing fitted dresses, stylish purses draped over their shoulders.

She set her jaw, rubbing her fingertips against her thumbs as she weighed her options.

'Excuse me?' An attractive woman poked her head through the door. She was in her forties, with luxurious dark hair and heavy makeup around her eyes. Gold hooped earrings swung from her ears. 'Are you Ms Johansson?'

Jamie's surprise changing quickly to mild displeasure. 'Maybe,' she answered dryly. 'It depends.'

The woman smiled, opening the door a little wider. 'Hmm.' She chuckled through closed lips. 'Your fiancé said you had a strange sense of humour.'

'My fiancé,' she parroted back. It wasn't a question. She knew who the woman was referring to. 'And what else did my fiancé say?'

'That you'd be by around this time to pick up the order he placed for you.' She smiled even wider now, holding the door open so Jamie could enter.

She didn't move. 'To pick up an order. Right.'

'He said you might need some coaxing. But come on, everyone likes to dress up for an occasion! And you don't get engaged every day, do you?'

'No,' Jamie said, trying not to look wholly pissed off. 'But you know, somehow it doesn't feel real. Like it never happened at all, even.'

'Oh,' the woman said, waving it off, 'it'll sink in eventually. And he picked a stunning dress for you – I should know. I recommended it.'

'Did you now?' Jamie stifled a sigh, picturing Alina. If she walked away, showed up to the dinner dressed in jeans and a T-shirt – the only things she had in her duffle bag, she wondered whether it'd jeopardise her chances of Elliot holding up his end of the bargain. She certainly thought he wasn't above holding his services to ransom. And it wasn't like he cared what happened to Alina. So, did she have much choice here?

'Come, come,' the woman beckoned. 'You'll want to try it on, I'm sure. Though I think by looking at you he got your measurements spot on.' She grinned. 'Rare in a man. You should count yourself lucky. He's a real catch.'

Jamie stepped forward reluctantly, refusing to take the woman's hand despite it being offered. 'Yeah,' she grumbled. 'He really is something.'

CHURCH WAS SULKING.

They were back in Cardiff now at the safe house, to ensure that Hallberg was still in the dark about the whole thing.

He was sitting on the couch pretending to watch television while Jamie got ready. Elliot had sent her another address, this time for a steakhouse in the centre of the city. A fancy one. Hence this stupid black dress that he'd bought her.

Jamie was standing in the bedroom in front of the full-length mirror, tugging down the hem. She could not fathom why they cut them above the knee. You had to keep your legs clamped firmly together and walk like you were trying to hold in a very volatile poo just to stop it from riding up your thighs.

Though walking normally in heels was no picnic either. Tottering was the word.

Jamie had never got used to them and she didn't want to. But, alas, even with her limited fashion sense, she still knew that her hiking boots did not go with this dress.

'Fuck it,' Jamie muttered, pulling the hem down once more and heading for the living room.

She kept her steps short to keep the dress from sling-shotting to her waist, and stepped from the bedroom.

Church quickly looked back towards the screen.

She brushed her hair from her eyes and tucked it behind her ears, begrudging the fact that it was down. She always kept it in a plait. A ponytail if nothing else. But to have it loose around her face – utterly annoying. A lot of womanly things were. Carrying a bag not big enough to put anything useful inside – namely her gun. Wearing shoes you can't run in. A dress that you can't fight in. Hair that blinds you. Pants that want to choke the life out of your nethers. The list went on.

'I'm going,' she announced. She didn't have to hide any excitement, because there was none.

'Nghh,' was all the response she got.

Yep, that seems about right, Jamie thought as she opened the door and stepped into the hallway. It closed behind her, the realisation that she was going to dinner with Elliot Day dawning on her. She'd had dinner with him before. Several times. But only once by choice – the first time. When he'd been assisting her with a case and she'd gone over to his apartment to discuss the home-less community, a community he was intimately familiar with, and the one in which a rather troubling murder had occurred. Little did Jamie know at the time that he was the one behind it. Hence it being the *only* time she'd gone there out of choice.

She didn't regard this as being by choice either. Just like the other times when he'd broken into her home and fixed dinner for her before she got there, or when he'd inserted himself into her case in Sweden, posing as her half-brother.

He did seem to like make-believe. Playing at being a good person, playing at being her brother, and now even her fiancé.

It was all mind games. Circling, looking for that jab to weaken the guard.

Well, Jamie had her elbows firmly together and she promised herself that tonight, nothing was getting through.

But he was slippery, he was smart, and he was quick. And Jamie couldn't help but feel naked in her dress. But no matter what she was wearing, she knew Elliot could see right through her. Every move she made was the one he seemed to want her to make. She couldn't surprise him, ever.

So, was there any point in trying?

BY THE TIME SHE REACHED THE RESTAURANT, HE was already there.

She stepped from the taxi to the curb to the door and headed in. She was greeted by the maître d', and shown to the table. They didn't even ask her name or who she was meeting.

This was becoming a pattern. Elliot was sitting

already, smiling softly at her in a way that made her look away and hope her cheeks didn't flush.

God damn it.

Thankfully it was dim in here.

The restaurant was busy, but the atmosphere was subdued. They were sitting in the middle of the room, with tables laid out around them. There were couples and groups, the place filled with laughter.

The walls were exposed stone, the ceiling wooden with hanging chandelier-style lights that kept the whole place bathed in a warm glow.

The maître d' pulled Jamie's chair out for her and Elliot stood, smoothing down the lapels on his suit. It was a pale grey, an open-collared white shirt beneath it. It looked like he had a respectable job, and had come from it to meet Jamie – his new fiancé in her figure-hugging black dress.

He said nothing as Jamie shuffled in front of the chair and sat, not meeting his eyes, despite them being fixed on her unabashedly.

When the maître d' left, only then did he speak.

'I wasn't entirely sure you'd come,' he said, his voice not loud, but still cutting the din.

He stared at her across the candle in the middle of the table, his elbows laid on the white tablecloth, hands gently clasped in front of his face.

Jamie readjusted herself on the chair. 'I wasn't either,' she said truthfully. 'But I'm here for Alina.'

'Naturally.' He cast around. 'Something to drink?' His eyes flashed back to hers. 'Non-alcoholic, of course.'

'Mhm,' Jamie said. She'd never drunk. And still didn't. But she guessed that the last part wasn't a guess. He remembered, and had likely somehow checked to see if it was still the case. If it wasn't, she figured her favourite wine would have been waiting on the table. Even if it wasn't on the menu. 'Water's fine,' she answered.

'Naturally.' His features were carved in shadow, the light of the candle flickering on his clean skin, his angular, shaven jaw.

'So, when do you think you'll be able to get Alina back?' Jamie asked.

'Straight to business,' he chuckled.

'Naturally,' Jamie retorted.

'Soon,' he said. 'I'm not saying it to be cryptic, or vague. I just don't know yet. I reached out to the Armenians, and I'm waiting to hear back.'

'You haven't got hold of them yet?' Her eyebrows raised. What the fuck was she even doing here then?

'It's not as though I have Aram Petrosyan's number to hand. And even if I did, you expect me to just call him and say ... what?'

'I don't know,' Jamie said. 'But you seem to be able to move heaven and earth when it suits you. Why not now?'

'You're just going to have to trust me. There's a way these things work. And I promise you it will be done. I'll get the girl back as soon as I'm able to do it safely. Not before, not after.' His words were certain, inarguable, but not sharp or cutting.

Jamie watched Elliot in irritated quiet. For one of the most wanted men in the country, he seemed perfectly at ease. Though that wasn't surprising.

'You think we might talk about something else?' he asked.

'What did you have in mind?' Jamie glanced around. 'I mean, what do you even expect to get out of this?'

He drew a slow breath, considering his answer. 'I just want ... a pleasant evening. I'd like to order food and enjoy it. I'd like to make conversation and enjoy it. I'd like to pretend, just for a night, that things are normal. That we're normal people. That you're not a detective hunting traffickers here under duress to rescue an adolescent girl from the clutches of monsters, and I'm not being hunted by every law enforcement agency from here to China.'

'You're wanted in China?' Jamie asked lightly.

'Only a little.' He held his index finger and thumb up.

Jamie smiled briefly, then hid it, clearing her throat.

'Give me that – just a normal evening, and I'll do what I promised.'

'And if I don't?'

'Then I'll still do it,' Elliot answered.

'Why?' She really was curious.

'Because you asked me to.' He settled into his chair a little. 'There's nothing I wouldn't do if you asked.'

'Oh, really?' Jamie laughed a little. 'And why is that?'

'Because we're friends,' he replied.

'Friends?' Jamie was shocked. 'Is that what you think we are?'

'What else would you classify our relationship as?' His brow creased. 'We know each other intimately. You call when you need help with something. And despite your best efforts, you enjoy my company. As I enjoy yours.'

'I ...' she began, ready to protest. She stopped herself. It was just them here, no one else around. No one to overhear. And with Elliot, she could be herself. 'I don't *dislike* your company. When you're not trying to interfere in my life, at least.'

'Or when it's invited, is what you mean.' He smirked a little.

'Friends are welcome at my home. But not when they break in.'

He leaned forward. 'Good friends have their own key.'

Jamie leaned in too. 'That requires implicit trust.'

'And we don't have that?'

'I don't trust you as far as I could throw you.'

'And yet you ask me to go behind the back of Interpol to break who knows how many laws to help you get what you want? And to not say anything about it. To keep your confidence. What would your friend Julia Hallberg say if she knew you were out to dinner with a wanted man?'

'You're threatening?' Jamie asked coolly.

'Never. I don't make idle threats. I just tend to ... do. I find if you tell people your intentions before you execute a plan, it's more easily scuppered.'

'That's ... a fair point actually,' Jamie said.

He tipped his head a little. 'So, tell me, how's your mother?'

'My mother?'

'You tend to repeat my questions back to me a lot, you know that?'

Jamie gave him a tentative smile. 'That's because they often come as a surprise.'

'I didn't think anything I could do could surprise you anymore.'

'You'd think I'd have learned by now.' Jamie laughed to herself a little. 'Oh, jeez, uh, my mother ...'

'I know you left Sweden at her behest. Left your job at the NOD behind. How does that all feel?'

'You want me to lie on your chaise longue for this?'

'I know you hate therapy,' Elliot answered, smiling. 'I'm just making conversation. It's what people do.'

'What friends do, I bet.'

'Sometimes, sure. I don't often get the chance for honest conversation. To take my mask off. I like to make the most of it when I can.'

I can appreciate that, Jamie thought. 'I wish she'd

never called,' Jamie said then. 'Life would be simple. I'd still be in Sweden. Still be happy.'

'Is that what you were?'

'Thought this wasn't therapy?'

'It's a question. Do you feel like it's something a psychologist would ask?'

'Yes.'

'Interesting,' Elliot said, smile widening.

'Don't read into it.'

He held his hands up. 'Alright, noted.'

Jamie exhaled, picking up her train of thought. 'Life would be easier, I know that much. But, despite resenting her for the call, I don't regret coming. Alina is worth it. Getting her out, saving the girls that we did. That feels good. It's a little sour right now. For obvious reasons.'

'Don't worry, I'll get her back,' he said, voice bordering on warm.

It gave her reassurance, at least. Elliot didn't say things he didn't mean. She knew that much about him.

A waiter appeared at the table then and Elliot ordered some sparkling water and himself a steak, medium-rare. Jamie asked for the same. It's what she was intending to order anyway. But she hoped Elliot wouldn't think it was just because he had done. Or that it meant anything.

When the waiter left, he waited for Jamie to go on. She obliged after a few seconds.

'As for my mother ... well, things sort of blew up.

Her husband being arrested probably didn't help our relationship.'

'Well then he shouldn't have fucked his case up so badly.'

Jamie watched him. 'You know something? Was he corrupt? Colluding with the Armenians? Or was it the NCA?'

Elliot seemed amused by the peppering of questions. 'I don't know. I never met the man. I can only go off what I read. I'm not psychic.'

'And *how* did you read about the case exactly?'

'Ah, well, I may not be psychic. But I'm very, very good.'

'At getting information?'

He shrugged. 'At everything.'

'Humble, too.'

'Comes with the territory. I'm also rich.'

'How rich?'

'Quite rich.' His eyes flashed in the candlelight.

'Must be nice.'

'It is. Makes this whole *being wanted in thirty countries* thing a little more bearable.'

'Beach houses on every continent? Private yacht to sail to them?'

'Sail? Flying is faster.'

'Private plane?' Jamie was surprised at that.

He held his poker face for a moment, then laughed. 'No, I wish. Not quite that rich. But I do have a boat.'

Jamie laughed too. 'You had me for a second there.'

They locked eyes, stared at each other for a moment.

Then, thankfully, the waiter arrived with their water.

Elliot poured Jamie a glass, and then one for himself.

'So, is this all tonight is? Just small talk, sparkling water, and steaks?'

'Would you be glad if it was?'

She shrugged, looking around at the other happy patrons. 'It's bearable.'

'What if I told you there was another side to tonight, that it could be more?'

'More?' Jamie stiffened, looking at him. 'More, how?'

'If I told you I had a gift for you.'

'A gift?' She put her water down. 'What kind of gift?'

'Not jewellery or anything so boring. Something you'll like. Something important.'

'I'm not sure I like where this is going,' Jamie said truthfully, folding her arms.

'How much do you hate Petrosyan?'

'A lot,' she said cautiously.

'You think about what he's done? What he does? The girls, the boys ... everyone he hurts.'

'I do.'

'And if I put him in front of you right now, what would you do?'

Jamie didn't answer that.

'Would you kill him?'

She remained silent.

'To get Alina back? To save just one girl? Would you kill Petrosyan?'

She swallowed, then spoke. 'In a heartbeat.'

'Then I think you'll like my gift.'

'What is it?' she asked, voice shaking.

Elliot sat back in his chair and turned, resting his elbow on the back. He nodded over his shoulder and then slowly turned his eyes towards the back of the room. 'See that man sitting at the table with his buddy and the four women?'

It didn't take Jamie a second to zero in on the guy. He was probably in his fifties and portly. He was Middle Eastern by his complexion and thick hair, wearing a black shirt, wearing a heavy golden watch. He had a friend with him who was leaner, wiry looking, with dark eyes.

The four women sitting around them were half their age and twice as attractive. They were of varying ethnicities and hair colours, but all wearing small, tight dresses that made Jamie's look like a nun's habit, their legs smooth and shining, and seemingly home to their date's grubby hands. Both the big guy and the thin one had at least one hand under the table inspecting the thighs of the women.

Escorts or just in it for the money, Jamie didn't really bother to guess. But the two men clearly had fat wallets. You don't get girls like that – and two apiece – just for a sense of humour.

Though they seemed to think their jokes were funny as they were practically roaring with laughter and slurping down wine.

'I see him,' Jamie said carefully.

'That's Babayan. Levon Babayan.'

'Should I know who that is?'

'Hallberg might. If she'd been doing her homework.' Elliot turned back to Jamie now. 'He's one of Petrosyan's lieutenants. Oversees the ... *care* of the girls that arrive in South Wales. Makes sure they get where they need to go.'

Jamie felt her fingernails drag across the tablecloth as she slowly clenched her fists, watching him.

'He likely dealt with Alina. He might even be overseeing her imprisonment right now.'

'What's your point?' Jamie growled. 'You want me to go over there and arrest him?'

Elliot smiled at her and placed his own hand on the table. It was loosely clenched around something. He turned it over then and unfurled his fingers, revealing a white pill. 'I don't want you to arrest him,' Elliot said, eyes fixed on Jamie's. 'I want you to kill him.'

CHAPTER
TWENTY-TWO

Jamie just laughed. Not because she thought it was a joke, but because it was plain insane.

Elliot kept his easy smile, kept his hand open, the pill there.

When Jamie ran out of air and finally stopped, Elliot's gaze, the weight of it, was enough to make her squirm. He was serious. Deadly serious.

Jamie shifted in her chair a little. 'I can't just kill someone.'

'Why not?'

'Because ... that's murder, and contrary to your belief system,' she said, reaching across and closing his fingers around the pill. 'Murder is wrong.'

'But you just said you'd murder Petrosyan in a heartbeat if it saved Alina.'

'I did. But I'm regretting it now.'

'No, you're not.'

Jamie looked away. 'I'm not doing it. Let's change the subject.'

'No,' he said flatly.

Jamie looked back at him. 'We're not having this conversation.'

'We are, Jamie. And you need to realise the game you're playing here. Whether you want to face up to the truth of it or not, that fat sack of shit sitting at that table there traffics little girls, he locks them in cellars, he sells them like livestock, and when the mood takes hold of his sad little penis, he—'

Jamie held her hand up and Elliot stopped. For a moment at least.

'I can tell you for a fact,' he said, 'that those women are older than his preferred demographic.'

Jamie let her eyes drift to the repugnant pig stuffing his face and fondling his dates. A wave of hatred rose through her.

'How many have you killed?'

'People?' Jamie looked at Elliot.

'Human traffickers.'

'I don't know. A few, I suppose,' Jamie muttered.

'And are they the ones you lose sleep over? Because I know you don't sleep well.'

'No,' Jamie answered. 'They're the ones that I think about when I want to sleep.'

'But you can only bring yourself to do it when they're shooting at you, I suppose?'

'That's one way to put it,' Jamie answered, sitting a little more upright.

'So, the desire is there, but it's the justification issue. Easily solved.'

'No, not easily solved,' Jamie protested. 'I don't have a desire to kill people.'

'Hmm, I disagree. Respectfully,' he added. 'What if Aram Petrosyan was sitting at that table and you had a gun? And I could *guarantee* you'd get away cleanly with no repercussions. Legal or otherwise?'

Jamie's mind flashed back to the water treatment plant. She had taken a shot then. Right at Aram Petrosyan, from the crowd. Unprovoked. The only reason he was alive was because the glass had been two-inch-thick safety glass. Enough to stop a 9mm bullet.

'I'd …' Jamie began, but stopped herself. She knew that lying would give her away as much as telling the truth. Hell, Elliot probably even somehow knew she'd taken that shot.

'If you'd kill Petrosyan with a gun, why not kill someone equally as heinous – worse even, if you're talking about actual physical interaction with the children he's dealing with – painlessly.' He opened his hand again, revealing the pill. 'Just slip it into his drink. It'll take hours to activate, and will present as a heart attack. By which point he'll no doubt be up to his eyeballs in cocaine, alcohol, and paid sex. It'll be no surprise to anyone when his heart gives out. And hell, his people won't even bother to call the police. They'll probably just dump his body in a river somewhere.' Elliot shrugged. 'Ten seconds of your time, no sleep lost, no repercussions to be had, and who knows how many lives you'll save?'

Jamie watched Elliot, his stare unwavering, his pulse slow and relaxed in his neck.

She let her eyes drift to Levon Babayan and settle there. She imagined him at work and it made her sick. One pill. In the drink. And he'd drop dead by the end of the night.

One less sick fuck in the world.

Jamie swallowed, then looked at Elliot and shrugged. 'It's a nice thought. But he's drinking from his glass every five seconds. I'd never even have a chance to get close. So, there we are.'

'That's not a problem. We just need a distraction.' His lips formed a pensive grin. 'Maybe your friend Solomon could help.'

'Church?' Jamie frowned. 'What's he got to do with this?'

'Well, I had hoped nothing. But it seems he found himself unable to give us any sort of privacy.' He leaned forward onto the table. 'Don't look now, but I'm fairly certain he's across the street sitting on the ground pretending to be a homeless person.'

'Jesus,' Jamie muttered. 'Seriously?' She looked out of the front window and, indeed, there was a large homeless man in a hoodie sitting against a door, his knees up in front of him. Hiding his watchful eyes.

'Am I wrong?'

'No.'

'So, then it's settled. Enlist the oaf's help, slip the pig the arsenic, and we sit down and enjoy our ribeyes. What do you say?'

'I say you're mad.'

'So you're going to let Babayan walk?'

Jamie bit her lip. 'I could call Hallberg.'

'And tell her what? You could lie, sure, maybe tell her that you managed to get the information out of The Surgeon, but you're stacking lies on lies. And honestly, in your mind, what's the worse crime? Killing someone you feel deserves it, or lying to someone who has your complete trust? One of your closest friends in the world, someone who continually sticks their neck out for you and—'

'Alright, alright, Christ, you're like a dog with a bone.' Jamie groaned. 'I can't believe we're even having this conversation.'

'And yet we are.' Elliot placed the pill in front of her. 'Don't do it, that's your choice. But know that he'll walk out of here and hurt people. And you could have done something about it.'

Jamie looked away, then leant down to pick up the handbag she'd brought. She fished her phone out and unlocked it.

'Hallberg or Church?' Elliot asked, smiling.

She just scowled at him. 'Shut up.'

CHAPTER
TWENTY-THREE

Jamie watched through the window as Church lifted his phone as covertly as possible into his lap. He seemed to pause then, staring at it. And then he risked a glance up under the brim of his hoodie.

Jamie saw him do it, and he quickly looked down again, hunching over further and sliding the phone under his hood.

'Yeah?' he said, gruffly.

'Hi.' Jamie rested her elbow on the table and put her head in her hand. 'You want to come in here a sec?'

He didn't respond right away. 'I can't ...' he said then. 'I'm out.'

'Out where?'

'Just walking.'

'I can see you.'

'No ... you can't?'

'No, I *can.* You're literally sitting across the street from the restaurant, right now.'

He laughed, quietly. 'No, I'm not.'

'You're the size of a prize bull. You sort of stick out a bit.'

'I'm not even anywhere *close* to the—'

'You want me to come outside? Because I will.'

He swallowed audibly. 'No ... No ... I ... Fuck.'

He hung up then, stowed his phone and looked up, pulling down his hood. He locked eyes with Jamie through the window of the restaurant, then got up and shed his hoodie, holding it in his hand as he crossed the street and entered the restaurant.

The maître d' who sat them held up her hand and said a few words to him. He muttered something back, then gestured vaguely to Jamie and Elliot. The fact he was in just a plain grey T-shirt and cargo trousers was probably enough to make the maître d' think twice about letting him in, but his sheer size and the look on his face was enough to make her think three times about refusing him entry.

She looked over at Jamie and Elliot, then stepped aside, allowing Church to approach.

He pulled a chair without asking from a table with a spare as he neared and put it down at theirs, sitting heavily, eyes fixed on Jamie.

'Mr Church,' Elliot said warmly. 'How nice of you to join us.'

'Fuck off,' he grunted.

Jamie let out a long breath, feeling like she should tell them to play nice. But realising that she was neither of their mothers, nor had any desire to get between them lest she get covered in piss from their match, she resisted.

'Firstly,' she said instead, looking at Church. 'What the fuck are you doing here?' Before he could respond, she cut him off. 'I don't even want to hear it. I know why you're here, and thanks, but I'm fine. Alright?'

'You know it's literally my *job* right now to be protecting you, right? From the murderous Armenian psychopaths that have marked you for death?' He fired a sideways glance at Elliot. 'Among *other* dangers.'

Elliot just smiled easily. The same smile, the same look in his eye Jamie had seen before. She could almost see the film role playing in his head showcasing all the ways he'd murder Church, grinning all the while.

She cleared her throat, pressing on. 'Well, it's good you're here, anyway. Because there is something I need you to do.'

'What is it?' he asked quickly, but with a certain amount of apprehension in his voice.

'You see this guy over my left shoulder?'

Church's eyes lifted for a moment and he learned all he needed to. 'The bowling ball in the silk shirt with his hand up that girl's dress? Yeah, I see him.'

'Good. I need you to distract him.'

'Distract him?' Church raised an eyebrow. 'Why? Who is this guy?'

Elliot fielded that one. 'He works for Petrosyan. He's a key player in his ... import-export business.'

Church's eyes flashed to Jamie's. 'And you want to lift his phone?'

'Not exactly ...' Jamie swallowed, then looked at Elliot. 'Elliot wants to ...' She took a second. '*We* want to ... make sure he can't hurt anyone else.'

'By arresting him.' Church's words were firm.

Elliot smiled, amused once more by the seemingly simplistic, black-and-white world that the 'oaf' lived in. Thankfully, he didn't say anything out loud.

'By slipping him a pill.'

'To knock him out, so you can lift his phone? Take him into custody quietly?'

Elliot did speak now. 'You're really not getting this, are you?'

'We can't,' Jamie said, pulling Church's glare away from Elliot and back to her. 'He's not on Interpol's radar, so we shouldn't know about him either. So, arresting him isn't exactly possible. And if we did, what would we say, we were out to dinner at this fancy restaurant and overheard him bragging about Aram Petrosyan and his work? And we just *happened* to be here out of coincidence?'

'We say The Surgeon tipped us off,' Church said flatly.

'He knew the intimate scheduling of one of Petrosyan's top lieutenants? And we *didn't* share that information with Interpol? They won't buy a word of it.'

She looked at Elliot, then back at Church. 'We shouldn't be here. We *aren't* here in fact. We never were. We never contacted Elliot Day, and we certainly didn't all sit down for a nice steak dinner together.'

'Ribeye,' Elliot added, smiling at Church. 'In case you were wondering.'

'Oh, you *really* need to shut the fuck up.' A vein bulged in his temple and he did his best not to look at Elliot, seemingly for fear that he might launch over the table at him.

'Church,' Jamie said, voice a little harder. 'There's no other way to do this. So, we either do it, or we let him walk. And if he does, you know where he's going? To hurt more girls.'

'So, we call in a tip. There are a million things we could do that don't involve murder, Jamie.'

Elliot seemed to weigh Church with his gaze. 'How many people have you killed, Mr Church?'

He clenched his jaw, didn't even look at Elliot.

'Ten? Fifty? A hundred? How many of those hadn't really done much at all to deserve it? But you were happy to put a bullet in them.'

'I was working,' he growled through gritted teeth.

'So, under the guise of professional obligation, murder is fine. But when it comes to making a moral choice, one which could actually *save* lives, prevent harm to others, that's a step too far. Interesting quandary to wrestle with there.'

He turned to Elliot then. 'I'll fucking murder *you* now if you don't shut up.'

Elliot's mouth widened into a smile. 'Mhm, I'd like to see you try.'

Church's fists balled on the table, his eyes flitting to the fork two inches from the knuckles of his right hand.

'You'd do it, wouldn't you? Kill me, right here in this restaurant if I kept pushing you? I can see it in your eyes.'

Church's hand twitched.

Jamie watched, breath held.

'So, what's the difference? You'd kill me, and in doing so would condemn Alina to a horrific fate. Would condemn yourself to a life behind bars. And would shatter Jamie's life into a thousand pieces, too. She'd surely lose her career, and probably face prison time for fraternising with a wanted criminal. And yet, that decision is already made in your head. No doubt about it. Because you *want* to do it. And nothing else matters.' Elliot sighed gently. 'But if you thought with your head, instead of your heart, you could act in a way that saves instead of hurts. Just go over there, jostle the man, spill a drink in his lap, make an advance on one of his lady friends ... no violence is necessary. Jamie will do the rest, and the pill will finish the job.' Elliot shrugged. 'Or, you could jam that fork in my eye like you're thinking about.' He stifled a yawn – Jamie wasn't sure if it was real or not. 'At least, you could try.' Elliot's head lolled to the side then and he looked at Jamie. 'What do you think? You want us to come to blows here in this restaurant, completely destroy your lives, and let this paedophile walk free out of this restaurant? Or ...' He let his stare drift back to Church, whose right hand was now firmly fastened around the dinner fork. 'Do you want to put your years of training to work, satiate that indefatigable sense of moral justice, and wipe a human stain from the face of the earth forever in one ... swift ... move.' Elliot gently cut the air with his hand, then rested it on the table so his watch was showing to the both of them, the second hand slowly ticking around.

Church's pulse throbbed slowly in his temple. 'This what you want?' he looked at Jamie.

'I don't know. But I know I'll lay awake tonight thinking about it if I don't do *something*.'

'You understand that this is all a game to him, don't you?' Church asked, trying to ignore Elliot once more. 'That he brought you here specifically because he knew this creep would be here. So he could do this – toy with you, twist you, manipulate you for his own gain. You said you knew what he was like, that you could handle it. Is this you handling it, Jamie?'

'I know,' Jamie said. 'I know, alright? You don't think I know all that?'

Elliot raised a hand. 'I'm sitting right here, you know.'

'But ...' Jamie went on, not looking at him. 'It doesn't make him wrong. And whether or not this whole situation is a setup, we're here now, and we can do something about it. About *him*.' She nodded backwards at the silken snake.

'And if we cut him down, another will spring up in his place,' Church said.

'So, it makes the act futile?'

'It just begs the question: where does it stop?'

Elliot raised a hand again. 'Oh, I know, I know.'

Church ignored him, but his knuckles did whiten around the fork.

Jamie drew a slow breath. 'When they're *all* dead.'

Church regarded her carefully. 'You got the stomach for that? The stamina?'

'I haven't stopped fighting yet. What about you? You want to throw in the towel?'

'I don't have that luxury.'

'Because you're still making up for past sins?' Jamie asked lightly.

Church sucked on his teeth and looked at the table. 'Fuck. I should have stayed at the apartment.'

'You should have,' Jamie said. 'But you didn't. So, you going to help me, or not? Put one more check in the plus column? It's why you took this job, right?'

He dragged his hands from the table slowly, then looked at Elliot with an expression so scornful she was surprised Elliot didn't burst into flames.

'I'll give you some time,' Church muttered, getting to his feet. 'But you'll need to be quick.'

'She is,' Elliot said. Unnecessarily. He just enjoyed twisting the knife.

As Church left the table, Elliot's hand appeared once more, opening to reveal the pill.

'It'll be quick, right?' Jamie confirmed.

'Relatively.'

'Will it hurt?'

'Do you want it to?'

She didn't answer. Instead, just took the little white tablet and squeezed it in her palm, then turned on her chair to watch Church make his approach.

And for her cue to get up, walk over there ... and kill a man.

CHAPTER
TWENTY-FOUR

What he was going to do, Jamie didn't know. But she didn't quite expect for him to do what he did.

He approached their table fluidly, carrying himself well, and swept up behind one of Levon Babayan's dates. The one who had her back to Jamie and Church. She was in a red dress, her exposed shoulders tanned and smooth.

Church stooped at her ear and whispered something before Babayan even realised what was happening.

She pulled away, shocked at first, but then stared up at his rugged features, his stare intense and heavy, and a smile spread across her face.

Babayan's face drained of colour and the whole table fell silent.

'What do you think?' Church asked her, not moving from her orbit.

She blushed violently.

That was enough for Babayan, who leapt out of his chair so fast that his stomach grazed the table and made all the glassware clink and shake.

Church pulled away from the woman slowly and stood.

'What the *fuck* do you think you're doing?' Babayan said, loud enough that the whole restaurant paused to look.

'I'm speaking to a woman far too beautiful to be here with a guy like you,' Church said easily. 'The last thing she wants is your stomach resting on the small of her back later tonight.'

Babayan went from white to red now, his ears turning the colour of tomatoes.

The final straw was when Church poked him in the gut and said, 'Boop.'

Babayan wound up for a haymaker and Church stepped to the side, walking casually into the space between the tables, forcing Babayan to turn to throw a punch at him. His fist sailed straight over Church's shoulder and he laced his arms under the fat man's armpits, almost lifting him clear of the ground as Babayan slumped forward onto him under his own momentum.

'Dancing, are we?' Church called, beginning to walk the man in circles. 'That a pack of Polos in your pocket or are you just happy to see me?'

The restaurant began to snicker around them.

A hand touched Jamie's on the table and she looked at Elliot. 'Go,' he said, his voice sharp and serious.

Enough to get Jamie out of her seat.

Luckily, she wasn't the only one.

Babayan's wiry friend was also on his feet now, trying to get at Church while he paraded Babayan around, swinging him in circles as he yelled out in anger.

Jamie went over quickly, trying to figure out how she was going to do this en route.

It came to her then.

She tried to intercede, grabbing Church's arm. 'Hey, hey, come on,' she said, loudly enough for everyone to hear. 'Sorry, sorry, he's had a little too much to drink, and—'

As they swung around once more, one of Babayan's flailing hands clipped Jamie on the side of the head, sending her sprawling.

She twisted through the air, crashing into their table, doubling over it.

When she managed to get to her feet, she was clutching the side of her face.

She said nothing more, instead just rushed back to her table gripping her face, tears in her eyes, grabbed her stupid little bag from the floor next to the chair, and then rushed for the door.

She heard Babayan's yells quell from behind her and could only assume Church had finally released him. There was another voice then, telling them all to calm down or the police would be called – manager, maybe? Then, the voices were gone, the door clapping shut behind her, the cool night air on her face, and a deep, rotting sickness in her gut.

The strike may have been fake, as was the reaction. But the tears were real.

A moment later, the door squeaked open and Jamie looked up to see Elliot stepping onto the pavement, clapping slowly.

She wiped the tears from her eyes and straightened. 'Can we go now?' she asked, not wasting time.

Elliot looked at her for a second, then turned and stared through the glass on the door back into the restaurant, as though waiting for something.

Jamie craned her neck, seeing that Babayan was now unhanded, was being calmed by a man in a suit, but was still gesturing violently towards the front of the restaurant.

A moment later, Church stepped through the front door, trying to smooth the creases out of his T-shirt. 'Happy?' he asked sourly, scowling at Jamie. 'I smell like a year-seven disco.' He grimaced at the aftershave now soaked into his shirt and skin.

'Nice work,' Elliot said, pocketing his hands. 'You ever act on stage?'

'How many times am I going to have to tell you to fuck off before you actually listen?'

'Mm ... At least once more. Maybe twice,' Elliot replied, smiling at him.

Church just grunted.

Jamie turned away from the door and began walking. They might have been complicit, but it was her that dropped the pill in his drink. That had pulled the trigger. Otherwise, they wouldn't be so chipper either.

'Jamie,' came Elliot's voice from behind her.

She slowed, turning back. 'What?' she asked tiredly. 'What else could you possibly want from me?'

'Nothing,' he said. 'I just thought you'd like to know ...' He took a few steps forward. 'That man wasn't Levon Babayan. And he wasn't one of Petrosyan's lieutenants.'

Jamie's blood ran cold. 'What did you just say?' she breathed, shaking with rage suddenly.

'And you also didn't kill him.'

Jamie did a double take. She was lost for words.

'Then ... Why? ... What? ... What did I ...'

'It was a laxative. A powerful one,' Elliot admitted. 'So, he won't be having a pleasant evening. But he'll survive ... most likely.'

Jamie stood there for a second, dumbstruck, and then she did the only thing she could possibly think of and punched Elliot right in the mouth.

Her hand rebounded off his jaw and she stepped backwards clutching it suddenly. 'Motherfucker!' she practically yelled.

A few passersby paused to look at them in astonishment, but quickly moved on. It was late and this wasn't a main drag in the city.

Elliot seemed mostly unphased, absorbing the blow

steadily. He straightened his head and rubbed his mouth, moving it around a little. 'Suppose I deserved that.'

Jamie still held her hand, but found words this time. 'So, who the fuck was that?'

'An old ... acquaintance. An arsehole who had it coming, believe me,' Elliot said, as though it excused what had just happened. 'I owed him one. Me, and a lot of other people in fact. So, you still did something positive. You can sleep well tonight knowing that.'

'You're unbelievable,' Jamie spat. 'All that for what? A joke? Just some fucking mind game?'

'No,' Elliot said, lowering his hand from his face. 'I wanted to see. See how much you cared. About this girl you're asking me to risk my life for. And now I know. And now I'll hold up my end of the deal. I'll make sure she's safe. And I'll get her out. You have my word on that.'

Jamie scoffed. 'Excuse me if that doesn't mean that much right now.'

Church breezed past Elliot then, hitting him with his shoulder, knocking him off balance. He stood next to Jamie, staring at Elliot, and the temperature dropped ten degrees between them.

'I think it's time you actually did fuck off now,' Church said, putting an arm around Jamie's shoulder.

Elliot lingered, licked his lips slightly, as though calculating, and then nodded. 'Sure.' He nodded to Jamie. 'Thank you for a lovely evening. I'll be in touch.' And then he turned on his heel and strode away.

As soon as he was gone, Church's hand dropped from Jamie's shoulder, and he too turned his back on her and walked away. Leaving Jamie alone in the street with her stupid little bag, her stupid little dress, a pair of pants that wanted to strangle her, and possibly – very possibly – a broken hand.

CHURCH'S LEGS WERE LONGER, HIS FOOTWEAR more appropriate, and his desire to get home that much stronger.

He walked to the taxi rank, got in the first one, and then they drove off.

Jamie thought about yelling out, but then decided against it. She wanted a few minutes to herself to process what had happened.

The taxi ride wasn't long enough, however, and she seemed to be at the front door to the apartment in seconds.

She paid the driver and got out, tired and shaking. She needed sleep, and she needed to decompress. The last few hours – hell, the last few *months* had been hectic.

Jamie kicked off her heels and padded up the steps to the top floor, where the apartment awaited.

She let herself inside, the interior dark.

For a moment, she thought that Church must have

already gone straight to bed. Or that he wasn't here at all.

But when he spoke, his voice echoing from the darkness, Jamie jumped a mile.

'Why him?'

'Jesus!' she called, slapping the light switch next to the door and drowning the apartment in light. 'Hello to you too.'

Church was sitting on the sofa, hunched over, elbows on his knees.

Jamie approached, dumping her heels and bag on the floor. She put her hand on her forehead, pushing her hair out of her face, and let out a long, exhausted breath.

'Why him?' Church repeated then, eyes fixed on the darkened TV, his brow crumpled.

'Why who?' she asked back, standing to the side of the sofa.

'Don't be coy,' Church replied. 'You know exactly who.'

Jamie nodded slowly, not really prepared for the question or a discussion on the subject. 'Uh ...' she began. 'I don't know, is the simple answer. It's not like I want him in my life.'

'You seemed pretty quick to reach out to him.'

Jamie let that sit for a moment. 'Not a decision I took lightly. And it wasn't exactly like I had him on speed dial,' she said defensively.

Church shrugged. 'We could have found another way.'

'You hate him that much?'

'You don't?' Church stood now, putting his hands on his hips, towering over Jamie.

'I do. When I think about everything he's done. Who he is. But ...'

'But what?'

'But there's something else. Something strange between us. There always has been. Ever since we met. We just ... get on. Despite everything. We know each other. In a way no one else does. And that ... that carries weight. For someone like me.'

'Someone like you? You talk about yourself like you're some ... total fucking weirdo.' He huffed, shaking his head. 'I don't get it. I really don't. He's a fucking psycho, and you're ...'

'I'm what?'

He just began shaking his head.

'I'm what?' Jamie insisted. 'What am I?'

'You're ...' He stopped shaking his head and looked at her, his face pained, lips bunched. 'You're ...'

She waited for him to say.

But he didn't say anything.

Instead, he just stepped forward, took hold of her face, and kissed her.

She stiffened in his grip for a moment, and then a plume of heat exploded deep inside her, riding up her spine like a lightning bolt.

She drew away, filling her lungs with a gasp, holding his elbows, his hands around the nape of her neck.

Jamie breathed hard.

Church looked down at her with his dark eyes – the colour of slate. 'Was that okay?' he asked.

Jamie just sort of blinked, her brain not seemingly connected to her mouth. It moved, but no sound came out.

Church took that as an answer, and moved his hands from the nape of her neck to her ribs, lifting her into the air and enveloping her in his arms, carrying her towards the bedroom.

Jamie's heart pounded, her arms around his neck, her nose touching his, his breath warm on her face, the smell of his skin invading her senses.

As he opened the door, she wrapped her legs around his waist, kissing him again.

And after that, it was all just a blur.

CHAPTER
TWENTY-FIVE

Jamie slept better than she had in a long time.

She roused slowly, pulling her face from the pillow, her body heavy, her eyes tired. Her hand spread beneath the covers into the empty space next to her, and then her mind jolted into action and she sat upright in bed, rubbing her eyes and looking around. The momentary sense of peace was gone and, suddenly, her heart was racing.

She was alone.

No one else in the room.

Door: closed.

Smell: sweat and sex.

Bedclothes: rumpled.

My clothes?

Jamie pulled the top sheet away from herself and looked down at her naked body.

Shit.

Shit. Shit. Shit.

She strained her ears, listening, the previous night coming back in flashes of entwined bodies, nails scratching on skin, fingers digging into flesh. Teeth sinking into shoulders, and ...

She shook the thoughts from her head. Focus! Focus!

She steadied herself. This was uncharted territory, and she had no idea what the hell she was going to do next.

There were pans clanging in the kitchen, cover enough for her to get up and get dressed, she hoped. She sniffed the air, then pulled the bedsheet away from herself again and sniffed under it.

Oh.

Jesus.

Okay, change of plan. Shower first, then dress.

She exhaled, slipped from the mattress and eased the door open, the smell of food reaching her nostrils. Her stomach grumbled, and the realisation that she never actually got to eat that steak dinner the previous night dawned.

But still, she needed to shower first, wash off last night. She hoped the memory of it would come off too.

She slinked from the bedroom into the bathroom and closed the door. Then she cranked the shower up as hot as it would go until the room began to fill with steam ... and then she sat on the toilet and put her head in her hands.

By the time she was done showering, there was no hot water left. Unfortunately, she hadn't melted down the plug hole as she'd hoped. So it seemed she'd have to face Church eventually.

Church. What a stupid name, anyway. Who the hell is called Solomon Church? What parent hated their child enough to call them Solomon?

She could ask him. But that would involve conversation. And that's the last thing she wanted to do with Church right now. Or ever.

But just then, there was a knock at the door.

A light tap with the back of a knuckle.

'Jamie?' Church's voice rang soft through the wood.

She froze, then mustered some words. 'Just a minute ... I'm ...' She looked around. 'I'm on the—' She cut herself off before she could finish that sentence, a flash of panic moving through her. 'I'm just finishing up.'

'Okay ...' he replied slowly. 'I made some breakfast. It's getting cold. You want me to nuke it for you?'

'No, no,' Jamie said, staring at the door, knowing she'd have to come out sooner or later. 'I'll be right there.'

JAMIE DIDN'T MOVE FROM THE BATHROOM UNTIL she was sure she could hear Church in the kitchen again.

She slipped back into the bedroom and dressed, and then with a few deep breaths, headed into the kitchen.

There was a plate of eggs and toast sitting on the breakfast bar and she slid onto the stool in front of it.

'Coffee?' Church asked, not looking up from the sink, where he was doing the washing up.

'Please,' Jamie said, staring at her food. She picked up the knife and fork and began eating, hoping if her mouth was full he'd allow her not to talk.

'How do you take it?'

'Splash of milk,' Jamie answered.

Church poured her a cup from the cafetière and brought it over, putting it down next to her plate.

He rested his hands on the kitchen counter then, bracing his weight in a large triangle.

She picked the cup up and slurped some coffee, keeping her eyes down.

'Jamie?' Church asked, his voice soft.

She looked up over the rim of the cup. 'Hmm?'

'You okay?' His eyebrows lifted gently.

She nodded. 'Mhm.' Then she shoved a big forkful of eggs into her mouth, pointing at them with her fork. 'Mmm. Mmm.' Then she gave him a thumbs up.

He couldn't help but smile. 'Jamie,' he said again, this time with a little more force.

She paused eating.

'Get out of your head.'

She swallowed loudly.

'We had sex. It's not that big a deal.'

She opened her mouth to speak, but he didn't let her.

'We're two adults. We did something adults do, alright? You liked it. I liked it. It doesn't mean I'm going to get down on one knee, and this doesn't have to be weird. Not unless you make it weird. Sex is a great stress reliever, and I know that last night … we were both stressed.' He shrugged, picking up her coffee cup and sipping out of it himself.

Jamie suppressed a wince at that, something that would always irk the living shit out of her. But she knew he was doing it to make a point.

'Now, I'm going to go for a run,' he said then. 'I've been neglecting my cardio. Would you like to join me?'

Jamie didn't want to risk saying any of the thousand things that were going through her head. She had a habit of blowing up her relationships, and though she barely knew Church, right now, she was relying on him to help get Alina back. So, if there was an option to *not* speak, *and* run instead, well that seemed like a good deal.

So, she just nodded and finished her eggs.

CHAPTER
TWENTY-SIX

When Church said a 'run', Jamie thought it would be a run – and not the Fan Dance.

She'd imagined maybe they'd run along the waterfront, or through the park as she had previously. But no. Church had seemingly requisitioned a car from Interpol that morning, and was intent on taking Jamie high into the Brecon Beacons to embark on something he – very casually, mind you – called the Fan Dance.

He'd said it so casually. So easily. With a shrug. The motherfucker.

It wasn't until they arrived on the western slope of Pen Y Fan, and Jamie stared up at the peak, did she begin to get an idea of what was going on.

As he limbered up at the side of the road, he explained; 'The Fan Dance is just a little selection exercise the army uses. Usually, they run it in full gear with weighted packs, so it's a breeze without.'

'Okay ...' Jamie said slowly, staring up the rocky path in front of them. 'And we're running to the top?'

He nodded. 'Uh-huh. And then down the other side.' He shook out his legs then, cracked his neck, and started jogging. 'And then back up again!'

Jamie took off after him. 'What did you say?' she called, the wind buffeting across the park and stealing his words, the sky moving in a solid grey sheet above them.

The hills were bare and green, the earth black where the grass ran thin.

'Church?' Jamie yelled as his long legs began carrying him up the steep slope.

But he didn't answer, he just kept running.

And all Jamie could do was try to keep up.

She learned later that the Fan Dance is indeed part of the selection process for the SAS, and that they do run it in full gear. But they also have four hours to complete it, and it's twenty-four kilometres long.

None of which Church mentioned. And none of which Jamie knew just then.

She was fit – very much so. She regularly ran fifteen or twenty kilometres, and was comfortable notching up a hundred kilometres a week. But, apparently, not all the road running in the world could prepare you for a slog like this.

Church was waiting for her at the top, and the many

hikers that summited the mountain every day looked over in surprise when she came over the ridge, red in the face and panting.

'Come on,' Church called, waving her towards him and their route down – the Devil's Staircase.

Mercifully, treacherous as it was, it was a little easier on the way down. On the lungs at least. The knees were less pleased.

Church jostled down in front of her, like an ibex chugging down a sheer rock face. Sure-footed and powerful.

She cursed him all the way down.

He did let her rest for a moment at the bottom, just to catch her breath. And it wasn't like he wasn't sweating or panting, either. If anything, Jamie thought he might just be pushing a little harder to impress her – or try and kill her. Both were plausible.

Though when he began looking at her, checking if she was ready to take on the second leg of this monster, she prayed to all the gods she never really believed in for something to stand in their way.

And then, mercifully, something did.

But it wasn't an act of godly intervention. More like one coming from the other guy.

Jamie's phone began buzzing in her waistband and she pulled it from the pocket on her leggings.

The number came through as blocked, so she knew it had to be Elliot.

She answered it, seemingly to Church's displeasure.

He had his fingers on his neck, measuring his pulse. It seemed to be slowing faster than he wanted by the look on his face.

'Hi, Elliot,' Jamie said, looking at him.

Church froze, then lowered his hand and stepped closer to listen.

'Good morning,' he replied. 'I trust you slept well.'

Jamie looked at Church, a little perturbed by that comment. Did he know? How could he?

She said nothing about it, hoping it was just coincidence. 'You found something? About Alina?'

'I did,' he replied, keeping his voice low. She didn't know where he was, but he seemed to be trying to keep to himself.

'Well, what is it?'

'I know where she's being held, and by who. The Nhang. The man who tried to kill you.'

Jamie didn't even bother asking how he knew.

Elliot went on, speaking quickly. 'They're holding her, and they brought The Surgeon in to make sure she was healthy.'

'Healthy? For what?'

'For what comes next. The Nhang doesn't know where you are. So, if you want me to get Alina out, you'll have to draw him away. Make yourself known and then deal with him when he comes for you.'

'Are you there with them now? You made contact? What's going on, talk to me.'

He seemed to consider that for a moment. His usual

jovial manner was gone. He was cold and serious now. Jamie glanced at Church, hoping that their dalliance last night wasn't the cause of it. Jesus, she never would have done it in a million years if she'd thought there was any chance of it jeopardising Alina's life. Hell, how could she even *think* of doing something like that while Alina was out there, being imprisoned by god-knows-who, having god-knows-what done to her.

'I've decided what I want.'

'What are you talking about?' Jamie urged him.

'In exchange for Alina's life.'

She just shook her head. 'No, I went to dinner with you, I slipped the guy the pill – that's it. You gave your word.'

'I promised that I'd save her. Not that I'd do it for free.'

Church's jaw flexed and he folded his great arms.

Jamie let out a long sigh. 'Fine, what is it? What do you want?'

'I want to be taken off Interpol's wanted list.'

She stared up at Church. 'I ... I don't know if I can do that.'

'You'll have to.'

'Hallberg will never go for it. What the hell am I supposed to say?'

'I don't know, Jamie,' Elliot said coldly. 'You'll just have to figure it out. And once you do, you can present this agreement to your friend, Hallberg: remove me from the most wanted list and cease any and all active investigations into me or my work, and I'll deliver Alina to you, safe and sound. As well as Aram Petrosyan.'

'Petrosyan?' Jamie repeated it, just to make sure she heard it. 'You'll ... how? Where is he? Is he in the country?'

'You've got two days, Jamie. I'll call back, and I expect you to answer – with good news.'

'What? No, wait a second—'

But he hung up.

'The fuck?' Jamie asked, lowering the phone and staring at it.

'He's playing his own game,' Church remarked. 'We can't trust a word he says.'

'No shit,' Jamie snapped, then looked up at him. 'Sorry, sorry. I just ... that's not like him.'

'Being a lying prick is out of character for him? Somehow, I don't think so.'

'No, something's wrong. He's a liar, yes, but he's never been like that. Never been ... cold.'

'The psychopath has never been cold. Hmm, that's interesting. Perhaps it's always been an act he's put on to manipulate you and get what he wants from you? And now he just doesn't see the point in it anymore. Ever thought about that?'

Jamie shook her head. 'I'm not having this conversation. I know Elliot, alright. I know you don't like him, but trust me on this. Something's off.'

Church drew in a long breath, then held his fingers to his neck again. 'Sounds like it's going to be a busy weekend then. Trap and kill The Nhang, somehow get one of Interpol's most wanted off the hook for crimes in a dozen countries, and then extricate a teenage girl from the clutches of the very same man we just exonerated. Oh, and nail one of the most powerful business magnates in Armenia and the head of a major international trafficking ring in the process. Easy pickings. Now, can we finish our run? I'm getting cold.'

'It sounds sort of crazy when you say it like that,' Jamie said, slowly pushing her phone back into the waistband of her leggings.

'Sort of crazy? Jamie,' Church laughed, setting off in a light jog, 'it's fucking batshit insane.'

CHAPTER
TWENTY-SEVEN

'Y ou really think this is going to work?' Church asked, leaning against the kitchen counter, sipping a cup of coffee.

Jamie shifted painfully on the bar stool, her legs aching and throbbing all at the same time. 'I hope so,' she said. 'I don't know how they kept finding us when we were in protective custody, but I can only assume that there were some communications being intercepted. The circle was never big,' Jamie said, shrugging. 'Just Hallberg, maybe a few others. Senior members of Interpol. Not weak links.'

Church didn't seem convinced. 'If that's the case, don't you think that they'll see through this? No contact for days, then just an email saying *Hey, here we are! Sure hope The Nhang doesn't read this email!*' He waved his arms for effect.

'Do you have a brighter idea?' Jamie asked, bouncing her knee under the stool.

'I just think we should pause for a second, take a breath. Think about this.'

'We don't have time to think about it. You heard what Elliot said. Two days to orchestrate this whole thing. Or he won't get Alina out.'

'You think he'd let her die if you don't hold up your end of the bargain?'

Jamie thought on that. She hoped that Elliot knew if he did, that Jamie would never forgive him. But then again, he hadn't seemed like himself on the phone. And that was scaring her more than anything.

'Talk to me,' Church said then. 'I can hear you thinking, but I don't know what about.'

'I don't think I want to.'

'If it's about Elliot, I promise I won't bite your head off.' He crossed his heart.

She took a breath, looking him dead in the eye. At least they weren't talking about last night anymore.

'It is about Elliot. But it's also about everything else.' Jamie shook her head. She couldn't quite put her finger on it.

'Meaning?'

'Meaning ... this whole thing has been off since the start.'

'You're telling me.'

'No, even before we met. When I first got back to the

UK, and I got tangled up with the NCA. It was the same thing – they knew where we were, where Alina was, how to get to us. It's not just a weak link inside Interpol.'

'You're not making sense.'

'My thoughts aren't making sense right now,' Jamie admitted.

'Okay, so let's work through this. From the top.'

Only one name came to mind. 'Catherine Mallory.'

'Who's that?'

'She was the NCA intelligence officer heading up the case before Interpol came in. She was all nicey-nice at the start, but that dried up pretty quickly when she realised I was keeping Alina's existence to myself.'

'People don't like to be lied to.' He shrugged.

'Well, I suspected that her way of paying me back was by selling Alina out to the Armenians. They found me and Alina in the middle of nowhere, and the only way that I could think that they'd do that was by tracing my phone. Then she took Alina from me, put her into protective custody with an old friend of mine – Nasir Hassan. He was working for Mallory, but once they were out of sight, she ousted him and put one of her other investigators on protection detail. A woman named Ash.'

'Okay ...? That doesn't sound too weird.'

'She also sent away the plain clothes police escort, and the liaison from Children's Services, moved them from one safe house to another.'

'Again, that doesn't sound too weird. She was trying

to keep Alina safe,' Church offered, playing devil's advocate.

'Maybe. Or, she was serving her up on a platter. I got a call from Ash, frantic, saying someone was watching the house and she couldn't get hold of either Hassan or Mallory. Hassan had just been chewed out for working with me, all but fired, so he was licking his wounds, searching for some sort of solace at the bottom of a bottle.'

'And Mallory?'

'I never got to ask her. I managed to wrangle Hassan and we raced out to the safe house but, by the time we arrived, the door was kicked through and there were three heavies inside, trying to take Alina. We managed to stop them, but ... Ash was killed.'

'Jesus,' was all Church muttered.

'If the plain clothes were still there, they could have called for backup. Hell, Ash tried to but Mallory didn't answer. It all just stinks to me. The Armenians tried for Alina twice, and knew exactly where she was. Twice. And twice is too much of a coincidence for me to choke it down willingly. But even if I wasn't so close to this, I'd be pointing the finger in the same direction. There's only one person with the means, and the opportunity, to feed the Armenians information.'

'You think Mallory's playing both sides.'

'I don't know. But I know she knows something she's not saying. And that she's still got her fingers in this. Interpol is partnered up with the NCA, and

Mallory is still running her side of the investigation. I don't know what they're working on or if they're making headway, but Mallory's got her own agenda here, I'm sure of it.'

Church brought it around full circle. 'So, you think she was clipping information from Interpol about your protective custody, and that's how The Nhang found you at the hotel.'

'Do you have any other ideas?'

'I don't. But then again, I'm not a big *idea* guy.' He knotted his arms. 'I'm more the *I'm going to ask this question and I'm only going to ask it once,* kind of guy.'

Jamie just stared at him. 'Chilling.'

He shrugged. 'It's effective.'

'I bet.' She shook off thoughts of Church beating information out of people from her mind. 'My main concern is that even if we somehow manage to get Alina away from the Armenians—'

'And kill The Nhang.'

'And kill The Nhang,' Jamie confirmed. 'If we don't get Petrosyan, and Mallory's still in play, then who's to say any of this is going to stop? We'll be looking over our shoulders forever.'

Church tapped his lips in a show of contemplation. 'Maybe. You could go to Hallberg and present your theory, but you've got jack shit in the way of *actual* evidence.'

Jamie nodded slowly, the wheels turning. 'What if we could nail two birds with one stone?'

'What do you propose?'

'What if we *don't* email Hallberg with where we're going to be. But we *do* let slip to Mallory where we'll be. Then, once The Nhang comes for us, we'll have our suspicions confirmed, we'll take out the guy trying to take us out, and we'll have enough evidence to take to Hallberg about Mallory.'

'That sounds ...'

'Good?'

'Like a long shot. And it's riding on a lot of *ifs*. If Mallory is the leak. If she gives the information to the Armenians. If The Nhang goes for it. We could just be wasting our time here when what we should be doing is turning the tables on them. Find out where they are, and then go in there. Search and destroy. Take The Nhang out in his own house, then grab Alina and disappear into the night.'

'Just like that?'

'I've run more than a few smash and grab missions in my time,' Church said confidently. 'I don't see it being a problem.'

'I do. Firstly, we can't risk Alina. And secondly, there's Elliot.'

He laughed. 'I'm not worried about him. And if he gets caught in the crossfire ...'

'It's not his life I'm concerned about.'

Church's mouth curled up. 'Wait, you're worried about *me?*' He laughed now. 'With him? Jesus, if you'd have said the twenty Armenians and the pseudo-mythical hitman it'd have been one thing. But you think I can't take Elliot?'

Jamie didn't answer right away. 'He's smart. And ruthless. If you know you can beat him in a fair fight, then he does too. Which means he won't ever let it get to that.'

Whether it was the graveness of her tone, or just the look on her face, Jamie wasn't sure. But Church didn't seem to push the issue further.

'No. Elliot is ... he'll keep his word. We need to draw The Nhang away like he said, and we need to ... try to speak to Hallberg about getting his name scrubbed from the most wanted list. We follow his plan, maybe plug the leak at the NCA while we're at it, and he'll hand over Alina, and Aram Petrosyan. It's our best option.'

'And when he screws us?'

Jamie didn't answer. She knew it was a distinct possibility. She'd been walked into the jaws of death by this very man several times now, believing him to be on her side, when he wasn't on anyone's. While he was serving his own machinations. That rug had been pulled out from under her before, and this time she was going to watch her footing a little better. Luckily, it seemed like Church had no desire to let Elliot move a muscle without wanting to pummel him into the ground. So that made her feel a little better about going along with his plan.

She didn't want to think about what was going to happen to Alina if Elliot was lying.

She had no idea whether Alina was even within his grasp. Or if she was even still alive. She could be dead already and he might well be leveraging her supposed rescue to get what he wants. His freedom.

Jamie thought hard on that. It sounded crazy to her at first, but the more she thought about it, the more plausible it became.

But if everything did go right, would that be the end of it?

If they got Alina out, if they killed The Nhang, if they got Mallory dead to rights, and if they put Aram Petrosyan in chains ... would that be it? Would they finally be free of this and able to breathe easily?

It was a terrifying thought. Because there were so many steps between here and there. And one misstep would mean the end. They had to proceed carefully, and they had to do everything right.

They had two days. Two days to make the impossible happen.

Jamie just hoped it would be enough.

She pulled her phone from her pocket and dialled a number.

'Who're you calling. Hallberg?' Church asked, finishing his coffee.

'No,' Jamie said, chewing her thumbnail. 'I'm calling Hassan.'

CHAPTER
TWENTY-EIGHT

They met Hassan at a Starbucks.

He was already there when Jamie and Church arrived, sitting in one of the booths, looking at his phone. As they approached the table, Jamie thought he looked tired, older somehow than when she'd seen him just six weeks ago.

He noticed them as they approached and got up, coming towards Jamie with a big grin. His arms widened and enveloped her and he squeezed hard.

'Jamie,' he said. 'It's good to see you.' He held her at arm's length then and checked either side of her. 'Where's the little one?'

Jamie smiled back, but the sadness in her eyes seemed to be a giveaway.

'Shit, what happened?'

'The Armenians,' Jamie said. 'They caught up with us. They took her.'

'Fuck.' Hassan shook his head. 'That's rough. Anything I can do?'

'Funny you should ask.'

He stiffened, realising this wasn't a social call after all.

Hassan's eyes turned to Church then, and although Jamie had always regarded Hassan as a sizeable man, Church dwarfed him. As he did with everyone.

'Nasir Hassan,' he said, holding out his hand. 'NCA Investigator, former Armed Response with the London Met.'

Church took it and shook firmly. 'Solomon Church. Former SAS Operator, and current babysitter,' he added, looking at Jamie, the corner of his lip curling a little.

Hassan grinned, squeezing Church's hand. It was like watching two bull elephants meet in the wild.

'Alright then,' Jamie said tiredly, 'you two want to feel each other's biceps, or should we sit down and talk?'

They released each other's hands and Hassan clapped Church on the shoulder. He gave him a nod of mutual respect.

And then they sat.

'You manage to get what you needed out of Caroline Lewis?' Hassan asked.

Lewis was their contact at the museum during the fundraiser, the one that put them on to The Surgeon.

'We did,' Jamie said. 'Thank you for that. Was the USB she handed over as useful as you hoped?'

He sagged forward a little, putting his elbows on the table. 'Turned out to be useless. I passed it up the chain, but it came to nothing. Six weeks of work down the fucking toilet.' He shrugged then. 'But what can you do?'

'Considering what Lewis told us, I struggle to believe there was *nothing* of use on that drive.'

'What can you do, huh?'

'Question it, for one.'

Hassan laughed a little. 'Yeah, that'd go down well. Mallory's been working me like a dog since you decided to swing back into town, Hurricane Jamie.' He made a zooming motion with his hand.

Jamie shifted a little in her chair. 'That's what I actually wanted to talk about.'

Hassan was still. 'About Mallory?' he asked, his keen eyes searching Jamie's face.

Jamie just nodded. Church was silent, letting Jamie do the talking. Which she appreciated. He seemed to have that way about him – he didn't say anything unless he meant it. And he didn't mince his words. He was direct, and though it wasn't always what Jamie wanted to hear, it was often what she needed. And, honestly, it was just a breath of fresh air. No second-guessing with him.

'Jesus, you just love playing with fire, don't you?' Hassan laughed. 'You know she tried her damnedest to get you on a plane back to Sweden? She butted heads with Hallberg and Interpol, argued herself blue in the face to get you axed out of this whole investigation.'

'I wonder why?' Jamie mused, glancing at Church.

He remained stoic.

'Why? Probably because you lied to her, fucked up her investigation, withheld a material witness from her … the list goes on.'

'Or maybe it's because she's crooked.'

Hassan fell quiet.

'I know it's a hell of an accusation.'

He snorted. 'It's more than that.'

'You don't think what happened with Ash's death was suspect? The fact that she removed the police protection and the Armenians knew *exactly* where to find her? And she tried calling Mallory when she saw they were coming for her. And Mallory didn't pick up.'

Hassan leaned forward. 'She suffers with migraines. She took a pill, went to bed. And she ordered the police away because she was afraid the Armenians *would* track them down. She thought just having Ash and Alina together without anyone else there would be the safest possible place for them.'

'She had a migraine. She took a pill. She was asleep. While her biggest witness and the only person who could point a finger in court was under the protection of one of her investigators. You expect me to believe Mallory would be so fucking negligent?'

Hassan's cheeks reddened, his brow creasing. 'You didn't even know Ash,' he breathed, the anger clear in him. 'She was a friend, and we were all close. Mallory would never – I mean *never* – do something to put her life in danger. What you're saying, Jamie, it's not just wrong. It's fucking offensive. And if you brought me here to try to get me to turn on Mallory …'

'You've changed your tune,' Jamie said coolly. 'Six weeks ago, you thought she was dirty yourself.'

'Six weeks ago, I lost perspective.' He tempered himself, taking a breath. Perhaps it was Church's fierce gaze that was doing it. 'But since going back to work …' He spread his hands on the table, looking at them. 'I took the time to re-evaluate things, and … I trust Mallory. She's a good intelligence officer, a good boss, and she couldn't feel worse about what happened to Ash. I looked her in the eye. At Ash's funeral. I saw. You weren't there. You didn't. So don't begin to try to tell me that she made that happen on purpose.' Hassan was holding on to his rage well, but Jamie could still feel a palpable heat coming off him.

Jamie didn't know what else she could say. Except for what she came there for. 'Then let's prove it. Once and for all.'

Hassan set his jaw.

'I'm being hunted.'

'No shit,' Hassan said. 'You have the innate gift of rubbing people up the wrong way.'

'It's not intentional,' Jamie replied.

'But it is effective.' Hassan let out a long breath, softening slightly, but still on guard.

'He's called The Nhang, some Armenian hitman, a psycho with a hard-on for toying with his victims.'

Hassan's eyes twitched a little, as though he was connecting some dots in his head. But he said nothing.

'Seems I've been marked for death, and he already has Alina. We have a plan to get her out, but we need to draw him away first.'

'And that's why we're sitting in a Starbucks?' Hassan gestured around, his patience worn thin.

'Yes,' Jamie said coolly. 'I want you to let slip to Mallory where we're going to be. And if The Nhang shows up, then we know who leaked it to the Armenians.'

Hassan scoffed and shook his head. 'Jesus, seriously? You want me to try and set her up?'

'It's only setting her up if she is dirty. If she's not, then The Nhang won't find us, and Mallory's innocence will be proven.'

Hassan's eyes fell to the table again. 'What you're asking, Jamie. If she finds out why I'm doing it, or even suspects ...'

'She'll understand.'

'No, she won't,' Hassan said. And then he began sliding out from behind the table. 'I'm sorry, Jamie. This time, I can't help you.'

He got to his feet, his eyes resting on her for a moment. He looked at Church then, gave him a quick nod.

Church returned it.

'Next time,' Hassan said, pausing next to Jamie, 'I hope you wanting to *catch up,* is just that. It's hard to be your friend when you only ever call when you want something.' He rested his hand on her shoulder and let out a slow breath. 'I hope you get Alina back.'

And then he strode away, leaving Jamie and Church alone.

There was silence between them for a few seconds, and then Church got up and pushed the chair under the table.

'Well, I like him,' Church announced.

'Of course you do,' Jamie muttered, wounded.

'Come on then, you can sulk in the car.'

'I'm not sulking,' Jamie said, getting up.

Church stooped a little to catch her eye, staring at her. 'Yes you are.'

'I ...' Jamie began, but then decided it wasn't even worth arguing. So instead she just said, 'Fuck you.'

And then she walked away, with Church following her, smirking.

CHAPTER
TWENTY-NINE

hurch drummed his thumb on the steering wheel. 'So, what now?' he asked.

Jamie stared through the windscreen at the Starbucks, Hassan's words ringing in her head. She'd been so sure that Mallory was the weak link. But if she wanted to keep thinking that, she would have to believe that Hassan was wrong. Utterly wrong.

She hadn't gone to Ash's funeral. She'd not known the woman. But Hassan had, and he'd stared across her grave and into Mallory's eyes. And he believed her to be a woman of integrity. And was Jamie arrogant enough to think that a few passing interactions and a few loose suspicions were enough to outweigh Hassan's assessment?

'Jamie?'

'I'm thinking,' Jamie said.

Church nodded slowly. 'I think we need to call Hallberg.'

'I'm thinking.'

'About what? We're out of plays here. It's time to call Hallberg, and—'

'Jesus! What the fuck did I just say?' Jamie practically yelled. 'I'm thinking and—'

He turned so quickly in the seat that Jamie recoiled in shock, frightened for an instant.

His gaze was hard and cold, and Jamie all but shivered under it.

'You don't get to do that,' he said. 'I'm here by choice, and I'm pretty fucking sure that just going along with your plans at this point is putting me at risk of prison time. So, when I continue to try and help you, you don't get to rip my head off, okay? Or I'm gone, and you can fuck this up all on your own. Got it?'

Jamie swallowed, then nodded. 'Sorry,' she mustered. 'It's just, I'm ...'

'Forget it,' Church said, sinking back into the driver's seat. 'Just remember we're on the same side here, alright?'

Jamie quietened, resigned herself to thinking some more. Though she didn't know what the solution was. She hadn't considered the possibility that Hassan would turn her down. But the implication behind his reasoning had an even greater impact on things. Because if Mallory *wasn't* the leak, then who was? And how did they keep finding Alina and Jamie?

She released a large pent-up breath. She was out of options here. There was only one choice. And that was calling Hallberg and asking the impossible. Asking her to get Elliot Day's name scrubbed from Interpol's most wanted list.

She doubted Hallberg could even make it happen.

But did she have any other choice?

CHAPTER
THIRTY

B y the time they reached the apartment, Hallberg was already inside.

They entered through the door to find her standing in the middle of the room, facing away from them, hands on her hips.

She turned slowly, brow furrowed. 'Didn't there used to be a rug here?'

Jamie just shrugged. 'I didn't ever see one. You?' She looked at Church.

'Don't think so.'

Hallberg looked at each of them in turn. 'You know what? I don't even want to know.' She let out a long breath. 'I couldn't help but check the wardrobe though. Half expected to find The Surgeon bound and gagged somewhere here.' She glanced around. 'Where is he?'

'He escaped,' Jamie said quickly.

'Escaped?'

'Yeah, the meeting went south. He managed to stick Church here with a syringe full of anaesthetic.' She hooked a thumb at Church. 'Went down like a sack of shit.'

He folded his arms. 'Not exactly how I remember it.'

'You were unconscious.'

'I had to subdue him,' he said a little sharply, 'and managed to give him a taste of his own medicine.'

'He had a second syringe?' Hallberg asked, her tone a little accusative.

'He had a whole pharmacy in his bag. He came here to do surgery, remember?'

She just listened.

'I nipped out to get some supplies while he was down, but when I came back he was gone.'

'He was just ... gone?' Hallberg shook her head a little.

Jamie nodded. 'Yep.'

'So, a syringe full of ... something ... was enough to knock out Solomon for an extended period, but The Surgeon was up and about in, what, minutes?'

'Maybe it was a different substance. Maybe he had someone with him, came to check on him after they saw me leave.'

Hallberg just held her hand up, closing her eyes. 'Just ... just stop. I'm not going to ask, and I don't want to know. Just ... just stop.'

Jamie looked down, saying nothing more.

Hallberg let out a long sigh. 'So, what's so important that you couldn't tell me over the phone?'

Jamie looked at Church, but he seemed to want no part in Jamie's tangled web, and just sort of gestured to the floor.

She wasted no time. 'I have a lead on Alina. And I can get Aram Petrosyan.'

Hallberg's eyes widened. 'Petrosyan? We don't even know if he's in the country.'

'I don't have it all worked out yet – but there's a possibility we can get Alina back and nail Petrosyan at the same time.'

'How?'

'I have a contact. Someone who's well connected. Someone who says they can get inside Petrosyan's operation.'

'Who?'

'I can't say.'

Hallberg took pause for a moment, mind working furiously. 'You don't have any contacts that have connections to the Armenians,' she said plainly, as though she were fully aware of Jamie's entire network. Hell, she probably was. Hallberg was meticulous, and one of the smartest people Jamie had ever met.

'Like I said – I can't tell you more. But that's what we're working on.'

'Working on?' Hallberg repeated back. 'Jamie, you're a witness, not an asset.'

'You were happy to let us go after The Surgeon,' Jamie replied.

'Yeah, and now he's dead, isn't he?'

Jamie said nothing.

'Right. I'm not losing sleep over it, but let's all just be adults about this. I don't appreciate being lied to. Especially not when I'm going out on a limb for you. You know Catherine Mallory wants you ejected from this whole investigation? Put on a plane back to Sweden?'

'Yeah,' Jamie said, 'I heard.'

'And considering you have no badge, no authority, and now that Alina's not under your supervision anymore, no real need to be here ... It's not easy to keep finding reasons to argue against her. But I'm doing it, because I have a lot of respect for you, and I know your intentions are good, and though your methods aren't always conventional, your results are inarguable. But when it comes to killing key witnesses that could be *huge* assets for Interpol—'

'I didn't kill him,' Jamie cut in.

Hallberg's eyes went to Church.

He folded his arms. 'It wasn't intentional.'

Hallberg just sort of laughed incredulously and shook her head. 'Right. So, what am I supposed to do here, Jamie? Tell me. What is it that you want my help with, what can I even do at this point if you need something but can't give me anything? I should be telling you to sit down, do nothing, and wait. But I know you wouldn't. So please Jamie, just be honest with me, because this is my career on the line here, and I really, really care about it.'

'You're right,' Jamie said then, Hassan's words echoing in her head. 'I'm not being fair to you.'

Hallberg looked at her, a little surprised, but cautious all the same.

Jamie stepped forward and extended her hand to her friend. 'Thank you, for everything. You've already done too much, and I've already asked too much of you.'

Hallberg just stared at her hand. 'Somehow this is even worse.'

'I'll figure things out on my own. It's best that you have *some* plausible deniability here. Even if it's just the ability to say that this was the last time we spoke, and you had no knowledge of what my intentions were, and no opportunity to stop me.'

'Okay, now you're making me really nervous,' Hallberg laughed, holding her hands up and away from Jamie's.

Jamie lowered her hand. 'Alina's all that matters now, and if we don't get her back, then she's going to die. Likely in the most horrific way imaginable. And I know you've got lines to colour inside of, rules to follow. But me? I think ... I think I'm just past caring now.'

Hallberg measured Jamie, her gaze sharp and penetrating. 'Whatever you're mixed up in, Jamie, you need to tell me. The truth. All of it. And I don't know what I can do to help, but you know I will if I can.'

'That's just it,' Jamie said, resting a hand on Hallberg's shoulder, 'you couldn't if you wanted to.'

'Try me.'

'I need you to get someone's name scrubbed off Interpol's most wanted list.'

'Not a fucking chance!' Hallberg really laughed this time.

'Then this is it.' Jamie extended her hand once more.

Hallberg batted it away. 'Who's your contact?'

'I can't say.'

'But it's one of Interpol's most wanted?'

'I can't say.'

'I'll find out.'

'I'm sure you will,' Jamie said.

'So, you might as well tell me.'

'Plausible deniability.'

'We're way past that.'

'Maybe. Maybe not. Tell me to get on a plane. I'll tell you fine. And then whatever happens, happens.'

'Fuck, you're so difficult, you know that?'

Church chimed in. 'Tell me about it.'

Jamie smiled to herself a little. 'You can both go, right now. The door's right there.'

'Yeah,' Church said, stepping forward and grabbing Jamie by the shoulders. 'But then you'd get yourself killed, and we'd feel all guilty about it.'

Hallberg afforded a small smile herself then. 'You really think that this *contact* can get her back?'

'He's not let me down before,' Jamie said.

Hallberg chewed the inside of her cheek. 'And he can deliver Petrosyan?'

'He thinks so.'

'Well, the most wanted list thing is a non-starter. I'll tell you that right now.'

'I figured.'

'So where do we go from here? Is there anything I *can* do that'll help, but also not get me sacked?'

'Can you get word out of where we'll be in a way that the Armenians are likely to intercept it?'

Hallberg bunched her lips. 'Why the hell would I do that? It'll lead The Nhang right to you.'

Jamie glanced up at Church for a moment before looking back at Hallberg. 'Yeah,' she said. 'That's sort of the point.'

CHAPTER
THIRTY-ONE

Jamie saw Hallberg to the door, and when she offered her hand, Hallberg just embraced her instead, squeezing her tightly.

'You're the dumbest person I've ever met,' she whispered in her ear. 'I'm just glad you've got Solomon looking out for you. Otherwise, I think I probably would have you arrested to stop you doing this.'

'You could try.'

'I could try.'

'We'll be fine,' Jamie reassured her. 'Church hasn't stopped bragging about his many, many epic adventures and victories.'

Hallberg arched an eyebrow. 'I know that's a lie.'

Jamie smiled anyway. 'Just trying to lighten the mood.'

Hallberg lingered at the threshold.

'What is it?' Jamie asked.

'Nothing, it's just … You're risking everything for this girl. And do you even really know anything about her?'

'I know she's a child. And I know the things that have been done to her, and the things that *will* be done to her if I don't get her back. Isn't that enough?'

Hallberg looked at Jamie, her expression conflicted. 'I've been digging Jamie – still searching. For something, for anything. But she's a ghost.'

'Just a girl from rural Georgia,' Jamie responded. 'You said it yourself.'

'And now I'm saying … I don't know if *Alina* even exists.' She broke eye contact. 'I'm just saying that maybe she's not who she says she is. That's all. There are parts of her story that don't add up.'

'And that means she's not worth saving?'

'I didn't say that.'

'We're going to get her back,' Jamie insisted. 'And when we do, I'll ask her for the truth. And she'll tell me.'

Hallberg just nodded. 'Of course. I'm sorry I brought it up.' She paused for just a moment more. 'I'll, uh … I'll wait a few hours and then put out that memo. With some luck it should find its way into the wrong hands.'

Jamie smirked a little. 'That was good.'

Hallberg shrugged. 'I try. Okay then … this is it.'

'Jesus, you're acting like you're never going to see me again.'

'I hope I do, but you know what you're doing here is ...'

'Yeah, yeah, between you and him, it sounds like I should be in a mental asylum.' She dipped her head backwards towards Church.

Hallberg looked up at him now. 'Make sure she doesn't get killed, yeah?'

'Do my best.'

Hallberg lifted a hand then in farewell, and took off down the corridor.

Jamie closed the door slowly and turned to face Church.

He stared at her, great arms folded. 'You good?'

Jamie nodded.

'Stressed?'

She stared at him, then realisation dawned. She laughed. 'No chance. Not happening.'

He lifted his hands. 'Worth a try,' he offered. 'We might not see tomorrow.'

Jamie approached, rested her hand on his chest. 'Well, one more reason to survive then, isn't it?'

'So, you have thought about it then?'

'Shut up,' she laughed, stepping away.

But the humour, the fleeting joviality of the moment dissipated as quickly as it'd come. And the reality of the situation quickly set in.

Church's words were the truth.

Today could be her last day on earth.

And that terrified her.

CHAPTER
THIRTY-TWO

hurch already knew the perfect spot to lay their trap.

But it was going to be a long day of driving.

They headed north, following the route that they'd taken days earlier when they'd been ambushed initially. Church's Land Rover Defender was totalled following the crash, but had now been recovered and was sitting in the lot of an accident repair centre.

He'd instructed them not to begin work on it yet, and now, Jamie knew why.

They pulled into the yard and approached.

It was sitting on its own, the roof half caved in, the wheels buckled underneath it, the chassis twisted.

Jamie couldn't believe they'd walked away from it without serious injury. But judging by the rugged nature of the car, the oversized, knobbled wheels, the bull bars on the front, it was the reason Church chose the thing: because it was about as tough as he was.

They pulled the Interpol loaner to a stop – a newer model Hyundai in blue – and stepped out. The air was warm, the weather bright but brooding. Clouds stirred above in that slowly swirling way they did when the weather felt like it could turn at any moment.

Church didn't bother calling for help or letting the garage know he'd arrived. Instead, he just walked towards the Defender, leafing through his keys. Jamie kept an eye out, reading Church's slight caution, his sidewards glances to ensure no one was watching.

He went to the back door and pulled at it. The warped frame of the vehicle had it jammed. He muttered to himself, taking it in both hands and ripping it open.

It came free with a scrape of steel on steel and Church stared into the interior of his car.

'Fuck,' he mumbled.

'Everything okay?' Jamie asked, coming and leaning on the rear wing.

'Yeah,' he said, leaning inside and pulling up the mat covering the floor of the boot. 'I just really liked this truck.'

'I'm sorry,' Jamie said. And she really was.

He'd already given up a lot to stick this out with her, and he was about to risk a whole lot more.

'Don't mention it,' he called, his keys jangling. She heard him slot one into a lock.

'No, seriously, I really appreciate everything. The second we got rammed off the road you could have left. It says a lot that you didn't.'

'It probably says I have a few screws loose,' he laughed, pulling a big black duffle bag free of the vehicle and laying it on the floor. He did so with care, which told Jamie what was inside. And the clinking of metal-on-metal confirmed it for her.

'Here,' he said, stepping around the Defender and handing Jamie a ballistic vest. She took it, shedding her jacket and slipping it over her head.

Church did the same with his, pulling the straps tight around his midriff, his long-sleeved shirt, rolled to the elbows, rumpling around his ribs.

He knelt then, opening the zipper of the bag, exposing the contents. Guns. A few grenades – the flashbang and smoke kind.

He ran his fingers over the contents, doing a mental inventory.

Jamie was very interested in guns, always had been. 'M4 Carbine Compact?' she asked, staring down at them.

'L119A1,' Church corrected her, touching the larger assault weapon in the bag. 'UCIW,' he added, touching the smaller counterpart. 'Both run on the Colt platform though.' He looked up. 'Good eye.'

Jamie shrugged, unhappy she didn't recognise them. 'SAS standard issue I presume?'

He nodded. 'Yup. 870 Remington,' he finished, pulling a pump-action shotgun free from the bottom of the bag. 'Boom-stick.'

'They call them that?'

'I call them that,' he said. 'Breaching rounds go *boom*.'

'I bet they do.'

'Should be sufficient.' He pulled the Remington shotgun into the air by the forestock and jerked it up and down. The forestock slid towards the action with a satisfying click and then Church pulled it against his shoulder, sighting down the barrel.

'Ahem,' came a nervous voice from behind Jamie.

She turned to see a freckle-faced shop helper, probably no more than sixteen or seventeen, wearing an oily overall, with gingery hair and a few scraggly whiskers on his top lip, standing at the bumper of the Defender.

Church slowly lowered the shotgun and stared at him.

'The, uh ...' the helper stammered, voice quaking, eyes fixed on the gun. 'Dave asked if, um, if we can, um ... get to work on this yet?'

Church put the weapon back in the bag and got to his feet, dusting off his jeans. 'Sure,' he said then, as though it was the most normal thing in the world. 'I doubt you'll be able to get the chassis pulled out, but you can try.'

'Uh ... okay?' the kid said, still staring at the bag.

'They're fake,' Church said then. 'Toys.'

The boy took one look at Church, the tattoo on his arm, the look in his eye, and knew it was a lie. But he'd have had to have been utterly mental to argue. So instead, he just nodded and turned to leave.

'Kid?'

He stopped, looking back.

Church didn't need to say anything, he just held his finger to his lips in the universal 'Shh' sign.

The boy visibly swallowed, then just nodded profusely and ran back inside.

'You think he'll say anything?' Jamie asked.

Church pulled the bag into the air with one hand and slung it over his shoulder. 'Ha,' he grinned, walking towards their Hyundai. 'Who'd believe him?'

THEY HEADED SOUTH, THE DAY WEARING ON. There was an old country hotel on the coast that Church knew about. He described it as a certified shit-hole. It had little more than a dozen rooms, half of which had been under renovation for the past decade, and the other half of which were damp and dated and not fit to be lived in.

He knew the old woman who ran it, a cantankerous old bat, he said, that lived in the basement of the place.

She was a horrid host and a horrid woman, so the hotel remained empty pretty much the entire time.

Jamie wondered just how bad she and the place could be, but a quick Google search revealed the place was rated one star off twenty-odd reviews, and that most of them named the owner by name as just an awful human being.

The Gwair Gwyrdd Country Hotel was not a popular destination. But Church felt that, along with its geographical location on the cliffs of Pembroke, single entry road, and elevated position, it would make the perfect place to defend from an attack.

'How do you know about this place?' Jamie asked.

'I used to come here as a kid,' he admitted as they wound through Pembrokeshire, headed for St Davids.

'What was that like?' Jamie rolled down the window and leaned her elbow on the sill, looking out at the rolling green countryside, remembering her own childhood. The long drives into the Swedish countryside with her parents. Back when her biggest concern was how to stay up later than her designated bed time.

'It was fine,' he replied. 'Same as most, I guess.'

'Not the forthcoming type, are you?' Jamie said.

'Eh, not much to tell.' He let out a long breath, which said more than his words did.

'You get on with your parents? You close?'

'No.'

That told Jamie more. 'Siblings?'

'Sister.'

'Older?'

'Younger.'

'What's her name?'

'Mary. Is this really necessary?' He looked over at her.

Jamie shrugged a little. 'Just making conversation. Killing time.'

'I can put the radio on.'

'Nah,' she laughed, 'I think I'd prefer to hear the story of why parents would call their kids Solomon and Mary when they have a surname like Church.'

He let out another long sigh. 'There's not much of a story to tell.'

'Oh, I bet there is.' This was far more interesting than the radio.

'Right. Sure. Dad was a Catholic priest from Tel-Aviv.'

'Israel?' Jamie was a little surprised.

'Yep.'

'You're Israeli?'

'Half. Mum was British. She was on holiday there in the seventies, met my dad. They fell in love. End of story.'

'Sounds like the beginning of one. A good one.'

Church grumbled. 'Mum fell pregnant, they married quickly – though dad's church wasn't too impressed about the timeline of things. So they moved to England, had my sister, dad became a priest here.'

'You always had the surname Church?'

'Family name. I come from a long line of Catholic priests.'

'You didn't want to follow in your father's footsteps?' Jamie didn't know if she could imagine Church standing at the head of a congregation, reciting from the bible.

'He wanted me to be one. I didn't. Didn't go down too well.'

'That's why you joined the military?'

'No,' he groaned this time, as though to illustrate his disinterest in going over this once again, 'I joined the military because when I finally stumped up the courage to tell my father I didn't want to go to seminary school, he gave me a choice – live under his roof and continue my studies, or do neither of those things.'

'Jesus. How old were you?'

'Fifteen.'

'Fuck.'

'Yep. But I was big for my age. Managed to get my mum to sign a waiver to let me join up for the army at sixteen, and that was it. Didn't have a whole lot of other options, and the foster system didn't really suit me. Can we drop it now?'

Jamie could see that he was getting agitated, that this was still a sore subject for him. So, she just nodded. She had her own baggage, her own parental issues. And she didn't much like dredging those up if she could help it. 'I'm sorry,' she said instead. 'Parents can be bastards.'

'Can't they just.'

'Was he a good man, at least? Your father?'

Church's eyes never left the road, and though he

only said one word, it spoke volumes. After a long pause, he simply said: 'No.'

And they drove on.

CHAPTER
THIRTY-THREE

When they pulled to a halt outside the Gwair Gwyrdd Country Hotel, Jamie thought it looked abandoned.

There was a wide forecourt with no cars in it, overgrown – and, aptly named for it, she thought – green grass leaning over the tarmac, and wilted flowers in the beds to the side of the door. Perennials that had sprung up during the spring and early summer, but without water had wilted and now died.

There was no light coming from inside, and the doors looked to be locked.

Church pulled their car up next to the steps leading up to the building and killed the engine. They needed it to look like they *weren't* expecting some sort of onslaught, so parking away from the building would only rouse suspicion.

'Well, this is it,' Church announced, getting out. 'You ready?'

'To get bitten to death by bed bugs? Sure,' Jamie said cheerfully.

'I hope we're not going to do much sleeping,' Church replied, grinning and heading for the back of the car.

Jamie got out quickly. 'Hey, if you think we're going to be—' She cut herself off, realising her mistake. 'Oh, you meant because The Nhang is coming to kill us. Right.'

'What did you think?'

Jamie reddened despite her best efforts. 'Nothing.'

'Sure,' he smirked, pulling her overnight bag from the boot and tossing it to her.

She caught it as he shouldered his own and then hoisted the gun-filled duffle from the boot. She knew it to be heavy, but he still lifted it with ease with one hand and closed the boot without breaking a sweat.

'After you,' he said, nodding her on.

Jamie headed up towards the door, pulled it free and stepped into the lobby. Though that was being kind. It was a wide hallway with a door on either side, stairs at the back that doubled back to the left, and a small check-in desk next to it, tucked back against the wall.

The carpet was the kind you'd see in a Wetherspoons that hadn't been redecorated since the 70s, and the walls were all anaglypta wallpaper and crown moulding. They were yellowed with years of cigarette smoke from back when you could smoke inside, and cobwebs clung to the corners.

Jamie and Church approached the empty desk and waited. There was silence, and all the lights were indeed off. The place was deserted.

She reached out and dung the service bell, the noise ringing in the quiet.

'Looks like no one's home,' Jamie whispered. Speaking loudly seemed both redundant and a little uncouth considering how deafening the silence was.

Church shrugged. 'I booked online. Paid my fifty-nine quid and everything.'

'Fifty-nine pounds to stay in this place?'

'The Honeymoon Room. Best there was.'

'Honeymoon Room?' Jamie arched an eyebrow. 'That part of our cover is it?'

'If you'd seen the photos, you'd have gone for it too. It was the lesser of the evils, trust me. Plus, it comes with an ocean view.'

'I can go outside and look at the sea for free,' Jamie replied. 'Outside smells better too.'

'Outside also has worse cover, no bottlenecks to defend, can be attacked from any and all directions. Tactically, it's a nightmare.'

'Oh, darling,' Jamie feigned, 'how romantic.'

He bunched his lips. 'Place needs a makeover anyway. Few bullet holes might spruce it up a little.'

They were both joking to keep the mood light, but were aware that trained killers were likely bearing down on them already and that any joy that could be wrung from this place would be short-lived.

Jamie dinged the bell again. 'Where is this woman? Dead?'

Church chuckled a little. 'She was already old when I used to come here as a kid, so … maybe?'

As though it were rehearsed, a woman came shuffling from one of the doors behind them then. 'I hear ya, I hear ya,' she grumbled. 'Hold your horses.' She stopped, looking up at Jamie and Church. She looked at them angrily, clearly annoyed to be taken away from whatever she was doing. 'Whaddya want?'

'I booked a room,' Church said.

'No ya didn't.'

He blinked, a little thrown. 'I did.'

'I don't know nothing about that.'

'I booked online. Booking-dot-com?'

'Online?' She laughed as though it were funny. 'Oh no, I don't pay for no internet. Fuckin' scam, whole bloody thing.'

'The *internet* is a scam?' Jamie couldn't help but say.

The woman's eyes closed to slits and she homed in on Jamie. 'Aye, 'tis.' She looked at them in turn then. 'Pair of yous: English?' she asked, with some scorn.

'Swedish.'

'Israeli.'

'Mm,' she said, as though those answers were somehow worse.

The mean little woman was probably in her seventies, but she looked as though she was older, with deep lines around her puckered mouth that made it look like a cat's arsehole. The hair on her top lip only enhanced the illusion. She was wearing a faded dress and a tatty cardigan and her white hair was pinned loosely behind her head.

'So, the room?' Church said.

'Well, I haven't seen any money,' she said. 'So, you'll have to pay now if you want one.'

Church's jaw flexed a little.

'Tactically, it's the right call,' Jamie reminded him. 'Cover and bottlenecks, and all that.'

The woman stared at them. 'You two aren't into any weird stuff, are you?'

'Hardcore BDSM,' Church said, deadpan. 'Your ceilings are rated for sex swings, right?'

Jamie elbowed him in the gut. 'He's kidding,' she said to the woman. 'He's a joker.'

'Right,' Church said. 'So, fifty-nine pounds for a room?'

'Sixty-nine,' the woman said, adding ten pounds for his insolence.

'Sixty-nine?' Church repeated back, restraining a grin.

'Don't,' Jamie muttered to him.

'Come on, it's on a silver platter,' he muttered back.

The woman was losing patience. 'So, you want the room or not?'

'Yes, we do,' Jamie said. 'Ocean view, right?'

'If you got eyes,' she said tiredly, going around the check-in desk. 'How many nights?'

'One will be enough,' Jamie said.

The woman looked up at Church. 'Mm, don't know if I could even stick that. But, you know what they say ...' She shrugged and shook her head. 'Love is blind.'

THANKFULLY, ONCE SHE HANDED OVER THE KEY, the little old woman shuffled off from whence she came.

Church remarked it was likely under a bed somewhere so she could terrorise children as they slept.

When they reached their ocean view room, Jamie realised it was about the only thing it had going for it. The wallpaper was streaked with mould, the window frames peeling – with what looked like lead paint.

Church dropped the duffle full of guns onto the bed and the whole frame squeaked and rocked terribly.

He leaned in, put his hand on the quilt and pressed a few times.

Squeak.

Squeak.

Squeak.

'Well, the neighbours will know exactly what you're doing in here,' he joked. 'No such thing as privacy here.'

She knew he was trying to keep things light, but Jamie was growing a little tired of that kind of talk. Her mind was solely on the task at hand, and her lack of reaction to his jest, combined with the look on her face, seemed to alert him to that fact.

He unzipped the bag instead and pulled out the two rifles, laying them on the fabric.

Then he fished magazines, suppressors, and a cleaning kit out of there and began arranging it all.

By the time he was done, everything they had was laid out on the bed, covering it entirely.

The thought they'd need it all terrified Jamie, but she'd rather have it and not need it than need it and not have it.

'I'll get everything prepped,' he said. 'You want to take a walk around the place, get yourself situated, check potential ingress and egress routes? Get your mind right?'

Jamie stepped towards the window and looked out across the sea. The Atlantic stretched away before her, and in the distance to the left swam the distant shore of Devon.

There were wild grasses falling away to a rocky cliff, the waves washing white below.

She just nodded, the gravity of things setting in. She saw her reflection in the glass, but Alina stared back, all doe eyed and pleading.

The idea of killing wasn't something Jamie often thought about. When she entered into situations where she had to, it was never the original intention. She always wanted to get things done cleanly, but had defended her life on numerous occasions. And she'd found a way to reckon with that. Now, waiting for killers to come to her with the knowledge they were laying a trap, intending to kill them when they arrived … That was different. That felt different.

She wasn't looking forward to it. Knew how it felt to pull the trigger, and was dreading it. How many would come? How many lives would she claim? Add to her running total. How many fathers would she take from wives and children?

All to save one girl.

How much blood could be spilled to save one girl?

Could that be weighed, cosmically? Would it go against her when the curtain was finally drawn?

Would that be tonight? Outmanned and outgunned, were they inviting their death through the front door?

'I will take that walk,' Jamie squeezed out, her throat tight.

And she left the room without another word as Church pushed a metal brush into the barrel of the rifle, making sure it would fire right, shoot straight and, most importantly, kill easily.

CHAPTER
THIRTY-FOUR

The sun was still high as Jamie stepped from the front door and onto the stone steps.

She stared out at the space in front of her, an isolated forecourt hemmed in by trees on the far side that gave way to hedgerows and then fields. There wasn't another building for at least a half-mile around. And there was no other access road in. The hedgerows meant that they'd not be able to come in on foot, so they'd either have to drive right down the road to the hotel and into the car park, or what was colloquially known in military slang as the 'kill box', or they'd have to park some way down the road and sneak along it on foot.

The only other option was to come in via the coastal path. Jamie had her phone out in front of her, looking at the map. From the north it was about a four-kilometre hike along the cliffs from the nearest parking area. And from the south it was six. Jamie doubted they'd come that way. It offered no strategic advantage, with everyone having to move single file down a narrow path. A correctly positioned shooter would mow them down unless they were just going to run headlong into fire.

No, the straight-on approach offered them the most cover. If they came under darkness, which they would, they'd be able to sneak on foot to the edge of the unlit car park, hidden by trees, and then fan out across the tarmac to make their approach.

Jamie had already walked the interior. Downstairs, a large dining room and lounge area occupied the front of the building, with the back comprised of a kitchen and what Jamie suspected was the living quarters of the old woman. How they were going to handle that, she didn't know. Hopefully, at the sound of gunfire, she'd get out of the place entirely. Or perhaps Jamie and Church would just bar her door to keep her locked in while the fireworks went off.

Either way, there were only two entrances to cover – kitchen, and front door.

Funnelling them in front would be ideal, but taking them downstairs was going to be difficult. Too much area to cover.

The central staircase would bring them into a bottle-neck that was easy to cover and defend, and the only other way up was a rickety fire escape at the back of the building. For which Jamie already had an idea.

She let out a slow breath, taking in the beauty of the spot, the quietude of it. She'd gone away with her parents as a girl, but she thought this probably wasn't bad either. Church hadn't spoken highly of his father, but that didn't mean there weren't good times. And this seemed like a fine enough place to be dragged off to. Hunting crabs in the rock pools, swimming at the nearby beaches, playing on the grass with his sister.

Life was good sometimes. But it wasn't good all the time, and that was the unfortunate part. Fathers like Jamie's, ones who loved their daughters, died before they could see them grow up. And fathers like Church's, who were at war with their sons, weren't around to see the men they became. Unfair and cruel.

Jamie promised herself in that moment that Alina wouldn't grow up alone or shunned. Jamie would be there for her. And suddenly, the justification for all this became clear, and the answer to her earlier question dawned. Yes, it was worth it. Killing these men was worth it to see Alina safe and watch her grow up.

She looked at the road coming in. That's where they'd come from.

Above Jamie was a small stone Romanesque balcony – for show, but it was still opened onto by a set of glass doors that let light into the corridor above. The balcony posts were solid stone with enough space between for a rifle to rest, but enough width to provide solid cover. Jamie could set up there and they could hopefully thin the herd before they broke cover and made it to the building.

Church could cover the stairs coming up then, and they could hold them off from here. If they got inside, their only way up was the stairs.

And if they managed to get to the top, they could take cover in the doorways, make their stand.

Tactically, it didn't get much better. The solid stone walls would prevent bullet penetration, and the narrow hallways would mean that shots could be easily placed. And difficult to miss.

'Okay then,' she said to the empty car park. Her stomach began to growl. She needed to eat. Needed to fuel up.

She didn't feel much like talking or joking now.

All that was left to do was wait.

Wait for death.

The question was: would it be hers?

CHAPTER
THIRTY-FIVE

The day seemed to ooze by. Jamie walked the ground, familiarising herself with the place.

She walked the building ten times over, getting to know every inch, trying to outrun her thoughts.

Then she walked the entry road, seeing where would be a reasonable place to park and leave the vehicles. Whether they could see that from the hotel – and after some investigation, Jamie found that you could, if you hung out of the window of one of the far rooms that faced the front.

Where the stairs came up, a corridor ran front to back, but in the middle of it another corridor ran left to right, with three rooms in each 'quadrant', carved up by the corridors.

At the far end of one was the fire escape. At the far end of the other was a window overlooking what seemed to be a heavily overgrown garden of some kind, fraught with weeds and wild flowers.

Though they only had access to one of the rooms – their ocean view 'suite' – Jamie noticed that the keys to the other rooms were just hanging under the check-in desk. So she took the one they needed, giving them line of sight to a layby sizeable enough for several cars. The natural spot that the attackers would choose to leave their vehicles.

The old woman was nowhere to be seen, but at some time around dinner there was clanging in the kitchen, and a little after, a buffet tray was left out in the dining room with a very pale looking soup or sauce or something. It seemed to have no meat in it, though it smelled vaguely of the stuff in dog food. Some stale bread rolls accompanied the feast. But both Jamie and Church decided that perhaps ordering some takeout might be the better option.

There was a chip shop in the local village, and ten minutes there and ten back yielded two large bags of chips and a couple of pieces of soggy fish.

They sat in the dining room, their pistols holstered and loaded on their hips – freshly cleaned and operational thanks to Church – and picked at their dinner. Church ate on autopilot, pushing chips into his mouth slowly. He didn't appear hungry, and had grown distant. Psyching himself up, Jamie thought, because she was doing the same.

They exchanged a small smile when they noticed

the other one was peeling the batter from their fish too. But no words passed. They both just grazed on the white flesh, leaving the rest, and pushing two big globs of greasy paper and mushed chips into the bin next to the door.

Night began to fall afterwards, but time ticked by slowly.

Jamie told Church of her plan to take up position on the balcony, but he insisted that he would take that post. Firing on unsuspecting men was different from shooting back, he told her.

He said it with the kind of conviction that suggested he wasn't unfamiliar with the experience, and the kind of weight that suggested it wasn't something easily shrugged off.

As such, Jamie would be covering the stairs, and keeping lookout at the window for the headlights in the distance.

They retired soon after to make their final preparations.

Church built a rest to lie on and took his position while Jamie made her final preparations; unlocking the other doors upstairs and opening them to provide solid cover, checking on the fire escape and her work there, locking the back door leading into the kitchen, and then, finally, taking a poker from the fireplace and slotting it under the handle to the owner's quarters, meaning she'd not be able to walk out and straight into the firing line.

Then she went to the far room, pulled the wingback armchair to the window, and sat, the cushion sending up a gentle plume of dust as she did.

She took the strap of the UCIW – which stood for Ultra Compact Individual Weapon, the SAS standard-issue compact assault weapon that had replaced the MP5 in regular use – and pulled it over her head. She cradled the rifle for a moment, hands a little sweaty on its frame, and then leaned forward and laid it against the wall, suppressed muzzle facing the ceiling.

She settled in then, to wait, the ballistic vest tight around her ribs. It was all she could do. Her eyes were fixed on the roadway stretching through the fields ahead. She could just see between two trees as it curved away into the distance.

And it's down that road that they would come.

THE NIGHT WORE ON AND MIDNIGHT CAME AND went without any fuss.

Jamie's eyes were beginning to droop. She'd been sitting in the chair for hours and she was getting tired.

'Anything?' Church asked, his voice ringing through the little earpiece that he'd given her.

'Nothing yet,' she said.

She knew he wasn't really asking if they'd arrived. More just checking she hadn't fallen asleep.

Sleeping wasn't an option though, and she didn't

want to just dose up on caffeine. It made her hands shake, and that wasn't good for shooting true.

Jamie reached down to her lap and pulled up the other gadget that Church had furnished her with when he'd given her the gun. A night vision monocular. She held it to her eye, the range-finder function telling her it was forty yards to the end of the car park, and a lot further to the layby.

They didn't even know these people were coming. Hallberg had sent out a message to ... *someone*, letting slip where they were. But who knew if it was intercepted, if it reached the right person, or if they even took the bait. They could know it was a trap and be staying away. That would be the smart play.

But then, through the grainy yellowed lens, a flare of light appeared in the distance. It flitted through the mass of foliage, unclear but unmistakeable. Right on its heels was another flash of light, then another.

Jamie touched her ear, instantly awake. 'Three vehicles on approach.' She watched carefully. 'Pulling up at the layby, half a mile out.'

'Solid copy,' Church replied, voice even.

Not a hint of sleep there. Hell, he'd stay awake for a week if he needed to, Jamie thought.

'You good?' he asked.

'I'm good,' Jamie replied, pulling her weapon onto her lap. She ejected the magazine and checked it was loaded, then pushed it back into the body and pulled the slide, chambering the first round. Ready to fire.

She took a few steadying breaths, watching as the lights died in the distance, and their fate drew closer. And then she got off the seat and to one knee, resting the barrel of the rifle on the window sill, pressing her shoulder into the side of the frame so she was almost completely hidden by the wall.

She'd walked the road, and knew how long it took. About five minutes at a steady pace. They wouldn't run, but they'd move fast, staying low, split into two teams, each hugging one side of the road.

Three cars meant anywhere between twelve and fifteen guys. Maybe more if they really squeezed.

Fuck. That was a lot of guys.

Jamie had three magazines for the rifle – ninety rounds in total.

Her pistol had one spare magazine – thirty-four rounds total, the Glock 45 she'd got from Hallberg.

Church had the same number of rifle rounds, the same number of pistol rounds, along with seven in the chamber of the shotgun, and fourteen spares. Twenty-one total. Plus two flashes, and two smoke grenades.

And when Jamie did the mental maths, it sounded like a lot. But when Church said, 'Movement,' in her ear, 'I count twelve bodies. Armed. Rifles. Stay cool. Wait for my signal,' she thought that even 269 bullets wasn't enough.

Jamie readjusted her grip on her rifle and sighted through the holographic scope, struggling to make out any shapes in the darkness, let alone twelve distinct bodies. Though she trusted Church, and was awaiting his signal. And when it came, all she had to do was fire.

'They're splitting up, flanking,' Church said, voice barely a whisper. 'Three left, three right, six coming right down the pipe.'

The Nhang? Jamie wanted to ask, but she couldn't speak. Her heart was hammering in her throat, strangling her voice. She could feel sweat beading on her forehead and running into her eyes, could feel her hands slick around the gun, the muzzle pointed towards the ground in front of the front door.

'Dropping flash in three, two ...'

And then the whole car park exploded in light.

Jamie's eyes danced with stars as a burst of brilliance and noise filled the empty space.

She saw six shadows cut out in it, diving in every direction as the flashbang grenade went off right in the middle of them.

'Fire.'

The word was as cold as the act.

Jamie resisted the urge to close her eyes as she pulled the trigger.

She remembered her firearms training, and she remembered what Church told her. Squeeze gently on the exhale, keep the butt tight against the shoulder. Short, controlled bursts. Pick your targets.

She aimed for the one closest and squeezed off half a dozen shots, the fire-rate catching her off guard.

Faster than she expected, the kick harder than she had prepared for from a gun this size.

Church's bullets hammered them too and the six began scrambling for cover.

Jamie didn't think about it, just fired. And suddenly, only four were getting to their feet. Then three. One more fell before he made it five steps. And the last one disappeared, hugging the wall beneath them.

'Five down,' Church called out. 'Hang on – shit!'

Jamie didn't get to ask what the hell was happening before the silenced spit of gunfire began singing under her window, two of the three heavies that had begun to flank around her side of the building reappearing to lay down cover fire.

The chakka-chakka of the weapons was enough to tell Jamie they weren't looking to take prisoners.

Church's heavy breathing and grunts meant he was pulling back, going for cover as they fired on the balcony. The sound of smashing glass rang out in the night.

'I'm clear!' Church called to Jamie, signifying he was safe.

Jamie stared down at the shooters, sitting ducks right beneath her.

She didn't want to, but she knew she had to.

She sighted them through the scope, wiped off her brow, pushed the air from her lungs, and shot them both in the back, fighting to keep the vomit from clawing its way up her throat and spilling through her teeth.

'Both are down,' Jamie forced out. 'Pulling back.'

'Okay, regroup at the stairs,' Church said. 'Seven down. Five to go,' he reiterated.

Jamie did not need reminding. Of either fact.

She ejected the nearly-spent magazine and pulled a spare from her belt, slotting it into the rifle as she pushed to her feet and headed for the door.

As she reached it, pausing at the threshold, looking left and right down the corridor, a horrible screeching sound began to ring out from her left.

She looked that way, watching, as through the window the faint outline of the metal fire escape began to shake and then fall away.

A loud scream erupted from beyond the glass, and then a huge crash rang out as the whole construction hit the ground.

The scream was abruptly extinguished.

Jamie afforded a small smile, trying not to revel too much in the reality of what had just happened.

She could make out the bolts on the floor under the window – the ones she'd spent the afternoon unscrewing from the steel brackets. She'd left a few in the stone, loosened, but enough to keep the fire escape up ... until there was significant weight on it.

A simple but effective booby trap.

Eight down, four to go.

Jamie went right, towards the stairs. Church was standing there waiting for her.

'Good call on the fire escape,' he said, nodding.

'Mhm,' Jamie replied.

'Hey.' He lowered his head to catch her eye in the darkness. 'They're coming here to kill us. Remember that.'

She just looked away. 'Yeah, I know.'

'You good?' he pressed.

What could she do but nod?

His gaze lingered on her for a moment or two, and then he pulled back towards the stairs, hovering above the switchback so that he could hear anyone coming up.

He motioned Jamie to take cover at the corner of the corridor and then they waited.

Just four to go.

Church was a statue as they waited, one hand on his rifle, the other clamped around another flashbang. They'd gone over the plan, and when the Armenians were in the corridor below, he'd drop a flashbang over, and then execute them from above.

It was unfair, Jamie thought, but he was insistent on this being as quick and clean as possible.

He held up his hand, signalling that there was movement below, to hold fast. His rifle hung from the strap around his neck as his other hand moved to the grenade ready to pull the pin.

But before he could, something clanked on the floor

six feet behind him, hurled in through the open balcony door behind.

Jamie wasn't sure what it was, but Church seemed to know from the sound alone, screaming, 'Grenade!' as he launched himself forward over the railing onto the stairs below.

Jamie only had time to throw her hands up before it detonated.

The wall took the fragmentary force, but the shockwave was enough to blow her off her feet and send her spinning through the air.

Smoke filled the hallway and Jamie groaned, rolling onto her side. She was unsure if the ringing in her ears was from the blast or if the smoke alarm was going off.

She coughed and hawked, running her hands over her body to see whether she still had all her limbs. Miraculously, apart from a few bruises and maybe a perforated eardrum, she thought she was okay.

Still, everything was throbbing. She didn't know her skeleton could hurt.

'Jesus fucking Christ,' she groaned, trying to get to her hands and knees. She spat blood onto the carpet, tasting metal in her mouth. She didn't know where it was from – though the side of her tongue was swollen and sore, so maybe she'd bitten it. She couldn't think straight to make any kind of definitive assessment.

She realised she was staring at the back of her hands then. Where was her rifle?

'Church?' she called out, her voice hoarse. 'Church?'

She felt around for her weapon, but stopped, realising there was no answer.

Alert suddenly, she got to her feet. It was pitch black in here and now the air was thick with smoke and plaster. She couldn't see her gun anywhere and the floor was awash with debris.

Fuck.

Jamie drew her pistol and found cover against the corner, distinctly aware now that Church might not have got clear in time, that he might have taken the full force of that blast.

That he might be dead.

That it might now be Jamie against four of them.

Think. Think.

Shotgun, where was the shotgun?

In their room. Go for that.

Jamie swept from cover and made a dash for it, the blare of the smoke detectors covering her footsteps – but also the footsteps of the assailants.

As she reached the door a burst of gunfire rang out.

Three quick exchanges, then silence.

No voices, nothing.

Church was still alive. Or at least he was until then ... had they finished him off?

Jamie shut out those thoughts, muttering to herself the one word that was keeping her mind straight. 'Alina. Alina. Alina,' she repeated, moving inside and reaching for the weapon lying on the bed.

She picked it up, knowing it was loaded and chambered, and then turned back to the hallway.

As she reached the door, she froze, a creak on the stairs.

Someone was coming up.

Her heart hammered as she listened to the footsteps between the strobing of the alarm.

She tried to steady her breath, tried to keep her grip firm but not overtight, her finger light on the trigger.

Fuck! Fuck, fuck, fuck!

The footsteps closer now.

Almost to the door.

Three, two ... now!

Jamie twisted from the doorway, shoving the barrel towards the figure in front of her.

She pulled the trigger and all at once, muzzle flash lit the space.

Church's face was cut out in the darkness for a moment and shock surged through Jamie.

But when the artefacts cleared from her vision, Church wasn't blown to a bloody pulp. He had one hand on the barrel, holding it upright between them, plaster raining down from the hole in the ceiling onto their shoulders, smoke curling from the barrel. He'd snatched it from the air just as Jamie fired, driving it upwards.

His other hand was pressed to his ribs, his fingers bloodied.

He opened his mouth to speak, but before he could

get a word out, Jamie threw herself at him, hugging him tightly.

Church grunted, then hissed in pain.

'You bastard,' Jamie muttered, letting him go. 'I thought you were dead. Why didn't you answer me?'

'I was a little busy,' he muttered, peeling his hand away from his side.

Jamie couldn't see the extent of the damage, but she guessed he'd been nicked or grazed by the bullets she'd heard earlier. Thankfully, he didn't seem to have taken a direct hit.

Though Jamie nearly just punched a hole right through him.

'I downed one,' Church said. 'Three left, but they took cover before I could get them. I don't know where they are.'

He swayed a little, then tilted forward, forcing Jamie to catch him under the arms.

His breathing was heavy and he sagged into the wall, eyes screwed up in pain.

'Jesus, are you okay?' Jamie asked, keeping one hand on the shotgun as she eased him down.

'Yeah,' he lied, 'just need to catch my breath.'

'What is it?'

'Getting shot might be part of it.' He bared his teeth as he hit the floor. 'My back,' he added then. 'I landed on the stairs.'

'You've got to get up. You have to.'

He just shook his head. 'I'll be fine, you just gotta

hold them off 'til I can … fuck,' he grumbled, straightening one leg.

'Until you can what?' Jamie asked breathlessly, looking down at him. 'Breathe without it hurting?'

'Don't think that's going to be any time soon,' he replied, wincing again. 'You've got this.' He nodded, maybe telling himself more than Jamie.

She held the shotgun in both hands, rattled off a shaky breath, and then pumped it, ejecting the spent shell.

She had this.

There wasn't really another option.

CHAPTER
THIRTY-SIX

Jamie had six shells in the shotgun, and three left to face.

'They're spread across downstairs,' Church said. 'You've gotta get down there. They're going to burn us out otherwise.' His voice was pained. 'They'll set a fire and force us out one way or another.'

'I ...' Jamie was about to say she couldn't, but she didn't really have another choice. The air was choking, still thick with dust.

Church dragged his pistol from its holster and awkwardly pulled back on the slide, kicking himself back towards the doorway of the bedroom. 'I'll cover the corner here,' he said. 'If they come up, I'll get them. But you have to get down there.'

'Yeah, yeah,' Jamie said. 'I heard you.' She tried to steady her breathing but couldn't.

She knew he'd keep telling her, keep insisting. So

she went. She thought about saying she'd be right back, or saying something meaningful or lasting, but that felt too much like tempting fate.

Jamie paused at the corner, glanced around at the staircase, saw it empty. No doubt they were covering it from below as Church was from above, waiting for her to creep down there.

She wasn't going to make it so easy.

Instead, she kept going along the corridor until she reached the far end, the fire escape and the collapsed stairway.

She neared the window and slowed, pressing herself to the wall next to it to peek out. She couldn't see anything, just the vague outline of the collapsed stairwell in a heap below.

Jamie figured there was probably a body underneath it, but she didn't really want to think about what a torso crushed by a tonne of steel would look like.

So instead, she just carefully unlocked the handles and pushed the windows outwards.

The flood of clean air filled her lungs and dust began pouring into the night.

She assumed by the very fact that she hadn't just been filled full of bullets that the three assailants were still inside.

Which was good. It's what she wanted – get to the ground, circle around, come in through the back, and catch them unaware.

The ground was a good twelve feet below, but on her

recce earlier and the time she'd spent on the fire escape getting those bolts loosened, she'd noticed that there was a stone ledge that separated both floors, a little piece of architectural flare that'd hopefully save her from breaking her ankles trying to get down.

'Here we go,' she muttered to herself as she hung the shotgun off her shoulder and mounted the sill. She turned around, hooked her fingers over the bottom of the frame, and reached down with her toe until she found the ledge, just a few inches wide, but enough to bear her weight.

She'd need to shimmy sideways so she'd be clear of the tangled metal below, but there was a drainpipe a few feet to the side of the window. She reached out for it, finding it with her sweating right hand.

Okay, now let go of the window.

She wobbled, almost falling, but then managed to get herself to the pipe, trying desperately not to think about how large the bolts holding the fire escape were in comparison to the measly screws holding the drain-pipe in place.

Deep breaths, don't fall, don't fall. Easier said than done. Fuck! Would a desk job be so bad? Clock in, nine to five, two weeks in Spain every year, lying on a beach getting a tan. Eating lunch with co-workers in the break room. After-work drinks with the office ... Actually, that sounded somehow worse than what she was doing.

Jamie crouched, getting a good grip on the drain-pipe, and then stepped back off the ledge. The metal whined and strained under her weight but, mercifully, held. Jamie climbed down carefully, getting purchase on the rough and misshapen stones.

And then she was down – far from her most harrowing climb. Her mind flashed back to the oil rig in the Norwegian Sea and the climb she'd had to make there. Compared to that, this was nothing. Jesus, how was she even still alive?

Jamie shut that thought down quickly, taking the shotgun from her back and stepping over the mangled fire escape and the half-buried body beneath it. The whites of the guy's eyes shone in the moonlight overhead, unmoving.

She looked away and pressed on, trying to ignore the fact that their attackers were clad in tactical gear and body armour with silenced submachine guns.

A shotgun at close range would be too much for their ballistic vests, but still – she'd have to be close.

The kitchen door neared, sitting ajar.

She stepped up towards it, nosing it open with the shotgun, praying it wouldn't squeak or screech. It didn't, and then she was stepping inside.

What little brilliance the moonlight afforded her disappeared the second she entered, and then it was just blackness.

The kitchen had a large island in the centre that Jamie knew was ahead.

Beyond it, a set of double swing doors led to the dining room.

She reached out until her fingers touched the cabinetry and then began tracing her way left around it.

As she neared the corner, she began to hear the voice of the old woman muttering behind the wood of her door, the fire poker still doing its work and keeping her in. She'd seemingly given up trying to get out, but had no doubt not given up the ghost.

'—yes, I bloody well know where I am, just get here faster! No, I can't get out. If I could, you think I'd still be inside? How am I supposed to know? Someone's blocked my bloody door! Sit tight? That what they're teaching the police these days? There was a bloody explosion! I don't know what kind. God alive, you better believe I'm staying on the phone—'

It was clear she'd wasted no time calling the police. Reporting explosions, possible gunfire, they'd be scrambling armed response, Jamie thought. That'd take a while, but not forever. How long ago she lodged the call, Jamie couldn't say, but the clock was ticking, and Jamie did not want to be here when the blues and twos screamed into the car park.

She circled the island, still half crouched, then froze.

A shadow moved across the old-fashioned porthole windows in the swing doors.

And then they opened.

Jamie stayed still, shotgun in hand, as one of the heavies stepped into the kitchen and looked left and right, listening.

The only sound was the voice of the owner ringing through the jamb.

The Armenian, face obscured by the darkness, turned towards the voice and approached, weapon raised.

Jamie listened to him come sliding around the island on her hip, staying as quiet as she could as the heavy went towards the door and leaned in, listening to the old woman talk.

Jamie went the other way, directly on the other side of the island. Her eyes had adjusted now and the faintest green glow from the 'Exit' sign above the back door was casting a ghostly light over the interior.

Pots and pans were outlined by it, along with a knife rack, and a heavyweight wooden butcher's block.

Jamie's eyes moved across them all.

If she fired a shot here, the other two would come running. But if she could take him down silently, she could take the odds to two-on-one. That was better.

Her hand crested the counter, going towards the knife block as the heavy began muttering into the door, cursing the old woman, no doubt. Jamie smiled slightly. If only he'd got to meet her, he'd probably be going in there right now to bash her head in.

Speaking of … Jamie's hand slowed. She didn't really want to creep up behind this guy and slit his throat. That seemed too barbaric, even considering the circumstances. But that was her only option to stop him screaming. Either that, or she could plunge a blade into the side of his neck. She'd have to sever the windpipe regardless.

She grimaced now. No, that wasn't something she was up to doing. Shooting was one thing, but that …

Her hand lowered, resting on the butcher's block.

Heavy. Solid wood. If she could swing it, she'd no doubt knock the guy unconscious. A pot or pan was smaller, more room for error, and the noise would be loud – a dong that could well draw the others.

She laid the shotgun down carefully as the Armenian began jiggling the poker, ensuring it was secure. While he'd have no trouble killing the woman if he needed to, there was no need to do that, to execute her when she was old and frail and locked inside. He just wanted to make sure she wasn't getting out.

Luckily, the sound of the metal rattling against the handle and the woman's raised voice, now yelling at whoever was at the door to let her out, tell her what was going on, and to promptly remove whatever was barring the door and promptly insert it into their rectum, was enough to cover the sound of Jamie standing and pulling the butcher's block into her hands.

She weighed it, realising it must be ten kilos at least. It was eighteen inches by two feet by her estimation, and would swing fast, hit hard, and carry enough weight to do the job.

Jamie swallowed, making sure her grip was tight. And then she lifted it above her head, stepping lightly.

She crept forward, watching as the guy stopped

shaking the poker, watched as he nodded to himself and then whispered a curse into the jamb once more.

Six feet away now, so cautious of her steps, ultra aware of their weight and noise, the creak of her boots on the tiles. The bang of her heart on her ribcage. That's all she could hear.

Four feet now.

Her muscles tensed.

The guy stopped, alerted to someone else's presence by that strange sixth sense humans have sometimes.

He turned.

Jamie swung.

The block came down, whistling through the air.

She saw the whites of his eyes as they widened, his hands twitch as he tried to bring his weapon up.

But it was too late.

The block connected with a dull thwack, clubbing the man to the ground under its weight.

He flew to the tiles with a heavy thud and lay prone, legs splayed.

Jamie held the block in her hands, panting a little, straining her ears for any hint of movement. Of feet thundering towards her. Or of the man on the ground coming around.

Thankfully he lay still, unconscious, or maybe dead. Jamie'd hit him as hard as she could. She had to be sure.

She laid the block down on the counter with care and stooped, pushing her index and middle fingers against his throat.

His heart beat softly, but when she pulled her hand away, there was blood on the heel of her hand. It was running through the man's hair, but there was nothing she could do now.

She swallowed the bile rising in her throat and stripped him of his weapon, then felt around his person, emptying his pockets of his phone, taking the radio from the front of his ballistic vest.

There was a walk-in freezer to her right and Jamie pulled it open, wasted no time in dragging him inside and closing the door.

She tried to ignore the visible blood trail he left on the tiles – black like tar in the half-light – tried to tell herself he'd be fine, alive and just knocked out by the time the police found him.

Then she backtracked to her shotgun, picking it off the ground with bloodied hands.

Two to go, she thought, shouldering through into the dining room.

Just two to go.

CHAPTER
THIRTY-SEVEN

Jamie advanced through the hotel's dining room and towards the hallway. She expected the final two men to be close. And though there was no way to tell who was left, she knew deep down that The Nhang was one of them.

That he was a survivor, not liable to get caught in a trap. He would wriggle free, live to fight another day.

Jamie slowed, breathing steadily, a sort of strange calm descending over her. The blood had grown cold on her hands now and the lack of light had seemingly heightened her other senses.

There was noise in the hallway, not voices, but the rustle of material. Clothing.

The squeak of boots.

Jamie paused at the frame and peeked around, seeing the two final men at the foot of the stairs. One was ahead, on the second step, weapon tight to his shoulder, looking directly upwards at the banister above.

The other was behind, covering him.

He began to turn and Jamie ducked back behind the frame, breathing softly.

She pulled the shotgun up against her shoulder and took a deep breath. She knew she couldn't peek, she wouldn't be able to without being seen.

She'd only get one shot at this, and she needed to be patient.

When they were both on the stairs, backs turned, she could take them.

The thought sickened her – shooting anyone in the back, regardless of who they were, just didn't seem sporting.

Creak.

One on the stairs.

Creak.

Two on the stairs.

This was it.

Jamie wanted to close her eyes, but she knew she couldn't.

She twisted from cover, the shotgun rising, and pulled the trigger before she lost her nerve.

Fire lanced from the barrel like dragon breath, punching through the darkness, the sound so loud in the enclosed space that it made her teeth hurt.

The flash was bright enough to make her see stars, cutting out the scene for a moment, burning it onto her retinas before time seemed to lurch into motion again.

The second man on the stairs was blown forward into the one at the front.

Blood spurted up the walls.

One called out, fumbling his rifle.

It clattered to the floor and he slid back down the stairs on his side, screaming.

And suddenly, she found herself staring down the barrel of the first man's gun.

Jamie pulled the trigger again and the hammer fell on an empty chamber.

Pump action.

Fuck!

She dived for cover, chased by bullets, and felt as two connected, punching her in the gut, the small calibre stopped by the vest.

But it still hurt like all hell and Jamie couldn't stop the scream escaping her lips. Hers mingled with the man she'd shot, and they melded together into a bone-chilling cacophony.

She managed to get hold of herself, finding her breath as she scrambled for cover in the lounge area. The man she'd shot just seemed to mewl instead, quiet and pained, pleading in Armenian for help, asking for his comrade to save him, to help him staunch the bleeding, or—

And then his scream was extinguished with the quiet cough of a silenced round.

The crying stopped.

One bullet. A mercy. Or a merciless act. Jamie didn't know which.

She kicked herself backwards, searching for something to hide behind, finding only soft furnishings. Chairs and a sofa.

Not enough to stop bullets.

Slow footsteps reached her ears.

He was coming.

Jamie lay on her back between a pair of wingback armchairs and hoisted the shotgun into the air in front of her, ripping back on the mechanism to eject the spent shell.

Another slid into the chamber and she pointed the weapon at the doorway, waiting for the last man standing to show his face.

But he didn't step out. Instead, he spoke.

'You killed my men,' came a cold voice. It slithered into Jamie's ears and made her shudder.

'You took Alina,' Jamie responded, sweat running from her brow and into her eyes. It stung.

A low laugh echoed from the darkness. 'The girl? Who is she to you?'

'Who is she to you?' Jamie spat back, willing him to step out, to get blasted by the shotgun. For this to be over.

'No one. Just a job. As are you. Though, I will admit, I will take some pleasure in killing you. It is only a shame I won't be able to take my time.'

'We have time,' Jamie called through gritted teeth. 'Come in here. Let's make the most of it.'

'So you can shoot me with that Remington in your hands? I don't think so.' His voice was smooth and chilling, the accent almost a drawl, dripping from his lips. 'I think I'd rather play this with a little more intelligence.'

Jamie didn't know what was coming next, but just the way he said it led her to believe this wouldn't be a fair fight.

There was a metallic *plink* that made the hairs stand up on the back of her neck, and then the flash of a hand around the corner.

Something black careened through the air above her, a shadow in the darkness.

Her mind put it together. The *plink* of a pin being pulled from a grenade.

Fuck!

Jamie rolled onto her side and kicked herself away from the armchair as the grenade landed somewhere behind her.

She covered her head, waiting for the explosion, but it didn't come.

Though as she drew a breath, her throat tightened to a pinhole and her eyes began to burn fiercely. She coughed and spluttered, unable to see or breathe as a noxious green gas began to fill the room.

Tear gas.

Fuck! He was trying to drive her into the hallway, into his line of sight.

Jamie raked in one last hard breath, feeling the gas burn her lungs, and held it. She managed to get to a shaking stance, squinting through the fog. If she ran out there, he'd murder her. No chance she'd survive.

But what about the internal walls? Were they solid stone too?

She looked down at the shotgun in her hands, then pulled it to attention and aimed at the wall a foot to the right of the door, and pulled the trigger.

The weapon bucked in her grip, but she held fast, stepping forward, pumping the action, and letting fly with another shell.

The fire punched through the plaster, revealing brick and black mortar, but it looked old and weak. And the second shot proved it, digging a huge gouge in the wall.

Jamie pumped, moved closer, and fired a third time, sending mortar fragments flying, leaving a hole behind.

Breath was running short and she could barely see.

The Nhang would be hiding back towards the stairs now, Jamie knew that. She couldn't see him through the hole, but she hoped she could surprise him.

She took one final step and jammed the muzzle right through it, pulling sideways on the stock so that the whole shotgun twisted until it was almost parallel with the wall.

And then Jamie pulled the trigger once more, watching as fire lanced into the hallway, right towards the stairs.

Before the flash had even subsided, she was through the door, pistol drawn and raised, firing at where she hoped The Nhang was before she even got him in the sights.

But for an old man he was fast, and was already retreating up the stairs. Cut out with shot, caught in a strobe light, climbing fast, rounding the balustrade, and then flying up onto the landing.

Towards ... 'Church!' Jamie tried to call out, but found the words strangled by the tear gas. 'Fuck!' she coughed, pinning the crook of her elbow against her nose and mouth and rushing forward after her quarry. 'Church!' she tried again, the word barely making it out of her lips before a coughing fit seized her and forced her to her knees.

She crawled the last few steps to the first floor, pistol waving in her grip.

At the top, out of the miasma, Jamie managed to get to her feet once more, but The Nhang was nowhere to be seen.

The hallway stretched out in front of her, the cross-roads in the middle beckoning as a guillotine. An easy place to get ambushed.

But she had no choice. Church was lame and she couldn't let The Nhang get to him, finish him off.

She had to reach him before that happened.

With everything she had left, she gained speed and charged forward, lurching into the wall and pinning herself to the corner half blind and starved of oxygen.

Tears streamed down her face and her chest burned like pure fire as she drew wheezing breaths.

Jamie dared to peek, seeing an empty corridor stretching towards the ocean view room, and then stepped out, advancing with her weapon raised.

Where was Church?

Where was The Nhang?

Nothing moved, and there was no sound.

She kept going, kept listening. Had The Nhang escaped? Slipped out through the open balcony door and back towards their cars? Ready to regroup and live to fight another day?

Jamie neared the open bedroom door and slowed to a stop.

Was Church inside? Did she dare call out?

There was only one option, and it wasn't a good one.

She steadied herself and then spun from cover and into the doorway, pistol up.

But before she could even take stock of the room, two hands gripped her arms and drove them upwards, her heels dragging on the floor as she was driven back.

She felt the impact as she was slammed into the door opposite, seeing The Nhang's eyes flash in the darkness in front of her. He twisted her wrist hard and Jamie cried out, the pistol coming free of her grip and hitting the carpet beside her.

He could have shot her, could have killed her. But he didn't want it to be over quickly. She remembered that as his face drew close to hers, his other hand finding her throat, fingers digging into the flesh around her wind-pipe and squeezing until he almost made a fist.

He wanted to look her in the eyes while he choked the life out of her. See the light go out.

No! Not like this! Jamie had had her back against the wall before, and she wasn't giving up.

With everything she had left, she drove her knee upwards into the gut of The Nhang, the ghost who had marked her for death, and was now coming to collect.

It connected, solid muscle and bone against her patella.

His grip loosened for a moment and he let out a short, sharp gasp, but he still had Jamie's hand pinned to the door above her with his left hand.

And though he released her neck with his right, it was just to make a fist and fire a punch into her gut so hard that she wanted to double over.

All the air left her body, and pain rippled outwards from her solar plexus in nauseating waves.

Stars danced in her vision, and then her head was shoved back into the door once more with a deep thump, his bony, steel-like grip under her jaw once more, keeping her head still as he wrung her neck.

She couldn't move, couldn't breathe, couldn't do anything.

A wicked smile spread across his lips.

They parted slightly and Jamie felt the wash of his breath on her face, hot and rancid. 'Die for me,' he whispered. 'Don't look away.'

Jamie shut her eyes.

He jerked her, her skull rebounding off the wood of the door again. Pain. Her eyes snapped open.

'There,' he said. 'Look at me. Look at me.' His voice began to grow distant. Jamie could just see his outline, the whites of his eyes shining as his stare bore into her soul, waiting, just waiting for her to fade to nothing.

Her vision pulsed black.

Her heart beat wild and erratic.

Church.

Where was Church?

Alina's face appeared before her then, hanging there, floating in the darkness.

I'm sorry. I'm sorry. I tried. I'm sorry.

Jamie felt the meagre coolness of tears in the corners of her eyes and she watched as Alina began to fade.

A warmth began to spread. From her feet moving upwards. From her fingertips down.

From her stomach outwards.

And then across her face. Like the spray of the ocean on her cheeks.

Jamie blinked. Once. Twice.

And then watched as her hands dropped in front of her. Listened as her heart beat began to fade in her ears.

She lifted her now free fingers instinctively, touching her lips. She pulled them away wet, glistening black.

She didn't understand.

The Nhang swayed in front of her, his grip loosening from her throat, his strength now becoming a weight on her instead.

He collapsed forward and Jamie saw then. The hole in the side of his neck. The blood pumping from the wound, spilling over his shoulder and onto his black shirt and tactical vest.

Jamie. Jamie. 'Jamie!'

The voice wasn't in her head.

She turned to look, seeing Church loping down the hallway towards her, pistol in his hand.

'Jamie!' he yelled again.

She began to sink under the weight of the man that had nearly strangled her, and tried to shove him off.

He slid sideways, soaked with his own blood, and collapsed to the ground.

Jamie pulled in a breath, her skin alight with pins and needles as oxygen rushed into her lungs.

Her legs quaked and then buckled, but she didn't hit the ground.

Church scooped her in his arms and held her, cradling her head.

'Jesus, Jamie,' he panted. 'Are you alright?'

He took her face in his hands and moved it left and right, inspecting her neck in the near-blackness of the upstairs corridor.

The first rays of light were creeping into the sky now, bathing the scene in a bloody glow.

'I'm sorry, I'm sorry,' Church whispered. 'I should have been faster. But I had to be sure. I had one chance.'

Jamie just smiled at him. She had no words. And not the strength to form them.

'It's okay,' he said. 'You're okay.'

She found the sleeves of his shirt at his shoulders and clutched at the fabric.

He grinned down at her and she did her best to smile back.

And then she closed her eyes and felt safe as he held her against his chest, tears coming once more.

'It's over,' he said. 'It's over.'

But she knew that was a lie. In fact, it was just beginning.

CHAPTER
THIRTY-EIGHT

Time seemed to lurch forward in blurry flashes.

Jamie could still feel The Nhang's hands around her throat as Church laid her down on the landing above the stairs, the dead body of the man who had nearly just strangled her lying in a heap a few feet away.

Church disappeared, limping but moving fast, and then, one blurry flash later, he was passing Jamie with their bags in his arms.

He moved to the end of the corridor opposite the stairs and Jamie watched, massaging her throat, sitting on her hip, struggling to breathe, unable to talk, as he threw their bags from the balcony and into the car park one at a time.

And then he was back and helping her to her feet.

'Hold your breath and close your eyes,' he told her.

She did, as they descended back into the fog of tear gas, her arm around his shoulder.

He led her through it, the chemicals stinging her eyes and nose regardless, and then the cool embrace of the dawn air enveloped them.

Church coughed and hawked, eyes watering as he went to the bags and picked them up again.

The minute or so that Jamie had been given at the top of the stairs to recover was seemingly all that Church was allowing her.

'We have to move,' he called, picking up her duffle bag and throwing it to her.

She caught it numbly and stumbled back a step or two.

He clapped then, loudly and suddenly, and Jamie jolted.

'Jamie,' he said, voice hard and loud, the kind of tone she thought he'd have used during his service.

Jamie looked at him.

'Move your ass.' His eyes were wild and frightening. 'Nod.'

She nodded.

'Move!'

She began to walk forward, following him as he lifted the other two bags and headed for their car.

He blipped the keys, lifted the boot and threw the bags in. A quick glance at Jamie. He didn't bother waiting, just pointed to the passenger door and ran to the driver's side and got in.

Jamie opened the passenger door and climbed in with the bag on her lap.

He started the engine, tearing the bag from her grasp with his left hand and throwing it into the back seat.

'Belt,' he ordered as he wheeled backwards at speed and spun them around.

He shoved it into drive and sped out of the car park, heading down the entry road at speeds bordering on reckless.

The narrow country lane swooped and cut a waving line between the hedgerows, and had Jamie's throat not been throbbing and swollen, she would have asked him to slow down. But it was, so all she could do was put her belt on, as Church had requested.

In seconds they were flashing past the black SUVs parked in the layby and hammering out towards town.

The sky grew lighter with each passing second, a cloudless sky above turning from black to blue to purple to pink and yellow with each passing second.

'Come on, come on, come on,' Church muttered, stiff at the wheel.

Jamie looked across at him, understanding then.

He knew that the call would have come, that the police would be inbound, and though he didn't know where they were, his intention to beat them out of the country lane was clear.

As they approached the village, he didn't slow down but he did seem to soften, and at the first opportunity he pulled right off the widening road and onto another one, heading for Haverfordwest. The armed response would be coming from Carmarthen, and it was clear that Church wanted to be far away from the route that would bring them in.

Once they joined a two-lane road and began passing the odd car, Church slowed, immediately blending in.

He finally sighed with relief and wound down the windows, letting the cool air flow inwards, the sun rising on their left as they headed south towards the town.

Church reached over then and put his hand on Jamie's knee, squeezing gently. 'You okay?'

She swallowed, winced, and then nodded. 'Y-uh,' she croaked, trying to clear her throat and then immediately regretting it. 'Fuck,' she muttered. It hurt. 'Fuck,' she muttered again reflexively, gripping her own neck.

Church sucked air through his teeth a little. 'It's gonna bruise.'

'Great,' Jamie whispered. 'And I don't even have a turtleneck with me.'

'We can get you one,' Church said, seemingly bright and unphased by what had just happened.

The muzzle flash was still swimming in Jamie's eyes. The blood. The feeling of the vibration through her hands as she'd clubbed that unsuspecting guy in the kitchen.

'We had to,' Church said aloud then, as though

reading her mind. 'We had to do it. They were coming for you. To kill you.'

'I know,' Jamie muttered back, closing her eyes and holding her face to the flowing air.

'We did it for Alina.'

Jamie didn't even bother to answer now. She knew *why* they did it. They did it so that Elliot could get Alina out. But now that they'd committed the act ... the question of whether Elliot would hold up his end of things still remained to be seen.

'What now?' Church asked then. 'Call Hallberg? Tell her it worked?'

Jamie let her eyes open slowly. 'No,' she said. 'Not yet. First, I want to see Alina.'

'We don't know where she is. And all we have is the word of that ... that fucking ...' Church's mouth bunched angrily for a moment. 'Elliot.' He practically spat the word. 'What do you want to do, just *wait?*'

Jamie swallowed again, and winced again. 'Yeah,' she said, watching the sky brighten. 'We wait.'

CHAPTER
THIRTY-NINE

Jamie didn't like dodging phone calls. Especially not from Hallberg. But it's all she could do.

After the tenth call, Jamie hung up instead of letting it ring out to the answering machine. At least that way, Hallberg would know she was alive.

She sent her a text anyway, the guilt just too much. 'Alive. Working on something. Be in touch soon.'

Hallberg texted back almost immediately, and Jamie got as far as reading:

JESUS FUCKING CHRIST! WHEN YOU SAID YOU WERE GOING TO LAY A TRAP FOR THE NHANG, I DIDN'T EXPECT—

. . .

AND THEN SHE STOPPED READING. SHE DIDN'T much feel like getting the shit kicked out of her any more than she had already that morning. Jamie turned her phone over.

She was sitting in the front seat of the car, waiting for Church to get back from Tesco, hopefully with some coffee, something cold and edible for her throat and, with some luck, the aforementioned turtleneck.

She craned her neck to see the marks in the mirror. Her throat was almost entirely purple. She didn't even know if a turtleneck would cut it.

Jamie let out a long sigh, bouncing her heel in the footwell.

Come on, Elliot. Call already.

But he didn't.

Church returned with a bag full of stuff, including two coffees, a white chocolate Magnum ice cream, and a black turtleneck shirt.

Jamie thanked him with a nod and weighed up the coffee or the Magnum. She'd been up all night and felt like shit in every conceivable way. So, she held the Magnum against her throat, and slurped down the coffee. It hurt to swallow, but the caffeine was very much needed.

'No word?' Church asked, getting into the car. He lifted his own coffee to his lips, scratching at his beard with his other hand.

Jamie's silence would have to suffice.

'Fine,' he replied, starting the car. 'If we're just going to sit and wait all day, I at least want to have a decent view.'

He pulled away and Jamie drank in silence, holding the Magnum to her neck until she felt it liquify in the wrapper. She didn't have a sweet tooth, and just hoped it didn't leak through the plastic. She didn't have the energy, or the desire, to clean melted ice cream off the seats.

They headed for the coast and Church pulled to a stop overlooking the beach at Newgale.

He stayed in his seat for a few minutes, the water calm and clear in front of them.

'I'm going to swim,' he said then. It surprised Jamie. 'I got tear gas all over me and, honestly, I could use a clear head. You want to join me?' He looked over at Jamie for a moment.

She shook her head. She'd never been one for cold plunges, and though it was summer, the water would be *cold*. Instead, she held up her phone to signify that she was still waiting for it to ring.

'Right,' Church said, nodding and smiling, a little sadly it looked like.

He exited the car then and walked to the boot. He opened it and began fussing with his bag.

Jamie honestly didn't know what to make of him. She liked him, a lot. It wasn't tough to spend time with him – he was intuitive, and not overly talkative. He was strong when he needed to be, soft when it counted. He met her head on when she was being stubborn – she wasn't sure how much she liked that. But there was something to be said about it, all the same.

He closed the boot and walked around the side of the car and down towards the beach.

It was still early and the beach was empty except for a few dawn-treading surfers after the twilight waves. They bobbed between the waves in the distance, waiting for the right swell.

Jamie watched Church head for the shore, slowing short of the tide.

He was small, no more than a shape in the distance as he pulled off his shirt and then dropped his jeans, his little bundle of fresh clothes next to him.

She could barely make him out as he kicked his boots off and ran towards the water.

Jamie's eyes were heavy and unfocused.

And as Church sank beneath the waves, diving into the frigid ocean, she allowed her mind to drift. To thoughts of Alina. She could picture her smile most clearly. And it brought her comfort.

The waves washed onto the beach in the distance, their sound soothing. The rhythmic beating of the ocean on the sand calming.

So much so that it must have put Jamie to sleep. Because the next thing she knew, her phone was buzzing on her thigh.

She raised her head quickly, alert all of a sudden.

She looked around, felt sweat on her skin. The car was warm, the sun now up. How long had she been asleep?

She rubbed her eyes, searching for Church.

She spotted him on the beach a little way down, watching the sea. He had his elbows resting on his knees. He'd finished his swim and changed, seemingly. Had he come to the car and noticed she was asleep? Left her there to get some rest?

She picked up the phone instinctively, ready to silence it if it was Hallberg. But instead, she saw 'Blocked Number' and answered immediately.

'Hello?' she asked, her throat hurting as she spoke. The word came out husky and quiet.

'Jamie.' Elliot's voice. 'Are you alright?'

'Mhm,' she managed. 'Alina?'

He took a moment, analysing what he was hearing, but didn't say anything about it. 'She's safe,' he said then.

'Where is she?'

'Hold tight,' was all he said. 'We're coming to you.'

But before Jamie could respond, he hung up.

She got out of the car and opened her mouth to call to Church, realising then she couldn't muster the volume.

So instead she walked down onto the sand. As she got closer, he turned, alerted by the sound of her footsteps.

He looked up at her and smiled.

Jamie smiled back, tears coming to her eyes before she could stop them. 'She's coming,' Jamie said, grinning now. 'They're on their way.'

CHAPTER
FORTY

She did not know how long she would have to wait.

But as holidaymakers, surfers, campers, tourists, day trippers, and all manner of ramblers began to clog up the car park and make their way down onto the beach, Jamie began to grow nervous. Was Elliot really coming here? A wanted man with a girl stolen from the Armenians? They'd just fought off an army for this, and they were about to receive them in a crowded beachside car park?

Jamie and Church stood behind their car, leaning on the boot lid. Jamie was now in the black turtleneck to hide her bruises, and Church had his great arms folded once more, eyes scanning the crowd like an eagle hunting for mice from a tree branch, missing nothing, cataloguing everything.

They hadn't spoken in nearly twenty minutes. They just waited.

A continual line of cars queued into the car park, shuffling down the rows and filling them up. Jamie and Church were at the front, so their row filled first. Now, cars were filing into the back, the walk to the sand growing longer with each vehicle.

'This is taking too long,' Jamie muttered, narrowing her eyes and searching the sea of people.

'Takes as long as it takes,' Church said.

Useful, thanks.

She probably thought he was no stranger to just *waiting*. Countless operations spent crouching in swamps or lying in the desert. Sitting on planes to who knows where, or on boats or helicopters headed for missions. Waiting with an eye in the scope for a target to appear. Waiting for a signal. Waiting for anything, for everything. He was disciplined, and not shaken by much. This included.

Though any time Elliot's name came up it did seem to ruffle his feathers the wrong way. He wasn't bashful about his feelings. Jamie thought she liked that about him the most. That he said what he meant and what he thought in a matter-of-fact kind of way. It took the second-guessing out of everything.

The din of the beachgoers was loud. People laughing and talking as they hauled deck chairs and heavily laden beach bags towards the sea.

Children giggled and screamed with joy, running

about like chickens on a farm. Darting between the parked cars and skipping down onto the beach.

It took her a moment to pick the voice out in the clamour. Her name being called.

'Jamie!'

She pushed off the car and stood taller, looking around. Scanning the crowd.

'Jamie!' The voice grew louder, excited and accented. She knew that voice.

'Alina.'

'Jamie!'

She appeared then, shoving her way between a family dragging what looked like their entire living room with them.

The girl seemed bigger than she remembered, all curls and white teeth, rushing towards Jamie.

She was wearing different clothes to when they'd taken her – a summer dress, sandals. She looked clean, she looked healthy, she looked strong.

And when she ran into Jamie, she almost knocked her off her feet.

Yep, strong.

Jamie staggered backwards, Alina's arms gripping her so tightly it hurt.

But she didn't care.

She hugged the girl back, listening to her quickened breath, wondering if she'd ever let her go again.

Alina moved her hands to Jamie's neck and squeezed even tighter.

Jamie winced a little, the pain in her throat sudden and violent.

Alina released, noticing, and looked at Jamie quizzically, perhaps noticing the deep bags under her eyes, the bloodshot whites from the tear gas, or perhaps just smelling the smoke on her.

'Jamie – are you okay?' she asked in her perfect, stilted way.

Jamie nodded. It was all she could do. She thought if she tried to speak, she'd burst into tears.

And to hide that, she just hugged Alina again, only releasing when Church cleared his throat loudly, signifying Elliot's arrival.

Jamie let the girl go, but kept hold of her hand, finding the man in question walking towards them, looking the picture of a summer holiday.

He was wearing beige chinos rolled to the ankles, boat shoes, a white shirt with upturned cuffs and undone top two buttons, and a pair of dark sunglasses.

'Jamie,' he said, nodding easily at her. 'Solomon,' he added, giving Church a polite nod too.

Church just grunted.

'Elliot,' Jamie croaked, garnering a questioning look from Alina.

Elliot came closer, lowered his head a little to look at her. 'A bit warm for a turtleneck, don't you think?' He paused, just a step or two away, and seemed to notice the bruising just beneath her jaw. His hand lifted, reached out. 'Let me take a look at that.'

Before his fingers got close, Church's hand shot out like a viper's head and took his wrist from the air, fingers coiled tightly. 'Keep your hands to yourself,' he growled.

Elliot's eyes flashed to his. 'I'd suggest you do the same.'

Church threw his arm back at him, the finger marks bright white on his tanned skin.

Elliot pocketed his hand without missing a beat and looked at Jamie again. 'All went well with our ... mutual friend, I'm guessing?'

The Nhang. Jamie nodded. 'He's ... not going to be a problem anymore.'

'How did you know where to find us?' Church interjected then.

'I have my ways,' Elliot said easily.

'What ways?' Church pressed.

Elliot looked into the distance, as though bored of the line of questioning. 'You know phones? The thing everyone has in their pockets? Well, they have this magical thing called GPS, and if you're clever enough, and you try really, really hard, you can use that GPS to find people.'

'Don't push me, psycho,' Church snarled this time, the muscles in his arms straining as Elliot toyed with him.

'Then don't ask stupid questions,' came the quick reply.

Church pushed off the car then to square up with

Elliot, and though Jamie meant to intervene, it was Alina who got there first.

She jumped between them and shoved Church in the chest, which seemed to surprise him.

Alina stood right in front of Elliot, looking fierce, brow cut into a deep V. She looked ready to fight, ready to protect him.

He laid a hand on her shoulder softly, and she glanced up at him.

'It's alright,' he said, 'we're just talking. I'm sure it's been a long night for them both.'

That seemed to ease Alina's concern, but she didn't move.

Jamie looked at her, then at Elliot. She knew how quickly he could get under your skin, how much he could make you like him, trust him.

And she didn't like whatever the fuck was going on here.

She reached out and took Alina's hand again. 'Thank you, Elliot, for holding up your end. I really appreciate it. But we have to go now.' She began to pull Alina by the wrist, but the girl pulled back, looking fiercely at her now. 'Come on, Alina, we're leaving,' Jamie said.

'No,' Alina replied, pulling her hand free of Jamie's grasp altogether.

'No? What do you mean no, we're going. Now,' Jamie insisted, making another grab for her wrist.

This time Alina whipped it out of reach altogether and then retreated behind Elliot.

'What the hell are you playing at?' Church snapped, coming forward a step. 'What did you say to her?'

He held his hands in the air innocently. 'I didn't ...' he looked from one to the other. 'I think it's best if Alina explains it.'

He stepped aside, then looked at her and gave her a nod of encouragement.

She stared back at him, her big brown eyes sparkling in the morning sun.

A few days. That's all she could have known him. And she was staring at him like he was what, a friend, her father, a fucking god?

Jamie held her tongue. Barely.

Alina swallowed, steeled herself, then addressed Jamie and Church as best she could.

'I am ... not ... alone,' she said, fishing for the right words.

'Of course you're not,' Jamie said, smiling and holding out her arms. 'You have me. I'm here.'

'No, that is not ...' Alina shook her head.

Jamie was confused.

'There are other ... girls. Like me.'

Jamie stared at Alina, at the look of pain on her face. She let her go on.

'They are ... there,' she said, turning and pointing in the direction they'd come from. 'They are ...' She trailed off, not knowing the words, then looked at Elliot, said, *'galiebshi gamok'et'ili.'*

'Locked in cages,' Elliot said, giving her the words she was asking for in Georgian.

Jamie didn't even want to know how he spoke it.

'In cages,' Alina repeated, looking at Church and Jamie in turn. 'Girls like me.' She put her hands on her chest. 'In cages. There.' She pointed into the distance again. 'You know?'

'Understand,' Elliot corrected her.

'You understand?'

Jamie's heart was pounding. 'I understand.' But she didn't.

'I go,' Alina said then, nodding to Jamie. 'I go. I help them. I ... save.'

Jamie shook her head. 'No, no, you're coming with me.'

Alina smiled at her but didn't come forward. 'I go.'

'No, you're coming with me. You have to.' Jamie began to get choked. 'I just got you back. I'm not letting you go again.'

'Jamie ...' Alina said, in that same, perfect, stilted way. 'I go. I save.'

Jamie scoffed this time, incredulous, verging on tears. 'Do you know what I had to go through to get you back? I'm not letting you go anywhere!'

'Jamie.' This time it was Elliot, voice like silk. 'It's alright. I'll look after her, I'll make sure she's safe—'

'You'll not do shit,' Church interjected now, taking

another step towards Elliot. 'You've poisoned her mind, and there's no fucking way I'm going to let you leave with her.' His hand shot out once more, going for Elliot's throat this time.

But either he seemed to expect it, or he was just a lot faster than Church expected, because his hand rose up so quickly, Jamie didn't even see it.

He drove it through Church's wrist in an upwards arm block, and then slotted his left foot forward, kicking Church's right ankle out from under him, putting him off balance.

Before Church could recover, Elliot just sort of pulled him forward and moved out of the way so that he stumbled past him three or four steps before he regained his balance.

He was back to his normal languid self then, addressing Jamie while Church managed to steady himself on the back of a Volkswagen Golf, shocked by the exchange, and now visibly enraged.

'This isn't me, Jamie, I swear,' he said, looking at her but aware that Church was at his flank.

Jamie held her hand up, stilling Church from knocking Elliot's head clean off his shoulders.

He came forward a little, but then stopped, hands locked in fists at his side like the loaded shotgun in the boot of their Hyundai.

'No?' Jamie asked back. 'She came to this conclusion all on her own, did she? You expect me to believe that?'

'I do,' Elliot said cautiously. 'Because she's right.

She's not the only one. There are others. Girls. Boys. Older, the same age ... younger.'

'How much younger?'

Elliot seemed troubled by the very thought – but then again, he was a wonderful actor. 'A lot younger. And there's lots of them.'

She felt like there was another tall order coming.

'But ... with The Nhang out of the way, there's a chance we can do something. Something big. Something that will help a lot more than just Alina, and something that will really hit Petrosyan and his whole operation where it hurts. Cut the head off the snake.'

Jamie watched him, searching his face for any hint of this being truth, or a lie.

'We have a chance,' Elliot said then. 'I know why they wanted The Surgeon, what they have planned.'

'Speak,' Jamie ordered him.

'There's an event, a big one. People coming in from all over the world by the sounds of it,' Elliot said. 'Being held in a few days' time. I don't know where yet, but I know it's something that makes that little exhibition you broke up in the water treatment plant look like a school yard tussle.'

'What are you saying?'

'Those fights, they're not just for entertainment. They're exhibitions. Of skill. They're warm-ups for the main event. That's why they wanted The Surgeon on hand. To make sure that the fighters are fit, are healthy. And to ... keep them going for as long as they can.'

Jamie's eyes went to Alina now. She was staring right back at her with a look of utter determination in her big eyes.

'No,' Jamie said then. 'Not a chance. I'm not letting her go anywhere near that place. She's not fighting. Not ever again.'

'I won't let it go that far,' Elliot said. 'I promise she'll be safe.'

Could she trust him?

'I don't know where it is yet. They're cautious of me. Naturally. They think I'm the one that offed The Surgeon in fact. And now with The Nhang mysteriously disappeared ... they won't be any more trusting. But they'll take me there, to wherever this is being held, and once I know, I'll send you the details.'

Jamie's lips quivered. 'And then what?'

'And then ... and then you kill Aram Petrosyan.'

'Kill him?' Jamie repeated it to make sure she heard him right.

'He's the one who wants you. And he's the one who wants Alina. And until he's dead, this won't stop.'

'Why don't you do it?' Jamie asked then, the anger rising in her as well. 'You have access to him. You're fine with taking a life when it suits you.'

'I don't have access to him,' Elliot said coolly. 'I'm with Alina. Making sure she's safe.'

'Convenient,' Church muttered from behind Elliot.

'Not convenient at all, actually,' he said back, a little strained. It was the first time she'd ever seen a flicker of uncertainty in him. The same she'd heard on the phone. Like he actually cared enough to be put off balance by something. 'In fact, it's pretty inconvenient, because if they suspect for even a moment what I'm doing, they'll put a bullet in my head. No questions.' His eyes burned into Jamie's with an intensity that made her uncomfortable. 'This is the plan. Trust me. I'll keep Alina safe, and when I know where and when it's happening, you find a way to get inside. You locate Petrosyan, and you put him down. For good. And when the dust settles, you'll be free.' He looked at Alina. 'Both of you.'

Jamie had no words.

Elliot seemed more on edge by the moment. 'I have to go. We have to get back before they suspect something. The Nhang leaving put a hole in their security rotation, but when Petrosyan gets wind of what happened to him, they'll double the number of guys watching us. And if that happens before we get back ...'

'So don't go,' Jamie said then, the words coming before she could think. 'Just stay. Leave Alina with me. I can keep her safe. We can keep her safe.'

Elliot stared at her for a second, his expression soft. 'And the others? The kids who are going to be forced to kill each other for blood sport before being sold off like cattle and used for fighting or worse until they're dead? What about them?'

'I don't care about them,' Jamie whispered, looking at Alina.

'Jamie,' Elliot said, voice sharp enough for her to

look at him now. 'You do. And you'd never be able to live with yourself. You know this is the right call.'

Her throat had all but closed to a pinhole.

'You can count on me,' he reminded her. 'To look after Alina, and to make this happen. I promise you that.'

She closed her eyes, knowing if she looked at Alina, she'd never let her go again. And then she nodded. Forced herself to nod.

She heard Elliot breathe a sigh of relief, and then Alina was hugging her again.

Jamie kept her eyes screwed closed, but hugged the girl back with everything she had.

It was only when Elliot pulled her away did she let go.

'I see you soon,' she said, her voice fading as she moved away.

But Jamie could neither open her eyes, or say anything back.

She just let them go, doing her best not to run after the girl.

After an age, Church's footsteps on the stony ground beneath them told her he was right there. She felt his hand on her shoulder, his grip gentle but firm.

'Come on,' he said, 'let's get out of here.'

Jamie let him steer her towards the car and climbed in when he opened the door. He circled around and climbed in the other side.

She pulled the sun visor down and looked up into

the mirror there, seeing her cheeks puffy and red, her eyes bloodshot, and tears rolling down her cheeks.

'Fuck,' Jamie said, punching the dashboard so hard she nearly broke her hand. 'Fuck!'

Church just sat there, staring at the gently rolling waves, the endless blue sky, and the millions of diamonds twinkling on the water. 'Fuck is right,' he said, slowly putting the car in reverse and backing out of their space. 'Fuck is right … but it just doesn't seem to cover it this time.

CHAPTER
FORTY-ONE

When Hallberg arrived, Jamie wasn't sure what to expect.

A few hours had passed since Elliot and Alina had left, and Jamie and Church had left the beach, heading back inland. Where, they didn't know. Jamie felt like a nomad. Nowhere to call home. The last place she had was Stockholm. That's where her apartment was, in the city. It was bright and clean and came fully furnished. She had no keepsakes or mementos she would miss. She'd not amassed anything she'd want to grab if the place burned down. She thought, at the back of her mind, she'd always known it would be temporary, and that had stopped her from buying things she'd not want to leave behind.

She didn't know if that was the saddest thing she'd ever owned up to. But either way, wallowing in self-pity could wait. It would have to. They still had a job to do. And it wasn't going to be easy.

Hallberg met them at the roadside in the car park of an old chapel a little way outside Carmarthen. Jamie thought she might have gone to the hotel, knowing what she knew, but it looked like she was steering well clear of the place.

When Church pulled in, she was standing against her car, on her phone. She hung up as they came to a stop, and approached.

Jamie thought she'd begin chewing her out immediately but, instead, she hugged her tightly.

Jamie hugged back, but couldn't help but hiss a little at the pain as Hallberg's arm squeezed on her neck.

She pulled back and reached for Jamie's collar before she could stop her, pulling it down to reveal the deep purple marks.

She said nothing, just pursed her lips and gently put the fabric back.

Then she took a few steps towards her car, turning slowly, as though gathering her thoughts.

'Well ... I'm glad you're not dead,' she said eventually.

'That makes two of us.' Jamie smiled wanly.

'I had an inkling of what was coming when you asked me to *leak* your location, but I didn't think it'd be this bad.'

'Is it *that* bad?' Jamie asked.

'It's pretty much a waking nightmare. For everyone

involved. Police, NCA, Interpol ... and that's not mentioning the political firestorm it's kicked up. Home Office want to know why there was an Armenian kill squad on British soil, and the Armenians want to know why a dozen of their nationals were gunned down in the arse end of Wales of all places.'

'Maybe they should ask them.'

'Not the time to be glib, Jamie. Whether it was justified or not, murder is murder, and there should be inquisitions, investigations, arrests, trials, and retributions. Fuck, if my superiors even knew I was here ...' She tsked. 'You seem to have the uncanny ability to make me risk my job, you know that?'

'Frankly, Julia, I'm a little past caring.' Jamie didn't mean for the comment to come out barbed, but it did.

Hallberg stiffened. 'One phone call, Jamie. Remember that. It's all over for you, for whatever crusade you're on here.'

'How about one to save fifty kids?'

Hallberg's jaw flexed a little as she measured Jamie. She looked at Church instead. 'You want to tell me what the hell's going on here?'

Church looked from one to the other, and then just got back in the car.

'Great,' Hallberg said. 'I just don't know what to do anymore, Jamie. I don't know how long I can keep covering for you here. If they find out that I sent an email saying where you were going to be, and then that night, all this shit happens? That's my ass.'

'Surely it's the *agency's* ass,' Jamie insisted. 'If you sent an internal email saying where I was going to be, and the Armenians picked that up, it's surely not on you?'

'It is if I knew this was going to happen, which I did. This whole plausible deniability grey area you're operating in – spilling blood and then slipping out the back door before the shit hits the fan, relying on our friendship for me to get you out of the graves you're digging for yourself. It's not sustainable. And it's not working for me anymore.' Hallberg let out a long sigh. 'Apart from killing those men, there were illegal weapons found on site, and the owner – who was found barred inside her own flat – described you and Solomon pretty accurately. So, there's no denying it was you two who filled that place full of holes and dead bodies. Braun, my boss, already asked me what I knew about it? Why you had those guns, where you were now, why you hadn't come forward. Did I know it was going to go down like that?' She just started shaking her head now. 'And I lied, once again. For you.'

Jamie watched her friend, listened to her voice crack. 'I'm sorry,' Jamie said. 'I really am.'

'It's not good enough this time,' she said.

'You're going to turn me in?'

'What other choice do I have? If they ever found out we met, I'd probably go to prison myself, let alone lose my job.'

'I never wanted that.'

'I know you didn't, but these things have conse-quences. Ripples that reverberate through everything around them. Interpol and the NCA are running one of the biggest joint-ops in their history, and at the heart of it there are two vigilantes killing key witnesses and blowing up hotels in Pembrokeshire. And the tide is turning.'

Jamie narrowed her eyes. 'What do you mean?'

'They're siphoning resources and setting up a team, Jamie. To come after you.'

'Me?' Jamie asked curtly, resisting the urge to say, *but we're the good guys!* So, instead, she asked, 'Who's running it?'

'Catherine Mallory.'

Jamie scoffed a little. 'Seriously?'

Hallberg nodded.

Another thought occurred to Jamie then, her mind going back through the last few days at light speed. 'Mallory. You speak to her a lot?'

'A bit,' Hallberg said. 'She's our POC at the NCA on this.'

'And the email about where we'd be ... Who did you send that to?'

'A few people,' Hallberg said. 'A chain email.'

'Including Mallory?'

'Yeah ... Oh, shit, Jamie, you're not still on this whole *Mallory is crooked* train are you?'

'You know that she told Hassan that the information

we got from Caroline Lewis at the gala came to nothing? Total wash?'

'Yeah, I'm aware,' Hallberg said tiredly. 'So what?'

'Did you take a look at it?'

'NCA's op. I had to pull strings just to get you in on that.'

'Right, so Mallory's the only one who got eyes-on with it I'm guessing?'

'I just told you that all of the NCA and Interpol are forming a super team to hunt you down, and you're still flogging this dead horse?'

'It's not a dead horse,' Jamie said. 'And you can't tell me this isn't a pattern? Every time Mallory's been looped in on where we've been, the Armenians have shown up. It's no coincidence, and if you keep thinking it is, it's going to bite you. She can point the finger at me all she likes, but I know she's fucking dirty, and I'm going to prove it.'

Hallberg put her hands on her hips. 'Right, and this is *after* you save fifty kids?'

'Exactly.'

Hallberg rolled her lips into a line, staring at Jamie for a few seconds. 'So, you want to humour me with ... whatever the fuck it is you're talking about? Or do you want to just part ways here and take your chances?'

'Promise not to tell Mallory?'

'I'm not in the mood for jokes, Jamie. I've been up since four AM dealing with your shit.'

'Right.' Jamie came a little closer, hoping the intimacy would make for a friendlier reception. 'I saw Alina.'

'What? Where?'

'My contact, the one I told you about? He met us, with Alina.'

'Elliot Day.'

Jamie was taken aback. 'I ... How did you know?'

'Because I'm good at my job, and while you were off fighting your war, I was doing it. You mentioned Interpol's wanted list, a contact with ties to people like the Armenians? You've had a varied career, but you don't know that many people on Interpol's wanted list. Once I started going back through your life, it wasn't hard to see. Frankly, I'm surprised no one else figured out you were working with him while you were at the Met. A serial killer, seriously, Jamie?'

'Why do I feel like I'm being judged right now?'

'Because you are,' Hallberg laughed. 'You guys swap postcards?'

'You're not ... surprised? Shocked? Appalled?'

'All of the above. For a minute, at least. But then I said, *Oh wait, this is Jamie Johansson.* Nothing you do shocks me anymore. Though I do dread seeing your name pop up on my phone.'

That hurt. 'Want me to apologise again?'

'No,' Hallberg said tiredly, 'just ... just tell me what's going on. I'll be incredulous, tell you not to do it, and then you can just go and do it anyway.'

'Wow, you're really just laying into me today, huh?'

'I'm lacking my usual patience for your bullshit, yes, so you'd better speak quickly, and clearly. And don't lie to me. Or I *will* arrest you.'

Jamie nodded. 'Got it. Elliot is ... a friend, I guess. For all his faults—'

'Murdering people and selling their organs for money?'

'Right ...' Jamie said, looking away. 'He's helped me out of a few binds, and always been reliable. I trust him.'

'Then you're a fool.'

'I seem to be hearing that a lot, lately,' Jamie said, glancing back at the car.

'There's probably a reason.' Hallberg folded her arms. 'Go on.'

'He's managed to get in with the Armenians, and he found Alina. We agreed that he'd get her out, but she doesn't want out. Not alone.'

'Fifty kids?'

'I don't know. Maybe less. Maybe more,' Jamie said. 'All locked up, being prepped for some sort of event, Elliot said. Something that goes down once a year. Scumbags bring in their fighters from all over the world, pit them against one another to the death. Big money changes hands, I guess. Kids bought and sold like meat.'

Hallberg's jaw flexed again. 'Where? When? Details? I can vet the information, run it up the chain, see if we can scramble an op—'

'No,' Jamie cut in.

'Why did I know that was coming?' Hallberg closed her eyes.

'I don't know any of the details yet, but what I do know is that if they even get a whiff of us knowing about this ahead of time, they'll cancel it and scatter.'

'So what are you proposing here exactly?'

'I'm going in there to get Alina out. But I'm trying to be straight with you here. I can't rescue fifty kids on my own – I know I need your help, the agency's help. I just … I have to make sure Alina is safe first. Once I'm sure of that, Interpol can have it. Though if you want to get there without them being alerted, I'd suggest you keep Catherine Mallory out of it.'

'So, you want me to just sit on my hands while you potentially disrupt the largest gathering of traffickers … ever. Knowing full well it's going on. And then, after I get your call, scramble … a strike team? Armed response? Military intervention? Helicopters, riot vans, an army of officers and agents? All on a moment's notice?'

Jamie looked at her, weighing the woman in front of her. 'To score the biggest bust of your career and cement your position at the agency for life?'

Hallberg's eyes twitched a little.

'How long would you need?' Jamie asked.

Hallberg's nostrils flared. 'An hour. But I'll need footage. Actionable intelligence. Enough to sway Braun to pull out all the stops.'

'I can do that.'

'Fuck!' Hallberg muttered. 'You're going to be the death of me.'

'Or I'm about to deliver you tenure.' Jamie cracked a smile. 'And once you don't have a boss to answer to, you can say I've been on the payroll this entire time and collect all the credit.'

'Ha! And let you get away with everything you've done? Fat chance. No, you're going to owe me one for this. Hell, you already owe me ten.'

'I'll owe you everything if this comes off,' Jamie promised. 'I'll worry about Alina, and once we give the signal, you come in and mop up the rest.' Jamie held out her hand.

Hallberg stared at it. 'And if I can't make it happen? If I can't scramble an army?'

Jamie held her hand there. 'Then at least we'll save one. And it'll be better than saving none.'

Hallberg thought on that, and then took Jamie's hand. 'I'll do my best to make it happen.'

'I know you will.'

Jamie made to let go of Hallberg's hand and walk towards the car, but she wouldn't let her. She held on firm.

Jamie paused and looked back.

'What does he want?' Hallberg asked then.

'Who?'

'Elliot Day,' Hallberg said. 'For helping you get Alina out. He asked to be taken off Interpol's most wanted list.

That can't happen. So, what else? What else does he want from you?'

Jamie swallowed. 'I don't know. Nothing, I don't think. He didn't say he wanted anything.'

Hallberg squeezed her hand a little tighter. 'He wants something, Jamie. They always do. And if he's doing this for you, then you're giving it to him.' She let Jamie's hand go and pocketed her own. 'Whether you know it or not.'

CHAPTER
FORTY-TWO

'That seemed to go well,' Church said as Jamie climbed back into the car.

Hallberg pulled around them, gave a small wave, and then drove off.

Jamie watched her go in the wing mirror before she spoke. 'Yeah. Now comes the easy part. All we have to do is get inside what's sure to be an extremely heavily guarded, private event, filled with mercenaries and trained killers, find Aram Petrosyan in the middle of it all, and then kill him.'

'And then get out alive,' Church added, holding his finger up and grinning. 'Don't forget that part.'

Jamie had to crack a smile at that, too. 'Does nothing ever phase you?'

He rolled his head side to side. 'Dinner with my parents. Conversations about commitment. The idea of raising children. When someone says that SIG Sauers are better than Glocks.'

Jamie smirked. 'I actually really liked my P320.'

He held his hand up and closed his eyes. 'Stop, stop. I don't have the energy for this argument right now.'

She laughed.

He laughed.

It was a moment of respite.

But it faded as quickly as it came.

'I think you'd make a good dad,' Jamie offered then.

He shrugged. 'I don't. Got a lot of baggage I'd unload on my kid, I know that much. And I don't think anyone deserves that.'

Jamie let the statement sit. She had her own baggage. And lots of it. And she'd never wanted kids. But the thought of looking after Alina didn't scare her. The opposite. The time they'd spent together, though short-lived and fraught with danger … Jamie had enjoyed it. It was nice to have a purpose other than just catching bad guys.

'So, what now?' Church asked then, breaking the silence.

Jamie shrugged. 'You got another bag full of guns hidden somewhere?'

'No,' Church said. 'You lost my only *bag full of guns,* unfortunately.'

'Me?' Jamie laughed. 'Joint effort, I think.'

'Debatable. But what else could I expect from a SIG-lover.'

'Hey, hey, I never said I liked them better than Glocks.'

'Yeah, but you said you liked them, so ...' He sucked air between his teeth. 'I just don't think we can be friends now.'

She huffed a little, then socked him in the arm. 'Just drive the fucking car.'

'Where to?' he asked, staring through the windshield.

'I don't know,' Jamie said truthfully.

'Alright then,' Church replied, starting the car. 'Lunch it is then. Steak?'

'Steaks? You want to get steaks now?'

'Yeah,' he said, pulling out onto the road. 'If it makes it any better, you can think of it as a last meal.'

'Weirdly,' Jamie huffed, 'it doesn't.'

AS THEY DROVE, JAMIE COULDN'T HELP BUT consider the scale of what they were about to do. That they'd be venturing into the viper's nest in order to cut the head off the snake. That a handful of armed men coming to them on their terms, on their home turf ... it was different from what lay ahead of them here.

Worlds apart, in fact.

'We need a second set of eyes,' Jamie said aloud, the thought forming as she spoke. 'Someone watching our back. Someone we can trust.'

'You have someone in mind,' Church said, a statement not a question.

'I'd say Hassan, but I don't know whether he'd go for it with Mallory in his ear.'

'I could make some calls,' Church offered. 'I know a few people.'

'No, I'd prefer Hassan. He's been in this since the beginning, and I don't like how we left things. I trust him with my life, and that list is pretty short.'

'I understand. The Mallory thing is an issue. One that will have to be resolved one way or another. Have you thought about how to prove her involvement in all this? Or her innocence?'

Jamie snorted at the last part. 'She's too smart to walk into a trap. If her activities have gone undetected this long, then she knows what she's doing. She's cautious. Though I still don't understand her motivations – I have no doubt Hallberg looked into her. And that she found nothing. If it's money, she's keeping it hidden somewhere – and that's no mean feat when you have Interpol breathing down your neck. But somehow, she doesn't strike me as the financially motivated sort.'

'If she is crooked, then she wants something. If it's not money, it's power.'

'They do seem to be the only two things, right?'

'And revenge.'

Jamie appreciated that, too. She'd waged her own wars without any mind for money or power. She'd labelled her driving force as justice, but she was old enough and cynical enough to call it what it was: revenge.

But she didn't say it.

'It's not something we can tackle right now. We have to be smart about it,' Jamie thought aloud. 'But in the meanwhile, you think we can convince him?'

'I do,' Church answered with a fair amount of surety. 'But this time, let me do the talking.'

'You don't think I can convince him?'

'I didn't say that,' Church answered flatly. 'But sometimes, you need the carrot, not the stick. And telling him his boss got his partner killed and he's stupid not to see it doesn't feel like the right way to play this.'

'So, you're saying I'm more stick than carrot?' Jamie asked coolly.

Church laughed aloud. 'Oh, Jamie. You're all stick,' he said, grinning at her. 'All the time.'

THE CONVERSATION WENT A LITTLE SOMETHING like this:

'Nasir Hassan – Solomon Church.'

'Hi,' Hassan said, a little cautious. Church had called from Jamie's phone, so it wasn't hard to surmise that they were together at the time. 'Everything okay?' he asked.

'We need your help.'

'Help? With what?' The air of caution was still there.

'We're running a covert operation under the purview of Interpol. Sanctioned but unofficial. Your ears only. We need a body for overwatch, no engagement. Just recon.'

Hassan was silent and Jamie was sure he was about to hang up. But then he said: 'No engagement?'

'Guaranteed.'

'What's the operation?'

'Targeted killing. Search and rescue. We're hitting Aram Petrosyan, then getting Alina out. Intel says other children will be held on site. Interpol are on mop-up after mission complete.'

'Why me?'

'Jamie wants you. She trusts you.'

More silence.

Then, he said: 'Okay. Send me the details.'

'Appreciate it.'

Hassan hung up.

Church handed the phone back to Jamie. 'All good.'

Jamie was gobsmacked. 'What the fuck?' was all she could muster. 'Seriously?'

'Seriously *what?*' Church asked.

'Seriously, you said literally nothing to him and he committed in a heartbeat. When the last time we spoke, he basically told me to piss off.'

Church considered that, then shrugged. 'Men are simple.'

'Men are simple? That's your answer?'

He chuckled a little. 'What do you want me to say?

Jedi mind tricks? Look, Jamie. Men are simple. All we want is respect.'

'Respect, right,' Jamie said. 'That still doesn't make what just happened any clearer.'

Church just shrugged again. 'I don't know what to say. Often asking a direct question yields a direct answer.'

Jamie shook her head. 'I'll never understand men,' she muttered. 'You have your own language.'

He harrumphed a little, amused. 'You think men are tough? Women are ...'

'Women are what?' Jamie asked coldly, narrowing her eyes.

'Yeah, on second thought, I'll keep my head attached to my body, thanks,' Church replied.

'I think that's smart.'

'Yeah,' he laughed. 'Me too.'

CHAPTER
FORTY-THREE

Waiting was the hardest part.

The day dragged on.

Jamie was tired, and though she had to assume Church was too, he didn't show it. They did get lunch. And afterwards, Jamie just sort of sank into a stupor, her mind wandering while she whiled away the hours waiting for Elliot's call.

And then it came.

And things began moving very quickly.

They only had a few hours' notice, and the location Elliot gave them was in the middle of Wales, in the middle of nowhere. An old country estate that Jamie never even knew existed.

Elliot said that the first fights were scheduled for ten at night, with the main event happening sometime around midnight. He didn't know when Alina would be making an appearance, but he assured Jamie he'd watch over her. He gave her the address then, told them to be in position for Alina's fight and wait for a signal, and finished the conversation with the words, 'Good luck.'

The wishes were ominous, and she felt like the phrase *'you're going to need it'* could easily have been tacked on the end.

Hallberg's warning echoed in her mind as the line went dead. What is Elliot getting out of this?

Frankly, the whole thing felt borderline suicidal. Especially considering they had no idea what they were walking into, when the fight would be, what the signal was, where their target would be, how to get to him, how to kill him, and then how to get out alive.

Interpol's arrival would also need to fit into all this. Somehow.

So, as they headed north, en route to the estate and their rendezvous with Hassan, Jamie's nerves began setting in.

'Stop chewing your fingernails,' Church said, not even looking over.

Jamie tucked them into the palms of her hands and laid them on her thighs. 'How are you not shitting yourself right now?'

'Who says I'm not?'

'So, you are?'

He smiled a little. 'No, not really. Funnily enough, years of training and active operations have sort of weeded fear and nerves out of me. At least when it comes to this sort of thing. When it happens, it happens. I'll be ready.'

'To die?' Jamie clarified.

'If that's what's in store. I find it best not to think about it. To just try ... not to. Be alert, be careful, don't take any unnecessary risks. I've been shot, I've been stabbed, I've been burnt, I've been blown up. None of them are fun. I've learned a lot of hard lessons about being careful.'

'Me too,' Jamie said.

'Mhm. I know. I spent a reasonable amount of time inspecting your scars, remember?' He raised an eyebrow, curled a little smile as he glanced over at her.

Jamie wrapped her arms around her body instinctively. 'Yeah,' she said sheepishly, 'I remember.'

Church smiled as though recalling it.

Jamie made more of an effort to hide her recollection. It had been nice. Probably the best she'd had. She'd never much liked sex. Though something told her it was likely because she'd done it with the wrong people. Either way, that night had been unexpected but, now, it was an island in her mind. A brief moment of respite to return to in what had been a hurricane of shit.

Church was a good man.

She didn't know how she'd live with herself if she got him killed.

But now wasn't the time to be focused on that. He was right in what he'd said – they just needed to be careful. To stay sharp. And to make sure that they accomplished their mission here.

Get in. Kill Petrosyan. Get out.

Simple. Right?

Right?

... Right?

She kept asking herself the question, but no answer seemed to come.

And they drove on.

THE AFTERNOON HAD WORN INTO EARLY evening, and the sky had paled to a soft summer yellow.

Church pulled off the road a few kilometres before the estate and pulled up the satellite view on his phone. He flipped over to the topographical layer and spent some time considering it before he marked a location and sent it to Hassan.

Then, they set off.

Jamie had to admit, it was nice to have someone with military experience doing this kind of planning.

Church guided them to the nearest village and then headed up a farm track until they came upon a little parking area that served as the trailhead to some hiking routes cutting through the wilds to the east of Tregaron.

There wasn't much out there – in fact the place was known as the Green Desert. The largest stretch of land in Wales with nothing in it.

From Jamie's own summation, they were about five

kilometres from the estate and the position that Church had marked for Hassan. It looked to be on a rise about a full kilometre from the house, about six-hundred metres outside the walls, and high enough up that they'd get a good overview of the place.

Church retrieved his duffle from the boot and laid it on the ground behind the car, taking a quick inventory of what was inside. The shotgun had been lost, but he'd managed to recover both of their rifles from the upper floor before they'd left. They still had their ballistic vests, too. Which Jamie was thankful for. She hoped she wasn't going to be shot. But … better to have it and not need it than the opposite.

'Ready?' Church asked, looking up at her.

Jamie nodded.

'Okay then.' He zipped up the duffle, shouldered it, turned, and headed down off the side of the road.

Jamie took one last look around, thinking how pretty the place was with its rolling hills, and how it was all just a thin veil draped over a bed of pure evil.

She'd had a taste of what lay ahead at the water treatment plant, but she knew this was going to be on a whole other level.

Decadence and evil in a scale yet unimaginable.

She let that thought sit, let it fester in her guts. Let it light her ire and burn in her chest.

Good, she thought. Burn. Burn hot and violent.

I need it to. Because tonight, I'm going to kill a man in cold blood.

· · ·

THE WALK WENT QUICKLY. CHURCH WAS marching at military pace, but even so, Jamie's mind was adrift. She was thinking of Alina, trying to think of her. Trying not to think about what was ahead. But it wasn't easy.

She could picture Aram Petrosyan. And though she hated the man, she didn't know him. He was a figure-head, a ghoul in her mind and not a person. She wondered if that would make it easier to sight him with her pistol and pull the trigger, or if it would make it harder. That when she did line him up, that she'd see him suddenly as a living, breathing creature. That when she looked in his eyes ... she'd choke. She wouldn't be able to do it.

Jamie had killed. But she wasn't a killer.

And this was premeditated murder. That's all there was to it.

Church slowed ahead, checked his phone, and then cut off the beaten path, trekking through the long grass.

Jamie followed diligently as he guided them over a series of rolling ridges, and then around the side of a hill. He slowed a little as they came to the crest of the final one and dropped the duffle from his shoulder. He rolled his arm around in circles and cracked his back. Though he wasn't showing it, Jamie thought he still must be in pretty bad pain from their ordeal at the hotel the night previous. It seemed insane to her that less than twenty-four hours had passed. But there was no time to dwell on that now.

Church was already digging around in the duffle bag for various bits. He pulled a rolled up mat from the bottom and spread it on the rise, then laid out a little folded up tripod and a zipped case. Jamie knelt beside him as he took out a rangefinder that looked like one half of an oversized binocular.

As he set up the tripod and began mounting the rangefinder, Jamie crouched down, looking over the valley below. They weren't terribly high up, but the ground fell away in front of them in a steady slope, giving way to a dense forest in the valley below. It stretched out for some distance before it abruptly ended and turned into a lush green lawn. It was cut out like a square, and in the centre of it was an old stone manor house. The front faced a long driveway that led down the length of the valley, a set of heavy gates inset in the stone wall – visible from even here – separating the grounds from what lay beyond.

Behind the house, a manicured lawn ran all the way to the rest of the trees, and little ants moved about, carrying what looked like chairs and other items, setting up for the garden party of all time.

If anyone else saw it, they'd think it was a wedding or some other summer event. But Jamie knew differently. That the elevated square platform in the centre wasn't a dance floor or stage, it was where they'd be setting up their ring to fight. It's where, in just a few hours' time, children would die at the hands of other children. While the filthy rich screamed and cheered and laid down vast sums of money, sipping on champagne and stuffing their faces greedily.

Jamie's fists clenched at her sides. Was Alina down there yet?

She could see cars trundling towards the gates, stopping, and then being let through. Any one of them could contain Alina. Or Petrosyan.

Elliot said people were coming in from all over.

All they could do was wait. For Hassan. For the party to begin. For night to fall.

And for their opportunity to strike.

HASSAN WASN'T FAR BEHIND. AND BY THE TIME that the ants scurrying about at the estate had finished setting up the garden for the main event, he arrived.

There was a gentle crunching of grass behind them and both Jamie and Church twisted, weapons drawn automatically.

Hassan stopped short, his expression stern, and raised his hands.

Wordlessly, Jamie and Church holstered their guns, and wordlessly Hassan lowered his hands and approached.

Church and Jamie both got to their feet as Hassan dropped the backpack he had slung over his shoulder. He kept the dissatisfied look on his face, but still took

Church's hand when it was offered, exchanging a nod with him before he looked at Jamie.

They stayed like that a moment, and then he afforded a small smile and opened his arms, scooping her up in a strong hug.

Jamie hugged him back, relieved that the coldness of their last meeting had seemingly abated.

'Good to see you,' he said, releasing her and giving her a once over, his eyes resting on her bruised throat. She was still in the turtleneck but the bruises had begun to spread now, and came right up to her jaw bone. 'I heard about West Wales,' he added. 'Glad you got out of it in one piece.'

'Barely,' Jamie smiled back. 'But we got it done.'

Hassan looked at Church and gave him another nod, as though in thanks for watching Jamie's back.

He returned it. Men seemed to say so much without saying anything at all.

'For the record,' Hassan began, stooping and opening his rucksack, 'I'm not excited about keeping Mallory in the dark on this.' He looked up at Jamie. 'So, I was never here, alright?'

'Of course.'

He looked up, his eyes lingered on Jamie's for a moment as he looked for confirmation in her face. When he was satisfied, he went back to digging in his pack, pulling out a pair of long-range binoculars. He held them up to his eyes, surveying the estate below them. 'Tell me what I'm looking at here. What are we doing?'

Jamie turned, arms folded, and looked down at the estate herself. Cars were now forming a line to enter at the gate.

'Aram Petrosyan's running an illegal fight event. Think Brecon, but times a hundred. Our contact inside says that they were just warm-ups, practice runs for this. Shitbags the world over are bringing in their prize fighters for a once-a-year event. From what we understand, it's going to be every major trafficker around with a taste for blood.'

'Fucking hell,' Hassan mumbled, still appraising the place. 'And Alina's in there?'

'Somewhere.'

'Who's your contact?' Hassan did lower his binoculars now to look at Jamie.

Church fielded it, but not in the way Jamie thought. 'It's need to know,' he said flatly.

Hassan looked at Church uneasily. 'But the intel is solid?'

'That's yet to be seen. But it's our arses if it's not. And you were never here, right?'

'Still don't want to see you two getting your heads blown off.' He went back to looking. 'So, you want me on overwatch here while you go in there and take out Aram Petrosyan. That about the sum of it?'

'Yep,' Church said then.

Hassan harrumphed a little. 'You know what I do for a living, right?'

'You knew what this was from the start.'

'I know,' Hassan said. 'I'm genuinely asking to see if you two sustained major head trauma last night.' He glanced at them both. 'From what I can see, this is a hornets' nest. Now, I can't say that I don't support the idea – hell, Petrosyan's operation has had me chasing my tail for the last six weeks, and I still owe that piece of shit for Ash, if nothing else. But I don't really see how this is going to work. There's two of you, and fifty of them.'

'We understand the scale of the task, we just don't really have much choice,' Jamie said, unable to keep the frustration from her voice. She didn't need Hassan reminding them of the odds here.

'Uh ... what about just calling Interpol in right now? That's the plan after you've killed Petrosyan, right? Call them in?'

'It's not that simple.'

'Enlighten me.'

'They wanted Alina, and they wanted me. And they won't stop. Aram Petrosyan is behind the order, so until he's in the ground, we won't be safe.'

'You believe that?'

'I have to,' Jamie said. 'We can't run forever, and next time they'll send more men, better armed, won't leave it to chance. We need to hit them where it hurts. Cut the head off the snake.'

Hassan reserved judgement on that. 'And what about Alina? You're getting her out afterwards?'

'Our contact is watching over her.'

'And you trust this person with her life?' Hassan seemed a little surprised.

Church snorted, which said what he thought about it.

'I do.'

Hassan measured Jamie, trying to figure out who this person was. Jamie didn't trust many people – that much was common knowledge. But who could she have on the inside here that she did?

Hassan seemed to draw a blank, not saying any more, just going back to his surveillance.

'Thank you for doing this,' Jamie said then.

'Don't mention it. I'm glad you called. I'd rather be here than know you're doing something like this without someone watching your back.'

'You can liaise directly with Hallberg. She's waiting for a call. She needs something actionable to muster a decent response from Interpol, so that's your number one priority. That and making sure we don't get killed.'

Church got down next to Hassan, on his mat, and began looking through the rangefinder again. 'This records in 4K,' he said aloud, 'pairs with your phone via Bluetooth. You can edit recordings, create a feed link and share it with whoever. If you give it to Hallberg, she can stream the footage live.'

He moved over and Hassan put his binoculars down

and began looking through the rangefinder now mounted on the tripod. 'Fancy,' he said. 'This some high-grade military kit you snagged from the SAS?'

'No,' Church laughed. 'Amazon. Free delivery with Prime.'

'Of course,' Hassan chuckled. 'Of course it fucking is.' He pulled back from it and drew a slow breath. 'Alright then,' he said. 'I'm all set, I'll give Hallberg a little tinkle and make sure we're singing off the same hymn sheet. So, I suppose you two should get ready. Night's coming and you've got a little walk ahead.'

Church set about laying out their vests and checking his weapon while Hassan got to his feet and offered a hand to Jamie.

'You sure about this?' he asked, his voice warm, concerned, his eyes questioning.

'I think so,' Jamie replied.

'You think so? You're getting into some pretty dark shit here, Jaim. You know what you're about to do, right?'

'I do.'

'Do you, though?'

'I do,' she said more firmly.

'Alright then, just checking. I know this whole thing has been ...'

'An ordeal?'

'Yeah. I just want to make sure your head is on square. That you're thinking clearly here.'

'I am.'

He stared at her for what seemed like a long time and Jamie did her best to hold his gaze.

'Alright then,' he said finally. 'Good luck. And say hey to Alina for me, would you?'

'I'll do that,' Jamie replied.

Just as soon as I've put a bullet in Aram Petrosyan.

CHAPTER
FORTY-FOUR

They headed down the hill as night began to close in.

From their elevated position, they were able to get a good sense of the layout of the estate.

It wouldn't be easy, but from their reconnaissance, they decided it was best to try to get in through one of the upper floor windows.

There was a balcony overlooking the fighting ring – prime position to view from, and to lord your power over everyone. Remind them by whose grace you were there.

That's where Petrosyan would be, they all decided. But how best to get there?

A full-length first floor window with a Juliet balcony looked to connect through to a main corridor, and that no doubt gave access to the bedroom they'd be viewing the fights from.

There was a single-storey section of the house attached to their nearside of the property, shrouded by trees. It would likely be some sort of laundry room that attached through to the kitchens – where deliveries were unloaded. That was confirmed by the fact that there was a refrigerated van parked there right now.

They could get over the wall under the cover of the trees and make a stealthy approach in darkness, then get up onto the van, onto the roof, and across to the main building. The Juliet balcony was just a few feet above and within easy reach. From there, they'd have a view of the fights, and once they were given the signal, they'd be able to get in through the window and get to Petrosyan before he even knew what was happening.

In theory it was a good plan. But it didn't take into account any of the armed men roaming the property, whether the window would be locked when they arrived, whether they'd be seen or heard climbing on the van and then the roof and, perhaps most importantly, what the signal was.

But as Church led the way through the dense forest, moving quickly through the undergrowth in the fading light, Jamie tried her best not to think about those things.

They slowed as they reached the wall and Church crouched there, leaning against the stone. It was streaked with moss, the grass long around it and the brambles arching and curving in long tangles.

'You good?' he asked Jamie, his eyes cold in the gathering darkness.

She couldn't help but be unnerved by him. By the way he changed when he was 'working'. He was always stoic and matter-of-fact, but when it came to an operation like this, what little warmth and humour there was in him just seemed to evaporate, burning off, leaving just this robotic husk that couldn't be tempered nor stopped.

But Jamie supposed that was the idea when it came to the special forces. The things they had to do were too much for mere mortals. And Jamie could attest to that. What had happened at the hotel, what was happening here, was beyond her imagination. And were she not arm in arm with Church, she would have buckled by now.

'Yeah,' she said quietly. 'I'm good.'

He nodded. 'Weapon loaded?'

'Yep.'

'Silencer?'

'Attached.'

'Spare magazine?'

'Got it.'

He kept reeling them off. 'Body armour?'

'Secure.' Jamie patted her vest.

'Earpiece?'

She touched her ear. 'Check.' It's how they'd get word to Hassan. And each other if they got separated.

'Alright then. You need to pee?'

'Excuse me?'

'Do you need to pee?' Church repeated. 'You won't have a chance once we're inside.'

'I'm good,' Jamie said, holding a hand up. 'But thanks for checking.'

'Hey, you only have to piss yourself once while waiting for go time for it to stick in your mind. No harm in checking.'

'I appreciate the concern.'

He afforded a brief smile. A crack in the ice. And then he beckoned Jamie towards him, interlacing his fingers in a platform on his knee. 'Up you go.'

She stepped forward, planting her boot on his hands, and was lifted with ease towards the top of the wall.

Jamie took hold of it and pulled herself over while Church jumped, grabbed the lip, and hoisted himself up without a hint of difficulty.

They dropped into the lion's den together and moved slowly, keeping low, the din of the party already rumbling from beyond the treeline. Music pumping, laughter echoing in the night air.

The fights had not started yet, but they would soon, Jamie thought. She could feel it. Could taste it. Like blood in the water. A strange feeling in the air, a whisper of death.

They forged onwards, the music growing and masking their footsteps.

Lights began to appear through the trees ahead, getting brighter as they neared.

Church held his fist up, signalling them to stop, and Jamie followed the order, mimicking his action as he pulled his pistol from the holster with a gentle slither.

He dragged the slide back carefully until a round clicked into the chamber, and then released it with as much care to mute the noise.

They were at the treeline, twenty yards or so from the van. It was dark and locked up, the back to the service door. Jamie could see now that there was the logo of a catering company on the side. How they managed to pass this off as anything innocuous was beyond her. But then again, with enough money you could do anything. And if a country manor house with a fleet of Bentleys and Rolls Royces parked in front of it screamed anything, it was too much money.

Jamie scanned the space in front of them.

Nothing was moving.

The summer was waning, but the nights were still bright enough and it seemed by now that the procession of cars had stopped.

Guests were being funnelled in through the front door, and there'd be no need now for anything to be moving at the service entrance. All the champagne and food would be out, security no doubt watching the party instead.

Church motioned for them to go forward and Jamie followed as he broke cover, strafing along the side of the wall towards the van. It was close enough that if they could get on the roof, they could make the jump to the building without too much difficulty.

They closed the gap, feet crunching on the stone, and then suddenly Church stopped, throwing his hand up again next to his head.

Jamie halted in her tracks, sweat beading her forehead, heart hammering inside her chest now.

What had he heard? What had he seen?

Jamie saw it too, then. Smoke curling into the night air above the van. Someone on the other side of it smoking. They couldn't have seen from where they were.

Fuck.

Church looked down at his boots, at the pea gravel beneath them. It was surprising that the smoker hadn't heard them already. But with each step closer, he would.

They were now just fifteen feet or so from the vehicle, but right in the open. They couldn't stay here. There was a light above the service door, and they were bathed in it. And there was no doubt what they were here to do in their body armour with weapons drawn.

Church motioned Jamie lower and she followed the order, watching as he got down onto his belly, very carefully supporting himself on his hands to get a look at the feet of the person – or people – they couldn't see.

He held one finger up, signifying it was just a single guard.

They'd have to do this quietly. Shooting out his ankle would give him chance to call out. Rushing him would give him chance to shout, probably get a shot off.

It was a tough situation, but they'd need to lure him into the open somehow and take him down.

The music was pumping from the other side of the house, but here, in the lee of the great manor, things were quiet. So, their options were limited.

Church let out a slow breath and eased back to a crouched position, leaning in to whisper to Jamie.

She lowered her head so his lips were next to her ear.

His breath was warm on her skin.

'You need to run,' he whispered.

'I'm not leaving,' Jamie argued.

'It's a distraction.'

She pulled her head away and stared at him for a moment.

'Turn and break for the trees. He'll come out to investigate, see you running, and when I have a shot, I'm going to take it.'

'That's risky.'

'So is sitting here braiding each other's hair. You're fast, he won't get a good look at you, won't know what he's looking at. I just need a second.'

Jamie set her jaw, not liking the plan. But knowing she didn't really have much of a choice.

Church laid a hand on her shoulder, a moment of reassurance. And then he was pushing her away.

Shit, not wasting time then.

'Run fast,' he said, smiling a little.

Jamie rose, cracked her neck, and gave him a nod.

And then she ran.

The sound of her heels digging into the stones was like someone ringing a damn church bell.

The soft surface absorbed the power she was putting through it, but she got her shoulders forward and head down, arms pumping. Honestly, it was good to have somewhere to channel the adrenaline.

It seemed like she'd only taken five steps before the spit of a silenced weapon echoed behind her.

One, two.

Crunch. Something heavy falling to the ground.

Jamie slowed to a stop and turned back just in time to see Church advance on the downed guard, cigarette still in his mouth and smouldering, and put two bullets into his skull.

Double-tap.

Jamie swallowed, grimacing a little, and started doubling back as Church took the guy by his feet and dragged him to the side of the van, rolling him underneath.

It would hide the body from easy view, but the blood stain was apparent on the pale stones.

'Nice work,' Church said, standing and dusting himself off.

Jamie just nodded, staring at the blood.

Church snapped his fingers, grabbing her attention. 'You still with me?'

She could only nod again. Her mouth only wanted to ask the words; 'Is all this really worth it?'

But she couldn't start questioning the plan now, not when they were this deep into it, and Alina's life was on the line.

'Let's go,' Church urged her before the doubt could set in any more. He once more interlaced his fingers, standing with his back to the van.

Jamie planted her heel for a second time and he popped her up nice and gently.

'Easy,' he muttered. 'In case there's an alarm.'

Jamie nodded, making her way to the back of the van, the roof ahead a few feet in front and about two above her.

She got a foothold on the back top corner, and then jumped forward, her toes hitting the stone tiles and immediately slipping on the lichen there. She lost balance and toppled forward onto her hands, nearly spilling her gun as she found purchase.

She stared down at the backs of her hands and could see them shaking. Jamie had lived through some tough nights, but this felt different. She wasn't just fighting for her own life this time, not for some vague sense of justice, or to liberate a stranger. No, failing tonight meant letting down someone she'd grown to really care for, someone she'd even grown to love.

Alina. Alina. Alina, she said to herself, over and over. This is for Alina.

Church landed on the tiles next to her, one hand coming down to steady himself.

He took Jamie by the elbow then and lifted her. 'Come on, home stretch,' he urged. 'You're doing great.'

He could read her like a book. Could see the insecurity there. She was a detective, not a soldier. But we are who we need to be, she thought. And I need to be strong.

Jamie clenched her teeth, raked in a few deep breaths, and then got to her feet, the ridge of the roof and a view of the party ahead.

They crept upwards together, prepared for what lay ahead, but not ready for what they were about to see.

CHAPTER
FORTY-FIVE

As they reached the ridge, they slowed, getting onto their bellies so as not to attract suspicion.

Though the people below them wouldn't have had less reason to look their way.

In the time it'd taken for them to make the journey down off the ridge, creep through the trees, and then get into the estate, night had fallen, and the evening's events had begun to unfold.

The raised stage in the centre of the garden was now bathed in bright lights. Around it, chairs and tables had been set up and were now filled with suited men and finely dressed women. Waiters and waitresses walked between the tables in white shirts and bow ties, serving champagne from silver trays.

All eyes, however, were on the stage, where two men circled each other.

At first glance, Jamie thought them seasoned fighters, but as her eyes adjusted to the harsh lights, she saw beyond the blood that they weren't men at all, just boys, maybe sixteen or seventeen. Lithe and half-starved, in filthy shorts with greasy hair.

They both strafed around each other, sizing the other up as the crowd looked on in seeming disinterest. There'd been no roars of excitement in the air yet, so Jamie guessed this was just the first fight. The first of many, she thought grimly.

Someone called out from the crowd in a foreign language and one of the boys turned his head to look in that direction – his owner, Jamie thought. There was no other way to describe it. These boys were put here to fight until they could no longer do so. And only someone who saw them as less than human would do something like that. Someone who saw them as property.

The second boy took the chance, his opponent's head turned for a moment, and lunged forward. He threw a savage punch, connecting with the first boy's cheek, sending him sprawling to the floor with a heavy thud.

It was over in seconds as the attacker descended on him, the crowd holding its breath as he mounted the prostrate body, straddling the chest, and began raining his fists down upon the unprotected face.

Jamie turned her head away, her mouth filling with saliva as nausea overcame her. Thankfully, the crowd's sudden eruption of cheers drowned out the thudding of bone on bone.

Everything in her wanted to rush down there and leap between them, but she knew she couldn't. But she'd never been more disgusted with herself for standing idly by.

When the howling of the wolves finally stopped, Church put his hand on Jamie's, curled around the ridge tile, and she finally looked up.

'It's over,' he said, voice barely a whisper.

She knew he hadn't looked away, but not even he could hide the glimmer in his eye from watching one child kill another.

'Use it,' he said then.

Jamie nodded. She'd been thinking just that. That this was all the work of one man. One man, one bullet, and they could stop all this. Aram Petrosyan was no more than a hundred feet from them, and tonight they had the power to end this.

She finally looked back down over the crowd, and saw that the boy who'd won had already gone, and the one who'd lost was now being dragged off the stage, leaving a trail of smeared blood behind him.

How many? Jamie thought. How many will die before Elliot gives us the signal. And we can end this.

Jamie swallowed the saliva in her mouth and raised one hand to her ear, touching the bud there. 'Hassan?' she asked quietly into the ether.

'I'm here,' he said quietly.

'You get that?'

'Mhm,' was all he answered. 'Hallberg too. She watched it live.'

'Fuck,' Jamie muttered, thankful for that. 'Okay. Let me know what she says. Whether it's enough.'

'How could it not be?'

'I hope you're right.'

Hassan didn't respond again, and all Jamie and Church could do was wait.

It seemed like almost immediately two more fighters were led out.

They didn't seem to be dragged, but they didn't seem excited.

Next to the ring were two middle-aged women, both looked lithe and weathered. Both looked determined, hair shorn short. These were seasoned fighters, unlike the first two.

No doubt they were building towards some 'main event'.

'It's okay,' Church said, turning his head to Jamie as one of the men who led them onto the stage told them to fight with a flick of the wrist. 'You don't have to watch, I'll let you know when we get the signal.'

'No,' Jamie said, steeling herself with a few deep breaths and dragging her eyes back to the action. 'I do. I should.'

Church stared at her in the darkness for a few

seconds. 'Okay,' he said, and they both turned their eyes to the fight and watched as the two women came together, their cries rising up in the warm night air.

Fighters came and went, some bouts going to the bitter end, others ending with submission and pleas of mercy, much to the dismay of the crowd. Boos echoed when both fighters survived.

As one more competitor was carried into the wings, moaning and whimpering, a hush befell the crowd and Jamie's skin suddenly became alight with gooseflesh.

Her heart began to beat harder as a figure stepped up on stage. A young woman, tall with bright hair and pale skin stepped under the lights and shielded her eyes, moving cautiously to the far side of the stage.

And then, a moment later, another figure emerged. A girl, shorter, with dark curls and tanned skin.

Jamie's heart seized in her chest altogether. 'Alina,' she whispered.

Church stiffened a little next to her and readjusted his position.

Jamie swallowed the lump in her throat and touched her ear again. 'Hassan?'

'I'm here.'

'You seeing this? What's Hallberg's status?'

'She's scrambling numbers as fast as she can. Wheels are in motion here, Jamie, I don't think I can ask her to wait.'

'Fuck,' Jamie muttered. If they came in too soon,

she'd never get to Petrosyan. If they came too late after they struck, then the net would be too wide, and who knows how many people would escape.

She couldn't think about that now, they had to be ready for the signal, whatever it was.

The Juliet balcony was to their right, within easy reach. They could be inside the house in seconds.

Jamie watched as Alina walked out, looking left and right, nervous it seemed.

Fuck! What was Elliot playing at? It was never supposed to get this far. They weren't actually going to fight? He wasn't really going to let her get hurt? She'd kill him. She'd ring his neck. She'd gut him like a fish if anyone laid a finger on Alina.

The tall girl sized her up, sinking lower into her knees, lifting her hands like claws, outstretched and ready to strike.

Alina came to a stop and assumed a fighting stance. But something was wrong.

She seemed sluggish. She was at an odd angle, her hands low and heavy. She was swaying on her feet a little.

But it didn't matter to her opponent. The tall girl rushed in, hands up, and grappled with Alina, grabbing her by the wrist and then taking a fistful of her hair.

Alina called out and before Jamie could even move, Church's hand was on her shoulder, forcing her into the roof, keeping her planted.

For a moment they stayed like that, locked in a death grip. And then something splashed on the mat between them and the blonde girl reeled backwards, throwing her hands in the air.

Alina doubled forward, clutching her stomach, and vomited again. Loudly. Violently. The liquid was shades of brown and red, bloody by the looks of it.

Volumes of it emptied onto the mat and then Alina stood up, coughing wildly before she stumbled backwards and lost her footing, falling flat onto her back.

Before she'd even settled, she began to convulse, the stage rattling beneath her as she seized.

Murmurs rippled through the crowd, the blonde girl looking around in confusion.

Jamie watched in horror.

Church's grip tightened on her shoulder and she glanced at him. 'The signal,' he said.

'But—'

'The signal,' he repeated. 'We move.'

Jamie's mouth flapped as she searched for the right words to argue. But he was right. This had to be it. Elliot's plan. The way he'd saved her from the fight.

Church was getting to his feet as all eyes fixed themselves on the girl seizing on the stage.

Jamie followed suit, unable to look away.

But as another person emerged into the lights, she felt a sudden wash of relief, seeing Elliot swooping in like a guardian angel, diving to the ground next to her to attend to his ward, putting one hand on her shoulder, the other on her forehead to stop her hurting herself.

He yelled something in Armenian to someone Jamie couldn't see, and then they were both gone, hidden by the corner of the building as Church dragged her towards the balcony.

She felt him jerk her arm then, pulling her towards him. He turned, catching her face with one of his big hands, his fingers around the corners of her jaw, holding her face painfully.

He stared into her eyes from six inches away, his cold look enough to send shivers down her spine.

'Focus,' he commanded her, digging in his fingers.

Pain.

But it worked, it centred her.

She nodded in his grip and he released, motioning her to go in front.

Jamie did so, moving quickly but carefully along the sloped roof towards the balcony.

Jamie jumped, taking hold of the rail, and Church helped her up, grabbing her heel and pushing it skywards.

His extra height and reach meant it was an easy scale for him and they mantled it together.

The upper corridor stretched out ahead and they were able to guess which door was their destination by the two armed men in black suits standing outside it.

'Ready?' Church asked.

Jamie let out a rattling exhale. 'Let's do it.' Before I lose my nerve.

He reached out, trying the glass doors.

Locked.

But they were old, single pane, wooden.

'This is going to get loud,' he warned her.

Jamie drew her weapon and chambered a round.

Church did the same, the pair of them cramped in the space between the rail and the glass.

He laid his free hand on the handle, taking a good grip, and looked at Jamie one last time.

'On three. We fire first. Shoot to kill.'

The words rang in Jamie's head, shocking and brutal. But it was their only choice.

She didn't get to think about it before Church threw his shoulder into the wood, splintering it.

Jamie rushed in after him, the two of them taking two steps and planting their lead foot, pistols rising through the air as the two guards at the door thirty feet ahead both turned at the noise.

Their eyes widened in shock, their black jackets flapping as they wrestled for their weapons.

Jamie pulled the trigger. One, two, three rounds. Squeezed off. Centre mass.

Church did the same, advancing quickly.

They struck true and the two men shuddered and fell to the ground.

Jamie tried to keep pace.

Church got there first, put a bullet in each, stilling

them for good.

By the time Jamie caught up, he was already at the door, hand on the handle.

He checked she was there, then twisted the handle and pushed inwards, rolling around the frame to cover the room.

Jamie knew the tactic, and did the same in the opposite direction.

Two more heavies in suits, on their feet.

Church took the one on the left down with deadly precision.

Jamie wasn't quick enough.

A flash from the second guard's muzzle danced in her eyes and she was punched in the chest, sent backwards into the wall with a thud, the bullet impacting her square in the vest.

She gasped, winded, but her gun was up, and the shot she returned was enough, blowing out the guard's shoulder and sending him spinning.

Church was already there, and put one through the side of his skull, sending him sprawling to the floor.

And all of a sudden, the room fell silent.

The regal wooden panelling, the expensive carpet, the four poster bed in solid oak. Double doors opened onto a full balcony overlooking the ring directly.

Two chairs were set up on it, high-backed thrones fit for royalty.

The two men who'd been sitting in them were now

standing up on either side, hands raised, eyes wide with fright, but they didn't beg for their life.

One was Aram Petrosyan. Jamie recognised him from the water treatment plant. He wasn't a tall man. His bald head shone in the light from the chandelier overhead and his sunken eyes were dark and loathsome. He stared at Jamie, lips turned down at the corners, dripping with malice.

The other man Jamie didn't recognise. He was younger, thirty or so, and tall. He had a thick shock of dark hair and finely manicured facial hair. He said nothing, but the tightly balled fists at his sides and the look of hatred in his eyes told Jamie that she shouldn't expect either of them to roll over and accept their fate.

Through the open door behind them, the deep chug of helicopter rotors began to cut through the droning music emanating from the garden.

Jamie and Church came shoulder to shoulder, pinning the pair of men in their sights.

Petrosyan's lips quivered with rage. 'You have no idea what you're doing.'

'Shut the fuck up,' Church growled. 'Jamie, do it.'

Petrosyan stared at Jamie, right in the eyes. He wasn't going to make this easy.

'It's the girl, isn't it?' he asked.

'Jamie,' Church urged. 'We don't have time for this.'

Petrosyan laughed now, but kept his hands raised. 'My God, you don't even know why she's so important, do you? Who she really is?'

'Jamie ...' Church said.

'Tell me,' Jamie demanded.

Petrosyan's hands began to lower.

Church took a step forward, pistol trained on Petrosyan's throat. 'Don't even think about it.'

Petrosyan's hands went back up and he drew a slow breath.

'Tell me!' Jamie yelled.

Petrosyan just laughed again.

There was noise outside the door now, footsteps clattering on tiles downstairs. Thundering on stairs. Lots of them.

'Fuck!' Church growled.

Muzzle flash lit the room and Petrosyan kept his slimy grin as Church's bullet found the space between his eyes.

The man toppled backwards like a falling tree, right into his throne.

He knocked it out of the way, spinning to the floor, and the other younger man dived to his aid.

'No!' the one with the facial hair yelled, scooping up Petrosyan with both hands.

Jamie didn't see what happened next as Church's arm took her by the waist and damn near threw her into the corridor.

He was right on her shoulder, already firing down the stairs, putting bullets in the wall to stop the heavies running up towards them.

'Go!' he shouted, shoving Jamie in the back, down

the corridor, back towards the Juliet balcony.

There were screams in the hallway behind them. Multiple voices. Jamie didn't know the words, but the tone was clear enough.

Shoot.

Shoot to kill.

Gunfire erupted behind them as they ran, sprinting towards the doors and the open night air.

Plaster and wood plumed from the walls and ceiling around them as they closed the distance, shielding their heads with their arms.

Jamie wanted to slow down, climb down onto the roof. But she knew she couldn't.

They were being chased, and they had one option.

Together, they leapt through the open door, hurdling the balustrade.

They sailed into darkness, the roof stretching out before them, sloped and mossy.

Jamie pulled in a hard breath, filling her lungs and tensing her body as they landed hard on the stone tiles.

She cried out in pain as she bounced and rolled, then slid down the roof. Her heel hooked on the gutter and sent her spinning, tumbling off the roof and plunging to the ground below.

She landed hard, everything going black for a moment. When she opened her eyes, she gasped, winded and weak, and scrabbled to her hands and knees in the rough stone.

Where was Church?

She looked around, panicked, seeing him next to her, scraped and dirty, but in one piece.

He swore, forcing himself to his feet, and staggered forward.

Jamie could only follow suit. They had to get out of here. And now. Which way?

It didn't matter, they didn't have time to decide.

Jamie and Church took off again, limping and loping as the beat of the helicopter rotors became deafening.

As they charged across the chipped courtyard, searchlights swung into view overhead, a maelstrom kicking up from the rotor wash as two choppers swung in low over the trees.

Sirens howled and a sea of blue flashing lights blasted through the front gate, fanning out across the lawn in a wave coming right at them.

Jamie and Church slowed, panting hard as one of the searchlights from above found them and drowned them in a white light from which there was no escape.

A black SUV with grille-mounted lights skidded to a halt in front of them while the other vehicles all barrelled deeper into the estate.

The other chopper circled above, the noise deafening.

Jamie could hear nothing. Just white noise.

They stopped now, their hands rising next to their heads instinctively.

Two figures got out of the SUV ahead of them, the headlights blinding.

Jamie couldn't see them, couldn't hear them, but the message was clear.

Get down on the ground.

And so she and Church did, pressing their faces to the cool earth, waiting for their arms to be folded up behind their backs, and for the consequences of their mission to finally catch up with them.

CHAPTER
FORTY-SIX

They rode together, but didn't say a word in the presence of the armed officers who had arrested them.

The car left the estate and drove quickly to the police headquarters in Carmarthen, where they were promptly escorted into the building in handcuffs, separated, and then shoved into whitewashed interrogation rooms.

One of the arresting officers undid Jamie's handcuffs and then left without a word, shutting and locking the door behind him.

She shifted in the metal chair, looking around and seeing nothing except four walls and a camera in the top corner of the room, the red light beneath the lens telling her that she was being watched.

She knew there was only one thing to do: wait.

But for how long?

And when the wait was over, then what?

JAMIE ASSUMED THAT THE MORNING HAD COME by the time the door opened and Hallberg walked in.

It had been hours. Jamie had slept a little. In patches, upright in the chair or with her head on her arms.

But it was how tired Hallberg looked that tipped her off.

She walked in, hair looking greasy, with deep bags under her eyes.

There was no acknowledgment or greeting as she came in. She just took off her grey blazer, hung it on the back of the chair on the other side of the table and sat, adjusted herself, laying the folder and the tablet she was holding on the table in front of her. She let out a long sigh, then turned to look at the camera.

Jamie did the same, unsure what was going on.

But when the red light blinked off and stayed dark, she felt a little relief, and then dread in turn. Was this going to be good, or bad? She couldn't tell.

So, she just waited.

'You okay?' Hallberg asked after an age, voice quiet and cold. 'They feed you, give you something to drink?'

Jamie shook her head. 'No.'

Hallberg raised her eyebrows. 'Probably because they think you're a human trafficker. What other reason would you have for being there last night?'

Jamie opened her mouth to reply but Hallberg held up a hand to stop her.

'You don't need to answer that. I think Aram Petrosyan's dead body says it all.'

Jamie stayed quiet.

Hallberg seemed to collect her thoughts for a long time before speaking again.

'That video – the one from Hassan ... It showed a live stream of two minors fighting to the death,' Hallberg said, the words slow. 'It showed two teenagers pitted against one another for sport, and forced to try to kill the other ... I've seen some things since I started this job. But that ...' She blinked, then shook her head. 'Trying to mobilise a response without that ... it would have been impossible. But with that video ... the final arrest count was over one hundred people. Some got away and some charges won't stick, but the people we do get will all be hit with trafficking or conspiracy charges. They're all well connected, too. And not just criminals – there were all sorts there. And they'll be happy to roll over on their contacts and sing their hearts out to stay out of the papers and out of prison.' Hallberg paused for a moment. 'And we have you to thank for that. This may be the biggest single trafficking bust in the history of the UK. And we didn't even know about this ring until two months ago.'

'You don't sound too pleased about that,' Jamie said carefully.

'You understand the concept of proper channels, right?'

'I used to.'

Hallberg chuckled a little, then pushed back from the table and got up. 'Come on,' she said. 'Let's get some coffee.'

'Coffee ... outside?' Jamie looked at the door cautiously.

'Yeah,' Hallberg said. 'Once again, you seem to have escaped the guillotine.'

'How?' Jamie asked.

'Direct order from the Chief Operations Coordinator for the UK, Human Trafficking Division.'

'Who's that?' Jamie asked, rising slowly from her chair.

'Now?' Hallberg smirked a little, opening the door and looking back at Jamie. 'It's me.'

THEY STEPPED FROM THE BUILDING AND INTO the morning sun.

'So, they promoted you,' Jamie said, smiling at Hallberg.

She nodded slowly as they came down the front steps, pausing on the pavement in front of the doors. 'Yeah,' she said slowly. 'Though it was a coin flip as to whether or not I was going to get fired, honestly.'

'What do you mean?'

'When Hassan gave me that stream link, I gave it

straight to Braun. But he didn't want to move on it. He said it needed to be vetted, analysed, all that kind of bullshit. Asked where it was coming from, where was the paperwork, blah blah blah.' She let out a long breath. 'That's the way it should have gone. An official investigation, all that crap, but ...'

'But?'

'But then I thought, *what would Jamie do?*'

'Uh-oh.'

'Yeah,' Hallberg laughed. 'I get that Braun was trying to cover his own ass, but what was going on there ... to turn your back on that because the T's weren't crossed and the I's weren't dotted?' She tsked. 'It was stupid.'

'So, you went over his head?'

She nodded. 'Yep, I went to his boss, and his boss's boss, got them to watch what I was watching, and told them we had to move fast, and we had to move hard. We'd get just one shot at it, and they asked what I needed. I told them it would have to be sweeping control of the operation and all the affiliated resources they had on tap – full tactical response. They conferred for a few minutes, naturally. While I sat by, wondering if I'd just committed career suicide. But then they came back ...'

'And gave it to you?'

'No, they asked me what my source was, where I was getting this footage.'

'And what did you tell them?' Jamie asked.

'I told them I had an asset on the inside. That I'd been running an under-the-table team, tracking down Petrosyan off the books as I feared a mole was inside the NCA or Interpol and I couldn't risk the Armenians finding out. They were sceptical, but when I explained to them that the asset was responsible for the West Wales Incident – what they're calling your little party at the hotel—'

'Hardly a party,' Jamie cut in.

'Still, they were unsure, but their choices were sit by and watch it all unfold, doing nothing, or give me what I asked for.'

'And that resulted in the biggest bust of its kind in the history of the UK.'

'Yep.'

'With you at the head of the operation.'

'Yep.'

'Because of your assets that you so cleverly brought in.'

'Yep,' Hallberg grinned. 'I figured you were going to continue to do stupid things regardless of what I said or threatened. So why not try and benefit from them? I rolled the dice,' she said.

'And you won.' Jamie shook her head a little, impressed with her. She'd always preferred to colour inside the lines. It was nice to see her unleash a little ambition and creative thinking. She just hoped she wasn't rubbing off on Hallberg too much.

'It was a play that benefited all of us. If they did fire

me, I wouldn't be around for you to twist my arm anymore – and honestly, that would have been a load off.' She laughed. 'But if it did come off, I knew it'd be a boon for my career, and it'd probably save you from some serious prison time.'

'I appreciate that. I really do.' Jamie drew a slow breath, revelling in her freedom. 'Church know?'

'Yeah, I sprung him before I came to get you.'

'Priorities,' Jamie snorted.

'Eh, after what you've put me through – now, and in the past, it was my pleasure to let you sweat a little.'

'Thanks for that.'

'Don't mention it.'

There was a lull for a moment as they basked in the morning sun.

'I honestly wasn't sure I'd ever see this again,' Jamie said then. 'When those choppers rolled in and the blue lights ...'

'You must have known there was a chance of that happening when you went in there,' Hallberg replied as she started walking away from the building.

'I did,' Jamie said, keeping step.

'So why did you do it?'

'Alina. If she could be free of it all, then it was worth it. I didn't really care what happened to me.'

Hallberg fell silent.

'What is it?'

Hallberg approached her car, blipped her keys to unlock it.

'What do you know?' Jamie pressed. Hallberg was clearly not saying something, and she couldn't help recount what Petrosyan had said in his final moments. That Jamie had no idea who she really was. Did Hallberg?

'I kept digging,' Hallberg said then. 'And I finally found the truth.'

'Which is?' Jamie folded her arms impatiently.

'Do you know where she is?' Hallberg asked.

'She's not in Interpol's custody,' Jamie said, more a statement than a question.

'We couldn't find her. We tried.'

'Then she's safe,' Jamie added, keen to get away from this tangent. If they didn't have her, that meant Elliot did. And she was safer with him than anyone else. 'What do you know, Julia?'

'Alina is ... Not Alina. Her name is Alaiana Darejani Katamadze.'

'Okay ...'

Hallberg took a breath. 'And the reason she's so special, why Petrosyan wanted her so badly, is because she's a part of the Georgian Royal Family.'

Jamie actually scoffed. 'I'm sorry, what did you say?'

'Not direct line, but she's the daughter of the cousin of one of the princes. Twenty-sixth in line to the throne, or something.' Hallberg waved it off. 'But her father is a major stakeholder in a host of big companies in the country, he owns vast swathes of land in the north, and holds a lot of sway with the government, especially with land rights.'

'Land rights?' Jamie homed in on the emphasis Hallberg put on that last part.

'Yeah, the kind you'd need sway with to ram through approval of a new oil pipeline, connecting Armenia with Russia.'

'Fuck,' Jamie muttered. 'So, Petrosyan abducted her?'

'We don't know the specifics of it. We haven't exactly reached out to the Georgians and said, *Hey, we found your missing princess. Bad news, though, we don't know where the hell she is.*'

'Point taken.' Jamie bit her lip. 'But he was using her to leverage her father into getting the pipeline approved.'

'And planning to use his construction companies to build it, effectively putting the monopoly on oil in Armenia and Georgia firmly in his hands.'

'He'd have a stranglehold on the entire country,' Jamie said, thinking about it.

'He would. We think that's why she was being kept separate from the other girls, why there was such a desire to get their hands on her. The fights placed her in mortal danger. Some video of your daughter being forced to kill or die in a fighting ring …? Enough to drive a father to do anything you asked, I'd bet.'

'Jesus,' Jamie muttered.

Hallberg watched her. 'Where is she, Jamie?'

Jamie looked up at her. 'I ...'

'Don't tell me you don't know. Don't lie to me after what I just did for you.'

'I don't know for certain,' Jamie answered truthfully. 'But I'll find her.'

Hallberg pushed her hands into her pockets. 'Alright,' she said then. 'Make sure you do. Because, you know,' she said, smirking a little, 'you work for me now.'

'Oh, do I?' Jamie asked, grinning back.

'You do,' Hallberg said. 'Officially. You're now an Interpol asset.'

'Tasked with what, exactly?'

Hallberg shrugged and then opened her car door. 'Catching bad guys, saving the world. You know, the usual. You want a ride?'

'Where are we going?' Jamie asked.

'Anywhere you want,' Hallberg replied. 'We have a few minutes until the shit hits the fan again. How about some breakfast?'

'Only if you're buying,' Jamie answered, circling the car and getting in the passenger side.

Hallberg laughed and closed the car door. 'You work for Interpol now, remember?' she said, starting the engine. 'I'll expense it.'

CHAPTER
FORTY-SEVEN

t took a little over thirteen hours to drive to Machir Bay on the western edge of the island of Islay in Scotland.

Jamie had first travelled here a few years ago now – but it felt like a different life altogether. After a particularly brutal case during her time at the Met, she'd needed to take a break to recover, to come to terms with what had happened.

She'd chosen the furthest place from London she could go. The furthest place from anywhere. Machir Bay was isolated, pristine, and silent. A stretch of white sand surrounded by grassy dunes with nothing but open ocean ahead.

It was where she came to be alone, but even here she couldn't escape Elliot.

She'd known then, that no matter how far she ran, he'd find her. Even there. And when he had, she'd put a gun to his head and promised him that if she ever saw him again, she'd put a bullet in him.

And yet, now, here she was, hoping that this was the place she would find him.

It's where she'd run to escape, and where she'd remained until the ghost of her father's work pulled her back to Sweden.

It was somewhere she'd been happy, or at least at peace. Where the noise wasn't all that noisy, and where she wasn't Jamie Johansson, wasn't a police officer, or a detective, or Interpol asset. She wasn't anything.

Jamie parked at the end of the road in the little dirt car park and got out. She'd set off at three in the morning to catch the ferry, and it was now mid-afternoon, the sun still high. Gulls wheeled overhead as she walked along the path towards the dunes, climbing in the soft sand until she reached the top, grasses gently rustling around her.

She stared down over the deserted beach, allowing her eyes to move along the shoreline slowly, her mind to cast back.

Even if they weren't here, it wasn't a bad place to be.

At first, she saw nothing, just an empty expanse of sand, and wave after wave after wave breaking in sequence.

But then, in the distance, a shadow. Just a dark speck near the water, flitting in circles, a second speck chasing it.

Jamie walked along the ridge, picking her way

through the grasses, heading down and then back up each dune, the shapes growing with each summit.

She could see a figure, a girl, running into and then away from the foaming tide. And in her wake, a dog, three-legged and awkward. Its barks now carried to her on the wind, followed by laughter and shrieks of joy as the water splashed her feet and wetted her legs.

Jamie let herself smile as she traversed the sand, closing in on a third figure standing on the rise, watching them.

He had his hands in the pockets of his dark jacket, the hem blowing in the sea breeze.

She walked up the final hill and stood next to him, watching Alina playing at the water's edge, watching Hati, her dog, jumping and frolicking with her. She hadn't seen the dog in more than eighteen months now. Not since Elliot took him from her in Sweden – though it was no love lost. He'd been a rescue, and had been no end of trouble for Jamie. Vicious and villainous. Though under Elliot's command, the perfect slobbering pooch. Elliot had a way with people, with animals, Jamie thought as she stood next to him on that dune. A way of getting what he wanted from them, always.

'I knew you'd come,' he said after a while.

'I knew you'd be here.'

He smiled a little.

'Is Alaiana Darejani Katamadze okay?'

'I was wondering how long it'd take you to find out.'

'So, you did know,' Jamie confirmed. 'You could have said.'

'Would it have changed anything?'

'I don't think so.'

'So what does it matter?' He looked over at Jamie for a moment.

Jamie thought on that, looking down over the bay. 'I suppose it doesn't. I'm just glad she's safe.'

'I promised, didn't I?'

'You did,' Jamie said.

The girl stopped then, a wave crashing over her feet. She stared up at Jamie, still tiny in the distance. And then her voice echoed on the wind.

'Jaaaaamieee!'

'Go on,' Elliot said. 'She's not stopped asking about you.'

Jamie didn't need to be told twice. And with a wide grin spreading across her face, she began sloshing down the slope towards the beach, sending rivers of sand down before her.

As she got onto flat ground, she couldn't help but break into a run, as happy as she'd ever been to see Alina do the same.

EPILOGUE

Jamie and Elliot walked slowly along the ridge of dunes, bracing against the incessant wind, watching Alina and Hati playing down below.

'You took care of her,' Jamie said.

'I promised I would.'

'You're a man of your word, I'll give you that.'

Elliot just took the compliment in silence.

'What happens to her now?'

'Well, if she lets Hati catch her, she'll probably get nipped,' he said, raising his chin towards them in the distance. 'But it'll be a good lesson for her.'

Jamie took a second to consider that, and couldn't help but wonder what kind of father a man like Elliot would make. No worse than her own, she thought, and then quickly shook that from her mind. 'I meant what happens to her in terms of her going ... home?'

He didn't answer right away.

'She's Georgian royalty,' Jamie said, her voice a little hushed as though someone might overhear despite them being utterly alone on the beach.

'She is,' Elliot answered carefully. 'But I've made some enquiries. Quietly. And ...'

'And what?'

'The Petrosyans abducted her and tried to use her as leverage against the Georgians. Her father is a hard man. And though there's a little speculation at play here – couldn't really go to him for a direct quote on the matter. But supposedly his answer was pretty cut and dry: he won't kowtow to threats. Especially those made against the royal family.'

'Meaning?' Jamie asked, hoping her first assumption wasn't right.

'He doesn't negotiate with kidnappers.'

'It's his fucking daughter!' Jamie hissed. 'You're serious?'

Elliot could only shrug. 'From what I understand, they're trying to track her down, trying to get her back. I assume that there are investigators, military personnel trying to locate her. It's why the Armenians were moving her around, I think. Every time they'd film her fights, they'd send the footage to her father, and then move her again so they'd never be able to find her. I suppose their thought was that watching his daughter fight to the death would leave him with no options; watch her be killed, or watch her kill to save herself.

Either way, the outcome is much the same. But he was seemingly unmoved by it.'

'That's ... well, I don't think *cold* quite covers it.'

'No, it doesn't.'

Jamie closed her eyes for a moment. 'So sending her back is off the table then?'

'If she's with us, we can protect her,' Elliot said with some confidence.

Jamie liked that option better. Regardless of how selfish it was. Her family obviously didn't want her back that badly. That was her rationalisation.

'It's settled then,' Jamie said. 'She stays with us. At least until all this is over and the dust has settled. Until it's safe for her to go home.'

'Safe.' Elliot said the word in a strange way, as though it was subjective in nature. Jamie thought it probably was.

They kept walking, in silence then.

After their tracks had stretched across two more dunes, Jamie spoke.

'You never did tell me,' Jamie said slowly, not looking at Elliot.

'Tell you what?' Elliot came to a halt, allowing Jamie to move in front of him and then turn.

'Why you wanted off Interpol's wanted list.'

He shrugged. 'Is it not enough to just want to not be looking over your shoulder every day?'

'You don't do that now. You're too smart.'

He smirked a little.

'And way too cocky.'

He let out a slow breath. 'Maybe I've turned a corner.'

'Turned a corner? Didn't realise you were a car. Petrol or diesel?'

He afforded a small smile, but for once didn't seem too interested in a back and forth.

'Weight of your actions finally set to crush your soul? The things you've done getting at your conscience after all these years?'

And then Jamie saw something she'd never seen in Elliot, and never thought she would. Discomfort. Like he was in a mild amount of pain.

'The things I've done ...' he began, the words coming quietly from his lips. 'They're ... I understand that they aren't ... *right.*'

Jamie restrained a scoff. Instead, she just listened, trying not to imagine, or remember them. Her hands weren't clean of blood, her own conscience not clear of lives. Some of them deserved it. Some of them seemed unnecessary. It was a difficult thing to reckon with, to wrestle with. You had to find a pit, deep down in the recesses of your mind, and that's where you had to shove them. Those thoughts. Those lives. Those bodies. You had to stuff them down into that pit and brick up the hole so you couldn't hear their screams.

'But ...' Elliot went on. 'What I did ... I could always justify it, to myself, at least. In some way, some form.' He looked at the ground over Jamie's shoulder, a slideshow of all his misdeeds reeling before his eyes. 'But these people, Jamie,' he said, breathless almost. 'It's different. The thing they do. To people. To ... to *children.*' His eyes flashed then, locking onto hers with such intensity that her skin erupted in gooseflesh. 'I never laid a finger on a child, I swear that to you.'

'I know,' Jamie said, the words squeezed in her tightened throat. 'I believe you.'

'But these ... these animals ...' He spat the words. 'They just ...' He shook his head, unable to comprehend it. 'I've always tried to remain neutral, to never pass judgement. I kept my professional integrity, and I traded lives, sure. But the balance always stayed even. These people, though ... They hurt for pleasure, for entertainment, for fun. They take joy in inflicting pain. In ways and of kinds you can't imagine. You don't want to imagine.' The contortion of his face told Jamie he didn't have to imagine. He'd seen. First hand. And it had changed something in him. Broken something. Unleashed something.

And it frightened Jamie.

Elliot Day was perhaps the most charming and most dangerous man she'd ever met. And if nothing else, she was always glad he was on her side – or at the very least, not against her.

'So you want to change sides,' Jamie said. 'That's why you wanted off Interpol's list?'

'I don't want to work for them,' he said,

harrumphing a little. 'Nothing so trivial. But there's only so much I can do alone.'

'You want to help them?'

'I want to help *you*. I don't want to just chip away at them, I want to gut them, like the pigs they are.'

She didn't want to ask if he meant figuratively or literally. Though she thought she probably knew the answer.

'So where do we go from here?' Jamie asked. 'What's next?'

Elliot turned to face the ocean, stretching away from them, dark and vast. A yawning chasm of the unknown hidden beneath the roiling surface. It was getting choppy now as the afternoon winds picked up, blowing the night in fast and inevitable.

'I don't know,' he said, with as much honesty as she'd ever heard in his voice. 'But this is far from over.'

'We got Petrosyan,' Jamie said. 'They're on their knees, the people scattered or in custody. They'll never recover.'

'You cut off a single limb. The body remains intact. The head remains intact.' His words were more decisive now.

'No, Petrosyan's dead. I ... *Church* shot him. Killed him. I saw it.'

'It's not him I'm worried about.'

'You mean the man that was with him? The younger man?'

'Petrosyan's son.'

'You think he'll be a problem? Step into his father's shoes?'

Elliot pursed his lips in thought. 'He's a pretender. Not ready for the throne. But ...'

'But what?'

'I'm still hearing chatter. I have backchannels into their world and ... the noise isn't stopping. Aram Petrosyan might be gone, but it doesn't sound like they've missed a beat. I don't know that we had the right target.'

Jamie's brow crumpled. 'What are you talking about? You said it. Aram Petrosyan was the head of the snake?'

'And yet ...' Elliot said, measuring out his words. 'I can still hear the hiss?' He looked at her and she couldn't help but shudder. 'Can't you?'

ALSO BY MORGAN GREENE

Bare Skin (DS Jamie Johansson 1)
Fresh Meat (DS Jamie Johansson 2)
Idle Hands (DS Jamie Johansson 3)

Angel Maker (DI Jamie Johansson 1)
Rising Tide (DI Jamie Johansson 2)
Old Blood (DI Jamie Johansson 3)
Death Chorus (DI Jamie Johansson 4)
Quiet Wolf (DI Jamie Johansson 5)
Ice Queen (DI Jamie Johansson 6)
Black Heart (DI Jamie Johansson 7)

The Last Light Of Day (The Jamie Johansson Files 1)
The Mark Of The Dead (The Jamie Johansson Files 2)
The Hiss Of The Snake (The Jamie Johansson Files 3)

WHAT'S NEXT FOR JAMIE?

Read on to discover the first three chapters of *The Hiss Of The Snake*, the next thrilling instalment in the Jamie Johansson Files!

THE HISS OF THE SNAKE

The Hiss Of The Snake is the third novel in The Jamie Johansson Files series, and the sequel to *The Mark Of The Dead*. After the showdown at the country house, and with Aram Petrosyan dead, the entire trafficking operation is in ruin. Multiple key witnesses set to turn evidence against the Petrosyan empire are under arrest and waiting to testify. But, before Interpol and the NCA can even catch their breath, three key people set to given testimony die in close succession, in their own homes.

The NCA are closing the cases faster than Jamie can even look into them, with Catherine Mallory strong-arming them into being ruled accidental deaths or suicides. But who has the reach and the influence to force the hand of the NCA, and to what end?

Jamie's new partner, Solomon Church, has been called away to fight his own war, leaving her to partner

394 THE HISS OF THE SNAKE

up with a very reluctant Nasir Hassan. Frozen out of the NCA, his only hope of keeping his career in one piece is to take an offer from Hallberg to work alongside Jamie as a Special Consultant under Interpol's purview. But that means working with Jamie, and against his former agency.

With alliances divided and their relationship on rocky ground, they must plunge into a dangerous cat and mouse game against a foe unlike any either of them have faced yet.

There's a viper in grass, waiting to strike, and Jamie is square in its sights.

Will she hear the hiss before it's too late? Or has Jamie Johansson finally met her match?

————

Read on to experience the first few chapters of *The Hiss Of The Snake*, the nail-biting, rollercoaster next instalment in The Jamie Johansson Files.

CHAPTER
ONE

The knock at the door was soft. Knuckles rapping against polished wood.

He knew better than to just let himself in. He would wait to be told he could enter, and if the signal didn't come, he would not. He would simply move away from the door, wait for an hour or two, and then return, regardless of how urgent the news was. And it was urgent. He knew she would want to know. But knocking twice was not an option.

The seconds ticked by, and despite the air conditioning in the office, sweat still beaded on his temples.

The man licked his lips, his clean-shaven face hovering just inches from the surface of the door.

Just as he was about to lose his nerve and scurry back to his desk, a voice echoed from inside. Not loud, which was why he was so close to the jamb.

'*Mutk'agrek,*' the voice said. Enter.

He straightened his tie, pushing it up into his Adam's apple to ensure it was proper, and then entered, head bowed.

'Madame,' he said, lowering his head further. 'I apologise for the interruption.'

When she didn't respond, he risked looking up, heart beating quickly in his throat.

The woman at the desk was small in stature, but he was under no illusions that she was anything but a viper ready to strike at any moment.

She was bent over a mountain of paperwork, her long, shining black hair tied up intricately behind her head, her cream dress a stark comparison to her tanned skin. Her elbow was rested on the table, hand raised, fingers rubbing together in thought as she read what was in front of her with an unnerving intensity. She had nails painted fiercely red and they shone in the white light that rained down from the LED bulbs overhead. To the right of her sprawling glass desk, the city lights glittered far below, visible through the floor-to-ceiling windows.

The man approached the desk briskly but paused six feet short, more than twenty from the door he'd entered through. And there he waited, hands clasped in front of him.

After an age, she picked her head up and looked at him. 'What is it?' she asked, her voice smooth and unhurried, but not suggestive of any patience.

'I have news, madame,' he responded, meeting her eye for a moment before looking down again.

She waited for him to speak.

'It's your brother,' he began, wondering what the next words would bring.

She stiffened a little in her chair, sensing his tone. 'What is it?'

'He's ... he's dead.'

She became still. Still as a statue.

He took that as his cue to back away quickly and leave the room.

The viper breathed softly, taking stock of the words, barely registering as her assistant made his exit.

Her outward display of rage was silent but vicious. Her fist balled, rings scratching against one another as her hand tightened, and then shot out. The diamonds and gold coiled around her fingers smashed into the screen of the computer on the edge of her desk with enough force that the screen shattered and sparked.

She pulled her hand back and looked at it, shaking now, blood running over her knuckles.

She studied it for a moment and then held it up in front of her, parted her lips, and licked the droplet of crimson liquid off her wrist.

And then she rose from her desk, letting her hand fall to her side, the taste of blood still in her mouth, and began striding towards the door. Her bloodied hand left smears on the hip of her figure-hugging dress. But she didn't care in that moment.

The door opened and she stood at the threshold.

'Who killed him?' she asked her assistant, her voice dripping with venom.

'I ...uh,' he stammered, all but losing control of his bladder at the sight of her.

'Was it her? The woman? *Johansson?*' She spat the name.

Her assistant swallowed, forcing himself to keep looking at her. He couldn't muster words. All he could do was nod.

Her jaw quivered and she had to clench her teeth to stop it. 'Have them ready the jet,' she growled.

He nodded again.

She made to turn back to her office, but paused, looking over her shoulder at him. 'And find me all there is to know about this woman. I want to know everything.'

And then she went back into her office, the door closing behind her.

In that moment, he wanted to ask her what she intended to do.

But he didn't need to. He knew all too well what happened to people who crossed Seda Petrosyan.

They died.

Slowly.

Painfully.

Horribly.

And though he didn't know this woman, this Jamie Johansson, or what she'd done ... He felt sorry for her.

Because Seda Petrosyan, the Viper, was coming for her head.

And she didn't even know it.

CHAPTER
TWO

Detective Jamie Johansson – or, *former* detective, Jamie Johansson, now *nothing* Jamie Johansson – or at least, she supposed, officially, *Special Consultant* Jamie Johansson as it would show up on the Interpol expense reports – stood behind Julia Hallberg, Interpol's new Chief Operations Coordinator for the UK as she sat at her desk.

Jamie was not alone in watching the computer screen over Hallberg's head. Nasir Hassan, formerly of the NCA – officially on leave, and unofficially booted out – was standing next to her. He too, was a 'special consultant'. The truth was, they were both outcasts now, bridge burners who'd stood against their own agencies, and were now orphans taken in by the only person they had left. Hallberg. And she was out on a limb for them, too. But, the results are inarguable. The bust at the manor had yielded over one hundred arrests. The single largest trafficking ring in the history of the UK brought down in one night. Over a dozen known traffickers that Interpol had been chasing for years were among them. Along with politicians, business magnates, celebrities, public figures, and a whole host of other people with connections both nationally and internationally. It was a smorgasbord, a feeding trough of information, names, dates, times, and reports of crimes that Interpol couldn't fathom.

Not like any of the credit went to the people responsible – namely the three people sitting in a dimly lit room in an all-but-abandoned office at a nondescript industrial estate in a town in South Wales that even people *from* South Wales would have to look at twice before figuring out how to say the bloody thing.

No, the credit went to the NCA and Interpol as a joint operation. Though, Jamie wasn't in this for any sort of glory. The only thing that mattered to her was that Alina, her ward, was safe once again. And that Aram Petrosyan, the piece of shit Armenian mastermind behind the whole cabal, was six feet under. When it came down to it, Jamie hadn't been able to pull the trigger. But Solomon Church had. Their time together had been short, but bloody. He'd saved her life countless times in just a few days, and she'd be forever grateful for that, but she hoped now that he'd rushed off to save the world elsewhere, that there'd be less blood spilt. Though, judging by what they were watching on the screen in front of Hallberg, it didn't look like it.

Just a few short weeks had passed since the bust, and though Hallberg warned them that a case of this magnitude would shed some skin as it rolled along, this was something else entirely.

They knew that some arrests wouldn't stick, that those with the means would throw money and high-priced solicitors at this, and charges would fall through. About a third of those initially put in cuffs were already walking free. Another handful just paid their bail and then fled the country. Another group managed to plead down, pay some big fines to stock the government's coffers, and then get off with a slap on the wrist.

Those who remained – the big fish; the politicians and business people with a lot to lose, those who could have their arms twisted, and who were well-connected enough to barter with information … they were the ones that the NCA wanted. That Interpol wanted. That they'd do anything to keep in their grasp.

But they also happened to be the ones who were dying.

'Fuck,' Hallberg muttered, leaning on the desk, elbow on the surface, knuckles in her cheek. 'What's that, three in a week?' she asked, knowing that it was.

Hassan had his arms folded. His mouth was bunched tersely and he was breathing a little harder than usual.

Jamie watched in silence as the scene unfolded.

The BBC was showing a home in the countryside surrounded by a sea of blue flashing lights. Two big vans were parked with their backs to the house and a fleet of figures in white overalls milled around while police officers set up a cordon.

The scene wasn't unfamiliar. And three in such a short space of time was more than coincidence.

The first to go was Mark Hughes, a politician who was potentially slated to make a run for PM in the next so many years. Until he was arrested and his name splashed across the front page of every newspaper. He lost his balance going down the stairs, fell and broke his neck. Unfortunate, but not impossible to swallow. He was out on bail, but the sweep of his house, along with his bloodwork showed that he'd been drinking a lot. An unhappy accident.

The second was Linda Harris, who sat on the board of a renewable energy company that had just been granted a tender to put a few dozen wind turbines along the border of the Brecon Beacons. She was found in the woods near her house, OD'd on pain pills her husband had been prescribed for his sciatica. Two was weird, but not a pattern.

The third, the most recent, was Simon Lloyd – a prominent thought leader and entrepreneur who had his fingers in lots of pies. He was well-regarded as a philan-thropist, very active in multiple charities, and his socials were awash with him doing fun runs, marathons, and other vanity challenges to raise funds for those in need. Why anyone would want to pay someone to climb Kili-manjaro to help support a UK-based charity was beyond

Jamie's understanding, but they did. But beyond the bull-shit charity schemes that were allowing Lloyd to check off bucket-list items, one thing was clear: the guy was fit, healthy, and not liable to go down with a heart attack.

Which is what had supposedly happened.

Jamie listened as the voiceover spoke. '... Lloyd was found in his kitchen this morning, having died of a sudden heart attack. Emergency services arrived on scene after a call from his wife, but Lloyd was pronounced dead at the scene. He leaves behind a wife, but no children.'

Good, thought Jamie. Not that he was dead – though she wasn't about to shed a tear – but good that he didn't have kids. Pieces of shit like Lloyd who presented themselves as heroes, just to go and bet money raised for charity on which child was liable to beat the other to death first at a party like Petrosyan's had no business walking the earth.

But to die from a heart attack? Suddenly? No fucking way. Three was a pattern, and this was foul play.

Though the NCA clearly thought so too, hence the SOCOs and police cars crawling all over the place.

'You need to get over there,' Hallberg said, turning to look up at Jamie and Hassan.

She looked tired. Jamie wasn't surprised. She was now in charge of coordinating every operation the Interpol was running in the UK. And though she was an expert delegator, that hardly freed her hands completely.

And what she was doing with Jamie and Hassan here was totally independent of any other oversight. She was handling it personally, along with everything else she had to do.

The NCA was heading up the case against Petrosyan's trafficking operation, as Interpol were, after all, only an advisory and intelligence force, and sub-contracted all of their fieldwork out to agencies like the NCA and regional police forces. But they'd already closed both investigations into both Mark Hughes and Linda Harris, ruling no evidence of foul play. Accidental deaths.

And Hallberg wasn't buying it any longer.

'You hear me?' she repeated, looking at both Jamie and Hassan.

They glance at each other.

'Is there a point?' Jamie asked, trying not to sound too blunt.

They'd already attended both previous crime scenes, to be told by the NCA that they were far from welcome. They'd even been escorted out of the first scene and forced to stand behind the cordon.

The second, they'd been allowed inside, but ignored by every NCA officer, police officer, and SOCO. It was as if they were ghosts.

So what Hallberg expected to find out, Jamie couldn't say.

The NCA had all but closed the doors to Interpol on

this case. And it was rubbing Hallberg up the wrong way.

It probably didn't help that Catherine Mallory, Hassan's former boss at the NCA, was the one at the helm. It wasn't surprising she didn't want Jamie and Hassan poking their noses in, but the way she was shutting these cases so fast was definitely not helping dissuade Hallberg of her corruption.

'The point is,' Hallberg replied coldly, 'that I gave you an order.'

Jamie liked Hallberg more than probably anyone else she knew. And she thought extremely highly of her as both a person and as a professional. But what Hallberg expected Jamie to wring out of a visit there, she just didn't know.

They were being stonewalled from the entire case. And there was nothing that could be done.

But Hallberg's expression, and her words, told Jamie there was no arguing.

'We'll go,' Hassan answered with a nod.

'Then go,' Hallberg said, the bags under her eyes visibly dark and deep. She turned back to the screen and killed the monitor, checking her phone for the time. 'Shit, I'm late,' she said, standing. 'I'll walk with you.'

Jamie and Hassan didn't really have a choice but to follow her. It wasn't an exaggeration to say that they were both ingratiated to her in a pretty serious way and she was pretty much the only thing standing between

Jamie and Hassan and a total loss of their careers, if not criminal charges.

Hallberg strode quickly for the exit and stepped out into the shared parking space in front of their industrial unit. The park houses six units in all. One was storage for a builder's merchants, another was a metal fabrication shop. One was a warehouse for a carpet company, another was a cross-fit gym, the fifth was storage for spare parts for plant machinery – buckets and the like – and theirs used to be the office for a timber company that had since gone under. There was no signage or any hint that it was being used for what it was. Which was just perfect. Because Jamie was sure that if anyone did know, they'd be shut down, or worse – targeted.

It was still early in the morning when they got outside – a little after eight. Apart from the cross-fitters who were congregating outside their roll-up door, getting ready to flip tires and yell at each other, the place was fairly empty.

Hallberg paused at the door of her Mercedes and looked back at Jamie and Hassan. 'Let me know when you get there, and if they give you any pushback. After the last time, you should have an easier go of it.'

'Here's to hoping,' Jamie said, albeit glumly.

Hallberg held her gaze for a moment, then nodded and got in the car. 'I'm not going to be reachable for a few hours, but I'll check back in when I have time. And if Mallory's there,' Hallberg added, 'Try not to piss her off, alright? I'm having a hard enough time justifying what you two are being paid for without you locking horns with the NCA every five minutes.'

'Do our best.'

Hallberg closed the door, wheeled backwards, and then sped out of the estate. Saying she had a lot on her plate was a pretty big understatement.

'Fuck,' Jamie muttered, listening to the exhaust noise fade into the distance. 'Guess we should get this over with.'

'Mhm,' Hassan replied, clearly not excited about it either.

Jamie looked over at him. Since he'd come to Jamie and Church's aid that night, Mallory had severed all ties with him. He was already on thin ice, being kept at arm's distance. But now, his career was shot. This gig was his only hope of staying in law enforcement. And though he was on the right side of things morally, and he'd had a direct hand in saving the lives of the children and teens liberated that night, Jamie couldn't help but feel that he blamed her for losing his position.

And she couldn't help but blame herself, either.

'You want me to drive?' she asked.

'No,' he said, not veiling the lack of affection he felt for her right now.

'Okay. You want to stop and get some coffee—'

But he was already walking away from her.

CHAPTER
THREE

J amie climbed into Hassan's car, measuring him as she did.

He was a little over six feet tall, with dark hair slicked back, a manicured beard that was short but thick, and dark eyes. She'd first met him back when she was working for the London Met when he was the captain of an armed response squad that had been involved with one of her investigations. Briefly, they were even partners when he made the jump across to become a detective.

Since, their paths had diverged and now by happenstance come back together.

It seemed like every time he was making progress in his career, Jamie derailed it all. He'd practically said as much. He wasn't happy to be in this position, butting heads with the people he used to work for, his life hanging by a thread.

Back when they'd worked together at the Met he'd been happily married, a father of two, his life on cruise control.

Now ... he was divorced, didn't get to see his kids, and his fresh start at the NCA had turned into a flaming repeat of history.

She wasn't quite sure she missed Solomon Church, the man who had come into her life like a hurricane and been the reason they managed to get to Petrosyan as they had. But ... right now, she would have taken his company over Hassan's. It seemed like the moment that they'd been turned loose and brought into Hallberg's fold, he'd been called away to attend to something else. Gone as fast as he'd arrived.

Jamie and Hassan fell into their current roles without much choice. Alina was still in play, the kidnapped Georgian royal that everyone seemed to want to get their hands on. And Jamie couldn't stop pursuing this until she knew for certain that Alina would be safe. And she didn't know that yet.

So here they were. Jamie and Hassan, reluctant partners, making enemies of the police and the NCA, and enemies of everyone else, too.

No wonder he was in a bad move.

They were on an iceberg together, drifting further from land by the second.

Hassan didn't wait for her to fasten her belt before he launched them out of the industrial estate and towards the home of Simon Lloyd.

But, on good terms or not, they had to discuss the case.

'Who's doing this?' Jamie asked, staring out of the window as they joined a B road and headed south towards Simon Lloyd's house just outside Cardiff.

Hassan just shrugged, keeping stoic.

'It has to be Petrosyan, right?'

'The man you killed.'

'Or his son,' Jamie offered, remembering the conversation she had on the beach at Machir Bay with Elliot Day. 'Narek Petrosyan is still alive. He's currently at the Armenian Embassy in London, seeking political asylum from Interpol.'

'I know where Petrosyan is,' Hassan said flatly. 'But he's a boy. We already looked at him. The kid might be as sick as his father, but he's not capable of running something as big as the whole operation. And nor does he have the stones to be killing politicians and public figures tied to his case. Nor do I think he would be that stupid, even if he was that bold.' Hassan sighed. 'I don't know who's behind this, but it's someone with a vested interest in seeing this investigation fall apart.'

'Or an interest in silencing those with something to say.'

'Same thing.' Hassan sighed again, and Jamie thought it was just for effect.

'Can we talk about the NCA?' Jamie hazarded. It was more than a touchy subject.

Hassan shifted uncomfortably in the chair, changing

which hand was on the wheel so that his back was practically to Jamie.

'Killing key witnesses is one thing – but regardless of who or why, doing it under the NCA and Interpol's nose is more than bold. If they have the ability to get to these people in such quick succession, then we have to assume that they have some sort of indemnity from the people looking into it.'

'And why do we have to assume that?'

'Because if they don't know they can get away with it, then they have to be acting under the impression that the NCA are too fucking useless to catch them.' Jamie tried to keep her tone light. 'So either Catherine Mallory is just terrible at her job, or she's crooked. And you know which one I think it is.'

Hassan stewed on that but didn't answer. He'd previously gone to bat for Mallory, defended her pretty passionately. But despite the jury being out on Mallory, Hassan wasn't an idiot. And the more time went on, the less he could ignore the things happening with Mallory at their centre. Every time something happened that stunk, Mallory was always right there. How many times it would have to happen before he finally just accepted it, Jamie didn't know. But it was really beginning to piss her off how hard a stance Hassan was taking on this.

With Aram Petrosyan dead, Jamie kept thinking about who would have the reach to make something like this happen. To kill an NCA and Interpol joint investigation into an international trafficking ring, and then right the ship afterwards. They wouldn't even have to kill all the witnesses. Jamie wouldn't be surprised if even now the ones who were still alive and intended to testify were rethinking that. Jail time didn't sound too bad when the alternative was being offed in your own home.

Her mind cast back to the beach once more, to the conversation she had with Elliot. When Alina was running around on the sand, laughing and playing without a care in the world. Elliot had warned her – he'd said that this wasn't over. That he had a feeling that Aram Petrosyan was not the one in charge after all. That someone else was the true head of the snake.

And that he could still hear the hiss.

Jamie didn't know if she could hear anything, but she could feel it: the coils tightening around her throat and chest.

Something was coming, she knew that much.

She looked across at Hassan again. Could she still trust him? She thought she could. But with her life? Those were the stakes in this game.

She thought about Church again. How much she'd like to have him with her now. Someone she could rely on.

There was Elliot, of course. But his priority was protecting Alina. That's where Jamie needed him.

So maybe this time she was on her own.

Her hands began to shake a little, the feeling of blood rushing through them causing pins and needles.

The coil around her body ratcheted tighter. Squeezing at her rib cage, forcing the air from her lungs, closing her throat.

Hassan drove on as Jamie slowly pulled her hands into fists, closed her eyes, and willed the feeling of nausea settling in her guts to go away.

But it didn't end.

In fact, she knew it was only the beginning.

ENJOYING SO FAR?

The Hiss Of The Snake is out on February 28th 2024. Find it on Amazon now.

Thank you so much for joining Jamie and I on this adventure. I sincerely hope you've enjoyed it, and are looking forward to the next one. But if you can't wait, or you want to see how the story all began, there is a whole series Jamie Johansson novels out already, chronicling her story from her first murder case while working for the London Met, through to some truly harrowing cases set in the heart of a wild and brutal Sweden.

You can find them on Amazon, available in paperback and on Kindle.

If you'd like to stay up to date with everything Jamie and the other novels I've written, you can find me on

Facebook as Morgan Greene Author, or you can visit my website at morgangreene.co.uk and join my mailing list.

Printed in Great Britain
by Amazon